Mr. Blackwell's Bride

A Good Wife Novel

SIENNA BLAKE

Mr. Blackwell's Bride: a novel / by Sienna Blake. – 1st Ed.
First Digital Edition: November 2017
Published by SB Publishing
Copyright 2017 Sienna Blake

ISBN-13: 978-1977530554
ISBN-10: 1977530559

Cover art & paperback formatting services by Romacdesigns: http://romacdesigns.com.
Cover art copyright 2017 Romacdesigns. All Rights Reserved Sienna Blake. Stock images: shutterstock
Content editing & proofreading services by Book Detailing.
Proofreading services by Proof Positive: http://proofpositivepro.com.

The characters and events portrayed in this book are fictional. Any similarity to real persons, living or dead, is coincidental and not intended by the author.

For Jennifer Ballam,

And all of you who loved Drake the most.

Chapter One

Drake

"What the hell do you mean, Carter's backing out of the deal?" I growled.

Roger, my second in command, was practically jogging at my side to keep up with me as I barreled through the corridors of Blackwell Industries' head office. Following close behind us were the heads of the analyst and legal team working on this deal.

A deal that I thought we had stitched up.

Roger rambled on about how this was unpredictable, it was one of those things, there were other companies out there to buy.

I ignored him. I wanted *this one*.

"Sam," I barked out as I approached my office.

My personal assistant's blonde head popped up from

behind her desk. "Drake?"

"Get me Carter on the phone. Now." I slammed open my door and strode into my corner office, a spacious and stylish space on the top floor with floor-to-ceiling windows overlooking the boxy cityscape of Los Angeles.

"Line two," Sam called.

It was game time.

I kicked a chair out of my way and leaned over my desk, pressing the flashing button to put Carter on speakerphone.

"Carter, buddy," I started, my voice friendly, even as I unbuttoned my collar and ripped my silk Hermes tie off from around my neck, throwing it across one of my expensive leather chairs. "What's this I hear about you getting cold feet?"

Through the speaker, I heard Carter sucking in a breath. I wasn't supposed to know yet. He'd only just decided to pull the plug. The truth was I had little birdies everywhere. Every-fucking-where. Sending information to me from all levels of every organization I was either competing against or looking to buy. *Especially* companies I was looking to buy.

"How do you know about—?"

"That's not important, Carter. What's important is *why* you want to back out of such a lucrative deal."

He paused.

"Come on, Carter. Talk to me. We're friends." I snatched my stress ball off my desk and crushed it in my hands. "What's going through your mind? Has someone else made you another offer?" I bet you it was Wright. I was going to kill that asshole sonofabitch. No, I would burn his company down and bury him in the rubble. Then I would kill him.

"It's…Jed."

"Jed?" I clicked my fingers at Roger and Sam, both standing at my doorway, mouthing, *Who the fuck is Jed?*

They both looked at each other, then shook their heads at me.

"My son," Carter clarified.

"Your son?" I repeated. That little brat barely out of fucking diapers? What the fuck did he have to do with anything? I inhaled slowly, then exhaled. *Stay calm. Stay in control.* "What has your son got to do with this deal?" The deal we'd spent six fucking months hammering out.

"Well, you see, I've been thinking." *Here we fucking go.* "About Jed. About his future. About what kind of father I want to be to him. He's my first boy, you know. The wife and I spent years trying. We had to go the IVF route."

Yes, yes, I fucking know this. And...? "It must have been a trying time for you both," I said, my voice as soothing as I could possibly make it.

"It was incredibly stressful for us, you know? I don't know whether Julie can go through that again. He...well, he might be our only child..."

I squeezed my eyes shut, fighting the urge to reach into the receiver and choke the living shit out of him. My voice, however, was calm and patient. "And that means?"

"If I sell my company to you, then I have nothing to pass on to him."

There it was. His actual objection to selling his company. A company that under his useless command was inefficient, turning over well below what it should be. The only reason why Carter's company grew to where it was today was luck. Pure dumb luck. Right product, right timing.

If I bought his company, I'd increase the profits by fourfold in the first goddamn year. I could already feel it shaping underneath my hands. I could see how and where I was going to trim all the fat. This company was already mine.

Not yet.

If I didn't figure out a way to get Carter to stick with the deal, then not ever.

Roger, Sam, all the heads of the project teams—Analysis, Legal, Finance—along with a bunch of other rubbernecking slackers were all gathered at my door. All waiting with a collective breath, wondering how the fuck I was going to convince this indecisive, toe-tapping man-bitch to get back on the train. Because we couldn't leave this station without him.

All that work for nothing.

I wouldn't let it happen.

I took in a deep breath and the faces at my door blurred. I exhaled, my mind focusing, thoughts sharpening.

"Carter, the best thing you can do for your son is to sell your company now. Put that money in a trust for him so he can build his own future. Who knows what will happen to the market in ten years' time? Who knows whether your company will even exist when he turns eighteen?"

"I…I don't know, Drake."

I gritted my teeth. This wasn't working. But I could make it work. I just needed to overcome his objections. One by one. I needed to turn his "nos" into "yeses." I changed tactic. "Buddy, I hear you loud and clear. You love your son. Am I right?"

"Yes."

"You want to do what's best for your son. To leave this earth knowing he's carrying on your legacy."

"Yes."

"You want your son to be *proud* of his old man."

"Yes," his trembling voice was barely a whisper.

"Carter, the best thing you can give your son is *not* your company…" I paused for effect. "It's *you*." My voice was smooth, the words flowing like silk now. "Your time. Your energy. Your love. *He* is the best reason to sell. You don't want to wake up one day an old man, your son all grown up, and realize that *you don't know him* because you spent your life, *wasted* your life, working your ass off to run a company that he may not want anything to do with."

Carter was silent on the other end of the line.

I kept going. "This is what great men know—we are not the product of *what we own*, but of *who we love*. This is your chance to be a great man, Carter. This is your chance to secure your son's future. And his son, and his son. Take the deal. Do it for him. Do it…for Jed."

There was a weighted pause.

We all held our breaths.

It was so silent you could hear a fly fart.

Carter cleared his throat on the other end of the line. "Well…okay then."

"Okay…what?" I asked gently.

"I'll sell you my company."

I pumped my fist in the air and gave out a little kick. "That's excellent news, Carter. I knew you'd make the right decision." I snapped my fingers at Siobhan, my head of Legal. "I'll get my head of Legal over there right away to get the papers signed." Siobhan nodded, a grin on her face, and she disappeared through the crowd.

Carter and I exchanged our goodbyes. I stabbed at the button, ending the call.

I spun on my heel, my arms held out to my audience, like *that's the fucking way it's done*. The crowd at the door erupted into cheers and hooting, their clapping echoing through my cavernous office.

I waved at them. "Alright. Show's over. Get back to work."

They dispersed with fading calls of congratulations and awe clear on their faces.

The adrenaline surging through my veins began to dissipate. Underneath I felt tired. Worn out.

I walked around my desk as Sam strode up, a bunch of notes in her hand, calls I'd missed.

A stab of pain shot through my chest. I winced.

"Drake? Are you alright?"

"Fine." I grabbed the notes and waved her out, calling out for her to shut the door behind her.

When I was alone I sank into my chair and clasped my chest, heaving in a breath. What the fuck was that?

Chapter Two

Noriko

Twenty more minutes.

Just twenty more minutes until I was—

"Norikooooo," my sister Emi's voice called through our house. "Where's my other schoolbag?" I could hear her rummaging through our cupboards. Morning light filtered through our *shoji* walls, panels of thin paper in wooden frames.

I let out a soft sigh as I finished folding the futons, the thin mattresses that my two sisters and I slept on, stacking them in the corner along with our comforters and pillows. Emi was thirteen. She just started high school, which meant she was now obsessed with her appearance. Which meant it's the impractical but so-hot-right-now choco-pink schoolbag or nothing.

"Have you checked near the front door?" I called out without bothering to turn and face her.

There was a pause, then the movement of feet across our thin mat flooring. "Got it."

Now that the whole family was awake, I slid open the *fusuma*, the sliding panels of our rooms, creating a larger space. I walked over to our small shrine in the corner of our living space and lit an incense stick for Mama. *I miss you every day,* I said silently to her as the spicy thick scent wafted around me. Then I squashed the worm of my anger wriggling in the dirt of the hole she left behind. The hole that I was now expected to fill.

Fifteen more minutes.

I hurried to the kitchen where the rice in the cooker was probably cooled enough to touch. "Your tie is crooked," I called to Tatsumi, my middle sister, as I passed her. She was putting on her sailor-style school uniform while dancing to Gwen Stefani, a western pop singer she has been obsessed with, blaring from the tiny player.

She cursed behind me.

"Language," I called back.

"Sorry."

In the kitchen I formed the rice into little balls around a small piece of leftover fish in the center, before rolling them in seasoning, my practiced hands moving quickly. I had four lunchboxes laid out. As I finished each *onigiri*, I placed them in alternating boxes.

"Can you do my hair, Nori-chan?" Tatsumi called.

"Only if you want an updo with rice bits and fish. Ask Emi."

"She can never do it as well as you can."

Tatsumi had always been concerned with her appearance. Lately it'd gotten worse. She admitted to me the other day she has a *boyfriend* at school. Fifteen is too young…too damn young to have a boyfriend. But I knew telling her *not to* would make her more determined to. I was hoping her crush was a phase. "Let me finish making lunch first," I called back to her. "You finish getting ready."

Footsteps ran up behind me. She threw her arms around my waist and squeezed. "Love youuuu. You're the best."

If my hands hadn't been covered in rice and smelling like fish, I'd have hugged her back. "I love you, too, little brat." I smiled, my chest warming. "Now go or you'll be late."

She ran off. I quickly finished our lunches, did Tatsumi's hair, then shoved the girls out the door so they could catch their bus. From the door of our house, I waved and called my well-wishes for their studies as they chased each other down the dirt country road.

I was alone.

At last. Alone.

My nerves tingled. I had this place all to myself. I felt like I could breathe again, the heaviness that hung around my neck like a metal collar, shrugged off. The door of the cage around me temporarily flung open.

I loved my sisters, I loved my father, but I yearned for the stillness of the house. No chatter, no demands, just the whisper of leaves against the paper walls.

I could just…*be*.

Instead of…*should*.

If only I could spend all my days alone. I wouldn't have to hide my secret. I wouldn't have to keep it wrapped up and tucked against my soul, constantly fearing that I'd one day drop it and it'd spill to the floor.

My secret…

You see, I was a bad sister. A bad daughter. Pretending to be a good one.

I was too selfish. I felt too much. I *wanted* things that I shouldn't want: to see all the galleries of the world, to spend my days making art, studying art. To be reckless with my life.

I didn't want to marry a stable man with a decent income and have his children like I was expected to. I wanted to run out screaming from behind everyone else's lives.

I dreamed—wild and shameful dreams—of being free, of being unburdened by all my responsibilities. It was like an ache that I swallowed, now sitting like an undigested stone in the base of my gut. I loved my family, even if loving them imprisoned me. I hated myself for wanting such selfish things.

I ran over to my drawer, my one personal drawer just for my use, pulling out the large sheets of paper and the tubes of paints my father saved up to buy me for my last birthday. He had handed it to me like an apology. "I thought you should have this. Before you finish your studies," he said, because he knew that once I went out to work, I'd never again have the time for it. Work. Marriage. Children. Death. It was what was expected.

Still, I'd promised myself one form of rebellion. I refused to marry unless it was for love, the kind of ageless love that one was lucky to find, even luckier to keep. The kind of love my parents have. Yes, *have*. Even though Mama has gone from this world, their love is still alive. It still crackles in the air around me. It still shines in my papa's eyes.

I spread the paper across the *tatami* mat floor and laid out my paints, the tubes bulging with magic.

Yes, I was much too selfish. Look at me now. Without anyone around, I was indulging in fruitless wants, in dreams as whimsical and thin as smoke. Who ever made a good living out of art? What a waste of my time. Laundry needed cleaning. Dishes needed washing. Dinner needed prepping.

All these things fell away as I lifted my brush. Every slash of color cut me free from the ropes around my heart. My soul mirrored every dot and stroke of vibrant paint. While I painted I forgot my responsibilities. I let go of my gray, dusty life. I lost myself in dreams and stardust. From nothing grew water lilies, then a lake and around it, a French garden.

I'd never been to France. I'd never even left Japan. I'd painted this scene from memory from a book on Monet I found in my university library when I should have been looking up a book on statistics.

I pulled back from my work, studying it with a critical eye. I shook my head slightly, a small smile on my lips. I could never get the light glinting off the water right. How did Monet do it? How did he capture sunbeams and press them into the canvas? Did he use magic?

Art is never finished, only abandoned. Leonardo da Vinci said that.

This work would definitely have to be abandoned. I sighed when I spotted the time. I needed to get ready for my lectures at university. Painting would not pay the bills. That's why I was studying something realistic—international business with a major in English—even though I was already fluent, thanks to my father.

The child inside me withered at the thought of a lifetime of working in this dry, dull field, my wild mind stuffed into a box, my future laid out. Endless hours in a cubicle in an anthill city, saving money to send back home.

I had no choice.

Papa wouldn't be an English teacher forever. At nineteen, I was the eldest and I was responsible for this family, even if I wasn't a boy. Perhaps it would have been better if I'd been born a boy. Or not born at all. My resentment hung out like an untucked shirt before guilt's hand shoved it all back in and straightened out my facade.

"Noriko," a familiar male voice called to me.

I looked up to see my father standing at the front door, slipping off his shoes, the dying light glinting in his silver hair.

"You're home from work early." I smiled. "I have some ongiri left over in the fridge, if you're hungry."

He didn't smile back. "I didn't go to work today."

Something jarred inside me. He didn't go to work? He didn't tell me that. He usually told me everything. I thought it was strange this morning when I woke up and he was already gone. "Where did you go?"

He ignored my question. "I need to talk to you."

"Can it wait, Papa? I have classes."

"No," his voice trembled. "It cannot."

I frowned as I looked closer. His face was drawn and pale. He suddenly looked ten years older than his forty-one years. Oh God.

Something was very, very wrong.

Chapter Three

Drake

"I'm afraid, Mr. Blackwell, you have a weak heart." Dr. Tao leaned forward in his chair. "And I'm afraid at the rate you're going…"

I'd given bad news before. I gave bad news all the fucking time in my position. I knew the longer he paused, the worse it was going to be. I began to count the seconds.

…three…four…five…

Fuck me.

"How much will it cost to cure me?"

Dr. Tao cleared his throat. "I'm afraid it's not that simple."

My eyes narrowed on his face. Was this some kind of lead-up? A windup where he buttered me up for a ridiculously expensive procedure? Or several? "Make it simple."

"It's not something that we can operate on. But with some lifestyle changes you can manage it."

"What?"

"You're putting yourself under too much stress. You work too hard. Slow down. Take some time off. Spend time with the ones you love."

I bristled. *Slow down? Take some time off?* Did he fucking know who he was talking to? "I'm not listening to any more of this bullshit." I shoved away from his desk and stormed out of his office.

In the elevator, alone, traveling down to the lobby where my driver was waiting, I caught sight of my face in the mirror. There were light smudges under my dark eyes. The downlights in this cursed tin can didn't help. My lips turned down at the corners. My tie was askew. At least my hair was still in place.

The withered face of my late father flashed before me. When had I started looking like him? I growled and turned my gaze away. I would never become him. Never.

Except at thirty-four my father had a wife and a son he could pass his company on to. What did I have?

Spend time with the ones you love.

A strange chasm seemed to crack out all around me. Somewhere in the distance, a clock began to tick. I didn't like this feeling at all. Not one fucking bit.

I would fix it. I was Drake Blackwell. If I could build a billion-dollar company, I could fix *this* little problem. I just wasn't sure *how*…yet.

Chapter Four

Noriko

"Cancer."

I blinked rapidly, staring at my papa. We were sitting alone in our tiny back garden underneath our favorite cherry blossom tree, his and mine, the dying sun casting a dim light across the world. In the distance the great figure of Mount Fuji stood watching over us like an old uncle.

"I don't understand," I said, my voice coming out like a ghost.

"I have six months. Eight if I'm lucky."

Inside me every cell had gone numb, drained of heat and life, prickles of ice skating across my skin, making the hairs on my arms stand on end. "B-but they can operate. The state will pay for it." Our healthcare system was excellent. The government wouldn't let him die.

My father pressed his lips together. "It's too late for that."

"No!" I cried. "There must be something." I found I was wringing my hands together.

"There is. But…"

Something. There was something. Hope. I grasped on to it like grains of sand. "What is it?"

"There is an experimental treatment. It will give me a chance…" I could hear the *but* in his tone. Unspoken, it clanged like a gong. "…but the state won't pay for it."

I felt like the ground underneath me was falling away and I was suddenly grasping for something—*anything*—solid to hang on to. "You have money saved."

"For you girls."

"We can use it—"

"It's not enough, Noriko. It's not enough."

My head spun and my chest squeezed as if a clammy invisible hand was crushing it. This cannot be happening. Not to Papa, the kindest, most loving man in the world. What kind of God would let this happen?

"I haven't told anyone else yet. Except you, *hime*." *Princess*, his nickname for me. The weight of his secret bowed my neck like a too-heavy crown.

In the background, I could hear my sisters banging through the front door, home from school, their voices muffled through the thin paper walls. I envied them. They were blissfully ignorant to the earthquake that had broken my world in two.

"When are you going to tell them?" I whispered.

"Soon. Tomorrow night, maybe. They'll have the weekend to…get used to it."

Get *used to* him dying?

Papa must have seen the horror on my face because he clutched at my knee. "They will be fine. They have you."

Who do I have if you die?

I shook my head as panicked fear shook my insides. "I can't be their role model. I'm too resentful of my responsibilities. Too outspoken. I selfishly want too much. I'm not patient enough. You're always telling me to have more respect."

Papa laughed softly, his eyes crinkled with affection, tears welling in the rims. He was trying hard to be strong. But he was close to breaking down. If he broke, I would too. "Hime, you are everything this family needs to hold together. Your heart is bigger than all of us."

I barely heard him. *You can't leave us. You can't.* My heart cracked and threatened to spill out all over my lap.

I should bow to him as my father, as my elder. I should accept what he was telling me. I won't. I couldn't.

"You can't leave me," I cried. *I'll never forgive you if you do.*

"I have enough saved that you can finish your studies, get a job."

No, damn him. He was talking like he was already gone. Like he had already given up. Like there was no chance left.

There was a chance, he said so himself. We just needed the money.

How would I get money?

"I won't let you die," I whispered, a promise to the gods that I would fight to keep him on this Earth. I would fight for him with everything I had.

Papa merely sighed, picking up a fallen petal on the ground and twisting it in his fingers. "Our lives are like these blossoms. Beautiful and short. We all must die, hime."

But not him. Not now. *Six months.*

I would not allow him to disappear, the only connection left with him through our *kamidana*, the small shrine we have inside our home. I *will not* light a daily incense for him. He will *live*.

My chest cavity filled with such hot, sticky resolve that it forced the pieces of my heart to remain in place. This absolute determination was the only thing keeping me from breaking apart.

In life we must either be the water or the rock. Up until now I had accepted that I was water, allowing myself to fit the container I was placed in, allowing myself to bend around the obstacles in my path.

Today I would become the rock. I would not bend. I would not flinch. I would stand in this solid faith, stubborn as stone. The universe around me would be forced to become water and to bend to me.

My father would not die.

I will find a way to pay for this experimental treatment. I would find a way to save him.

How? How does a nineteen-year-old woman with no degree make a lot of money and fast?

My mind turned to the curious foreign woman who approached me at my university several weeks ago.

"You are very beautiful," she said in accented Japanese. She was pale like milk with jade-green eyes staring back at me from under waves of thick hair the color of the tail feathers of black kites. She wore a tailored cream pantsuit and smelled of lilacs and money. "Do you have a boyfriend?"

I raised an eyebrow and studied her. "I'm not gay, sorry."

She laughed, the sound like clear temple bells. "I'm not asking for me."

I frowned. "Then who are you asking for?"

She ignored my question and studied my face. "Do you ever wish you could…leave? Get away from the constraints of your place in this society?"

I blinked at her but did not speak to confirm or deny. It was a lucky guess.

She continued, "You dream about seeing the world. Of seeing the Mona Lisa *in the Louvre in Paris. Van Gogh's* Starry Night *in New York. You dream of being an artist."*

"You're a witch," I choked out.

"No, just observant. You have paint flecks on your cheek." She brushed my cheek with her thumb, firm yet tender. "And your book on Italian impressionist artists is not part of this business school's curriculum."

I flushed, shoving the book in question—her window into my soul—further into my satchel. "Who are you? What do you want?"

"Direct. Confident." Her smile grew cat-like. "Unusual. I like that."

I bristled under her assessment. "You still haven't answered my question."

"My name is Isabelle Taylor. I own an international agency."

I frowned. "Modeling?" I often had people tell me I was beautiful. Nevertheless I couldn't see myself making a living out of something as fleeting as beauty. "No, thank you."

"Not modeling. Something more...exclusive."

I had no idea what that meant.

"I could make you very rich," she said. "I could give you the freedom you crave, the life you want."

I laughed but it came out like a strangled cry. Even so, a part of me lunged at the possibility like a kitten chasing a butterfly. I tamped that part of me down. "You're crazy."

Now it was her turn to laugh. She pressed a card into my hand, black with silver font. Her jade-chip eyes glinted with knowing. "Call me when you change your mind."

Sitting under the tree surrounded with fallen blossoms, I thought back to the black card still sitting in the bottom of my bag. For some reason I had not wanted to throw it away.

I could make you very rich.

Unease wormed its way through me. Rich. At what cost?

I shoved this unease aside. It didn't matter what the cost was. I would pay it. I would do anything to save my father.

Anything.

Chapter Five

Drake

That night I attended a fundraiser for one of the charities that Blackwell Industries supported. After my delightful appointment with Dr. Tao, I wasn't feeling up for people. Except I couldn't cancel last minute because I was the one who had to deliver the keynote speech.

Smile plastered on my face, I shook hands and made small talk with a blur of faces.

Through the crowd, I spotted Jared Wright, a blond-haired snake in a suit. Instantly my shoulders tightened, my lip curled up. Trust that fucker to be here. He probably had a litany of heckles ready for when I got on stage.

He caught me glaring and lifted his glass in a mock toast, a smug grin on his face, daring me to go over there and beat him to a pulp for the slimy trick he pulled last month, swiping the Mercer deal right out of my palm. I'd win, too. I worked out as hard as I worked. A weights room and shower adjoined my office via a connecting door. Exercise kept me sane. At least, until today. My hands clenched into fists as Jared's blood splattered all over my imagination.

Billionaire Drake Blackwell beats long-time rival, Jared Wright, half to death at a charity function

Wouldn't that make a nice headline for the papers?

"What are you looking at?" James asked me as he stepped into my line of sight, breaking through my violent daydream.

I turned my attention to James Firestone. I hadn't seen James in, well, it must have been several months. Probably at the last fundraiser. Here he was, looking like he'd spent a month in a spa—rosy cheeks, bright eyes, animated hands, making him look at least ten years younger. The bastard was even smiling.

But that's not what caught my attention. On his arm was one of the most stunning creatures I had ever seen: delicate limbs like porcelain in a long, shimmering rose-colored gown matching her marshmallow mouth, dark slit eyes that sparkled with intelligence. "And who is this?" I asked, curiosity and envy eating me alive.

James turned to the wide-eyed beauty. "This is Satsumi." His eyes flashed. "My wife."

"Your *wife*?" Two words stuffed with unasked questions.

James answered none of them. "Satsumi, this is Mr. Blackwell, one of the few men in this room who, dare I say it, is richer than me." He let out a boisterous laugh.

Satsumi bowed her dainty head. "Very pleased to meet you, Mr. Blackwell."

"Likewise."

"I was just saying to James," Satsumi said, "how interesting your speech was."

"Really?"

She nodded. "You make a good point about free higher education and the impact it would have on Americans living below the poverty line."

I raised my eyebrow. "You actually listened to my speech?"

"Well," she said with a glint in her eye, "somebody had to."

I let out a laugh. The three of us debated the topic until Satsumi excused herself to go the bathroom.

When she was out of earshot, I turned to James. "She is a find, isn't she?"

"Indeed."

"Where did you meet her?"

He paused. "Through a mutual friend."

"Last time I saw you, you swore up and down that you weren't giving in to your grandfather's will stipulations."

"Well, that was before…"

"I didn't think women like her existed. She's stunning, exotic and dear God, those eyes. They look like they're drilling right into you. She's intelligent, funny and she isn't intimidated by the Plastic Pack." I glanced over to the gaggle of twenty-something trust-funders and shuddered. I turned back to James. "Her only downfall is that she chose *you* as a husband."

He laughed and I caught the twinkle in his eye. There was something he wasn't telling me. "Careful, Drake, if I wasn't so sure you had no heart I'd say you were half in love with her already."

"I have a heart." Apparently, it'd kill me one day. "Just not for dodgy car salesmen like you."

James snorted. "A Bugatti is not just a *car*."

"I know. You sold me two already."

"Did I? Looking for a third? Perhaps one for your latest lady friend. How is the lovely…what was her name again? Katie? Kitty?"

I flinched when I thought of Kristie. "Let's not talk about her."

"Gold digger?"

I made a face. "That. As well as being insipid and culturally ignorant."

"You're too hard on them, Drake."

"She thought Jackson Pollock was an actor."

"Oh."

"And Salvador Dali was a pop band."

James chuckled into his whiskey before taking a large gulp and smacking his lips. "Welcome to LA," he said, waving his arms with a flourish as if he were a ringmaster in a circus.

Welcome to LA. I found myself gazing across the ballroom to where Satsumi was floating her way back through the crowd.

James seemed to read the envy on my face. "Are you even ready to settle down?"

"I don't know." I tore my gaze away from her. Dr. Tao's words echoed in my mind again. *Slow down. Take some time off. Spend time with the ones you love.*

"Marriage might do you good. I thoroughly recommend it. Even Clooney got married."

"Find me another Satsumi and I might consider it."

As Satsumi approached us, her sweetheart face smiling and radiant, her eyes only on James, he slipped a card into my hand and whispered, "Let's talk."

Chapter Six

Drake

I held the black matte business card in my fingers and stared at the crisp, stylish silver font.

GW Agency
Exclusive & priceless imports

Underneath was a number.
A wife.
I could procure a wife. One like Satsumi, polite, reserved and completely un-LA. Together we would produce a son or daughter, I didn't mind which. I'd have a family. I'd have an heir. Someone to groom in my shoes, someone to pass the company on to when I…
Something tightened in the pit of my belly.

Yes, this was a plan that could work.

I needed a wife. One that I didn't love. Nor her love me. Look how well *love* worked out for my parents.

No, my marriage needed to be ordered, efficient and productive. No mess. No emotions. A perfect business arrangement where both parties won and a productive synergy was created.

Using the GW Agency to arrange a wife would be perfect. Absolutely perfect.

Why were my nerves tangling?

My eyes flicked to the door to my office even though I knew it was locked. Sam was somewhere outside holding all my calls and keeping back the tidal wave of people who all wanted their pound of flesh from me.

I loosened my tie, which felt like a noose, as the ringback tone sounded in my ear. I wouldn't even be entertaining such a ridiculous thought if it wasn't for Dr. Tao and his fucking—

A clear, sweet voice filled my ear. "Good afternoon. How may I direct your call?"

"My name is…Pierson." I don't know why the fuck I used my father's first name. "Pierson White. I was referred by a client of yours…James Edward Firestone."

"Wonderful, Mr. White. Let me transfer you to Ms. Isabelle Taylor, our company founder and CEO. She handles all new customer inquiries personally."

I was placed on hold, the soft violins playing Mozart's Für Elise lulling me into a half-daydream. What the fuck was I doing? Shopping for a wife? I was rich enough that I didn't need to do it this way.

But the thought of navigating the Los Angeles dating pool made my head throb. God forbid the female public knew that Drake Blackwell was looking for a wife. That would be the equivalent of spilling blood in a sea of piranhas.

James was right. This method was precise, discreet and convenient, and if I could secure myself my very own Satsumi, marriage wouldn't be too hard to endure, would it?

The music in my ear halted. A female voice spoke—rich, luscious, with more than a hint of naughty. The kind of voice that made any man stiffen a little. "This is Isabelle Taylor. Thank you for waiting."

I made my decision right there. "I'm interested in using your service to find a...permanent companion."

"Excellent."

"I have standards."

"So do we."

"I want the best. Money is no object."

"And I shall personally select your shortlist once I know what will suit you."

"I want her to be—"

Her thick, rich laughter cut me off. "That's not how I work. We'll talk and I'll ask questions."

"It would be easier if I told you what I wanted."

"It has been my considerable experience that most men don't know what they want. I don't presume to challenge how you run Blackwell Industries. Let me do my job, Mr. Blackwell."

I stiffened. "That's not the name I gave you."

"I had your phone number traced." She paused. "What? You think I don't run background checks on everyone we deal with? As of this moment I know more about you than your doctor. How is Dr. Tao?"

I should have her hunted down.

Despite her blatant invasion of my privacy I found myself grinning. It took a lot to impress me. She had done it. I repressed the urge to inquire about *her* marital status. "Ms. Taylor—"

"Please, call me Isabelle."

"Isabelle, you're hired."

Even through the phone I sensed her smiling. "I thought so."

Chapter Seven

Drake

A few days later Sam stuck her blonde head in through my office door. Colleagues of mine always assumed I was fucking my assistant. She was attractive in an LA way: tanned and blonde, a standard beauty. I didn't get to where I was by being stupid or following my dick. I don't fuck around where I work.

I hired Sam because she was clever. Clever and very, very cunning. Many a time I needed information about what a competitor was doing that no amount of money could squeeze out. Sam was able to extract that information with a hair flick and a flash of leg. She was completely loyal to me. After all these years together, I had learned to trust her.

"Drake, there's a courier here with a package."

"Tell him to leave it at your desk."

"He won't." I could hear the annoyance in her voice telling me that she tried that already. "He refuses to leave it with anyone except for you and he won't go away until he delivers it." She screwed up her nose. "He smells funny."

I laughed. "You're mad because he won't bend to your will."

Sam made a face at me.

"Where is the package from?"

"A company called GW Agency?"

I froze. It was from Isabelle. "Send him in."

"Drake—"

"It's not a bomb. It's not anthrax. Send him in."

She stared at me. I knew she wanted more information on the GW Agency. I wasn't going to give her any. I also knew that the first thing she would do after sending the courier in was to look them up online. She could try. I already had. She would find nothing except for a website as simple and nondescript as their business card.

As the uniformed courier stepped up to my desk, I pushed aside the papers in front of me, starting to run red with my corrections. I grabbed a dark fountain pen. "Where do I sign?"

"You don't." The courier, a clean-shaven youth who looked more like a bouncer than a messenger, held out a machine about the size of a card reader with a shiny square screen in the center. "I'll need your right thumb and forefinger."

"Excuse me?"

"Your fingerprints."

I blinked. "Are you serious?"

"No fingerprints. No match. No delivery." He spoke with a calmness that relayed to me that this wasn't the first time he had to explain the deal to a surprised customer.

Ms. Taylor had my fingerprints now, did she? This made me even more impressed than before. And uncomfortable.

Isabelle Taylor was not someone to be trifled with.

I pressed my thumb and forefinger onto the screen. I was rewarded with two green ticks and a thin package about the size of a slim booklet. It itched under my fingers as the courier guy took his sweet-ass time repacking his machine in his backpack. *Come on. Why can't he do all that outside?* Finally, he saluted me goodbye and left my office.

I tore open the package. Inside was a slim silver tablet. I turned it on, tapping my fingers on my desk as I waited for it to load.

The screen lit up, *GW Agency* scripted across the center in silver lettering. There was a single file named Open Me.

Here we go down the fucking rabbit hole.

I pressed the file and the program launched.

Welcome Mr. Blackwell
Please tap to continue to your personalized catalog

I stabbed my finger to the screen. Four portraits in color laid out in a two-by-two grid appeared. Four faces. No names. Just the letters W through Z underneath them. My eyes darted from W to X to Y…

They were all beautiful. Indeed, Ms. Taylor only selected beautiful girls. There was something about this one…the one labeled X. There was something in her eyes. Something that held mine. Like two black holes drawing me in. While the other three girls smiled with their perfect teeth, this one's smile was serious and reserved. I sensed something deeper behind her expression. Something… complex.

It was like looking upon the face of the Mona Lisa. I was drawn in, not really knowing how or why. *Tell me, what's the sadness behind your smile?*

I spotted the text along the bottom.

Please tap on the individual photo to learn more about each candidate.

My eyes flicked back to the girl with the Mona Lisa smile. I didn't need to know anything more about her.

My phone rang. I picked it up without taking my eyes off the lovely X. "Yes?"

"Mr. Blackwell." I recognized Isabelle Taylor's distinct voice right away. "I trust you've received my package."

"I'm looking at it right now."

"Excellent. I would tell you to sleep on it but if I know you at all, I believe you've already made your decision."

I traced my finger across the face on my screen. "I want X."

"Excellent choice. Now if you—"

"I want to know her name," I interrupted, still staring into X's silent eyes. I needed a name to go with this face. *A name. Give me her name.* Like knowing her name would make her mine already.

"I'm afraid I can't do that."

"What?" I finally tore my eyes off X. Nobody said no to me. Nobody. I opened my mouth to yell when Isabelle spoke.

"Mr. Blackwell. I'm sure you understand what a sensitive matter this is. Protecting the privacy of my girls is as important as protecting your privacy. I'm sure you, of all people, would understand that. Only once the papers have been drawn up and signed will her name be released to you. You'll see all you need to know about your future fiancée in her dossier."

My fiancée. Something kicked in my chest.

Fear reached out through me like a clawing hand, trying to take back what I was about to do. I should pick one of the other girls, one who I wasn't so damn drawn to. It would be less complicated that way. Less chance of any complicated...*feelings* arising.

I almost snorted at my own silly thoughts. I was Drake Blackwell. If anyone knew how to keep their emotions in check, it was me.

"Fine," I said. "Send the papers through."

"Excellent. Congratulations on your engagement, Mr. Blackwell."

I hung up and traced my finger across her face again. Until then, my mysterious X.

Chapter Eight

Noriko

Several weeks later...

Most women faced their first day of marriage with an anxious, giddy excitement. I only felt trepidation scurrying around the insides of my body like a swarm of ants. I was the *only* passenger in my new husband's private plane.

Jesus Christ. I had never even been out of the country before...

Now I was hundreds of miles in the air, rocketing at incomprehensible speeds towards Los Angeles where my husband lived.

My *husband*.

I tried to make myself comfortable but the leather seat I was sitting in was too soft. I smiled nervously at the flight attendant—donned in a smart navy uniform, "Drake Industries" emblazoned across her pocket—and accepted her offer of a flute of champagne, something she called Moët, even though I was still too young to legally drink, both in the country I left and the country I'm headed to.

A private plane.

My own flight attendant.

Champagne.

I could have choked on my own disbelief. There was no point in even trying to pretend that I belonged among such blatant, outrageous luxury such as this. I took a huge gulp, my first sip of champagne, to steady my nerves and coughed as bubbles went up my nose, the fruity taste slightly sharp on my tongue.

Oh my God. I wasn't cut out for this.

What I wouldn't give to be back home in our simple house, us three girls all crowded on a single futon bed under a single blanket as father read out from his favorite novels. A pang of homesickness ripped through me followed by an aching longing to be back at my papa's side.

For my last night in Japan, I lay beside my father on his hospital bed in Kyoto, the closest city to our village. He was going into his first round of radiation tomorrow.

I'd already signed the contracts. No backing out now. Tomorrow I would be carried away to a new life.

My father gazed at me with such despair, his chocolate eyes glossy and wet. "Hime," his voice broke, "please don't do this. You don't have to marry that man for money."

"Your treatments..."

"I'd give up these treatments, surgery, everything. Just...don't go. Please, hime."

"No," I said, my voice coming out hard to counter how soft I was feeling, the backs of my eyes pricking. "I won't have you die. Not while I still can do something."

"My hime."

"I'll come back, Father, I promise." I lowered my voice so that the bodyguards outside wouldn't hear and report back to my new husband, excitement and hope filling my hushed tone. "I found a loophole. I can leave him and still keep the money. You focus on getting well and I'll come home."

"What? Is that legal?"

"He had it written into the contract. I'll be back in one year. I promise."

The tiny plane shuddered as we hit a patch of turbulence. I squeezed my eyes shut as the tears threatened to fall. I would not cry. I would not.

My thoughts turned to the secret package in the bag at my feet, the bag I refused to let anyone else touch. The way I would guarantee this loophole.

A sliver of guilt embedded under my skin. It was... deceitful, I know. But I promised Papa that I'd come back to him. My family needs me more than this stranger does.

What kind of man *buys* himself a wife?

I was surprised when Isabelle called me to tell me that he had singled me out. She showed me my new husband's clean criminal record and assured me that he was well-respected in his community, that I would be well taken care of.

It didn't matter how well taken care of I'd be. I wouldn't stay past a year. I wasn't the wife for him. I wasn't supposed to be anyone's wife.

I squeezed my eyes shut. I missed my family with a soul-deep ache already. They were the ground beneath my feet, the path the sun made across the sky, the predictable ebb and flow of the moon. Now I was on my own, a tiny boat in the midst of an unknown sea.

One year.

Four seasons.

Thirteen cycles of the moon.

I was already counting it down.

The plane landed in a private terminal at LAX, the Los Angeles International Airport. The captain announced right before we landed that it was almost nine p.m. The weather was gorgeous, a beautiful spring night to welcome me to California. As soon as the door opened a man rushed in. He performed my TSA clearance right there on the plane. My brand new passport was stamped and returned to me, the man bowing as he backed out of the plane.

I took the short flight of steps down to the lit tarmac, my feet wobbly even in my simple Mary Jane shoes. My hands were clammy as I gripped the balustrade, my precious bag over my shoulder, the only thing I brought with me.

A black stretch limousine waited for me at the foot of the stairs, a limo with tinted windows so I couldn't see in. My head spun. I'd only ever seen one of those in movies. Now I was going to be in one and it was going to take me to my new husband.

My new husband.

Just breathe, Noriko. Breathe.

A driver opened the passenger door for me. "Welcome to Los Angeles, Mrs. Blackwell," he said as he stared forward like an army officer at attention.

It took me a second for my brain to register that he was talking to *me*. I was Mrs. Blackwell. The name hung about me like an ill-fitting coat.

I guessed him to be in his early thirties, wearing a full suit and cap even in this heat, showing only his beautiful chocolate hands and twinkling brown eyes despite a serious set to his mouth.

"Sorry, I don't know your name."

The driver blinked at me a few times, clearing his throat before saying, "Um, Felipe, ma'am."

I smiled and bowed, a habit. "Thank you, Felipe."

Felipe frowned at me for a second before he bowed awkwardly back. Was it just me or did I detect a slight blush to the dear man's cheeks?

I clambered most ungracefully into the limo, my skirt flouncing ungracefully around me before realizing, to my horror, there was someone already inside. I thought it was empty. It was not.

A broad-shouldered man in a dark three-piece suit sat facing me in the center of the wide leather seat, one arm outstretched across the back, a gold watch glinting on his wrist. This must be Mr. Blackwell.

"Well, this is certainly an attractive option." His voice was deep and boomed around the cabin, resonating with power, causing a rush of goose pimples across my skin.

Was he calling *me* an attractive option? I wasn't sure whether to be insulted or flattered. I mean, really, what did I expect from a man who "bought" his wife?

"I don't care what Deloitte thinks. He's not the one with his ass on the line."

I frowned. Then spotted the small clip in one of his ears. He was talking on the phone.

The car door slammed shut, cutting out the wind and rest of the world. I was left alone with him—my husband—the silence between his words deafening.

I placed my bag beside me and leaned back in the seat as the limo pulled away. The seat was firm, the new leather smell still clinging to the overly air-conditioned air. The rest of the interior was wood paneling and chrome.

Outside, through the heavily tinted windows, street lights rolled by as we passed out of the airport. He continued to talk on the phone, his voice animated. I had time to study him.

He wore a tailored suit, open at the jacket to reveal a dark gray shirt underneath with a matching silver tie. I didn't know clothing brands well, but I could tell it was tailored, clinging to his wide shoulders. He had midnight hair that appeared disheveled, as if he'd run his hand through it a few times, a wide jaw that kept clenching in the pauses between his sentences. His cocoa eyes were hooded, deep-set. He stared right at me, a slight smirk pulling at his perfectly sculpted lips.

I was taught never to stare back; especially to a man I should be showing respect. I'd never been one for conforming. Besides, I couldn't seem to help it. He was mesmerizing, dark power rolling off him. This was a man who knew what he wanted and would not take no for an answer. This was a man who demanded the world and always got it.

As I watched him watching me, something foreign pricked at my lower belly.

"Call Mike. Ask him where that damn preliminary report for the Forrest takeover is. If he doesn't have it ready, fire him."

I frowned. We'd been driving for at least twenty minutes now. Was he going to talk on the phone the whole damn time?

I crossed my arms over my chest. His eyes dropped blatantly and unapologetically to my breasts. Small yet perky, they were being pushed together by my crossed arms. Something flashed in his eyes. My chest tingled at his heavy assessment. I wanted to uncross my arms but I was paralyzed, like he'd somehow pinned me with his stare.

"I don't give a shit. It was supposed to be on my desk by the end of last fucking week."

His cursing caused me to flinch. I'd never heard such blatant swearing. So foul. So rude. The prickling in my stomach turned...warm. Liquid. How strange.

His eyes snapped back up to my face, his voice growing more aggressive at the unknown person on the other end of the line.

I wanted to snatch that stupid earpiece from his head.

Instead I pressed my lips together, tilted my head and raised an eyebrow at him. I knew I shouldn't be displaying my disapproval—this was not the action of a *good wife*—but dammit I was jet-lagged, I hadn't slept for almost twenty-four hours, and I'd ripped myself from my family and married a stranger who lived on the other side of the world. It might as well have been another planet.

I felt like I might cry. I didn't want to. Especially not in front of *him*.

Instead I channeled all of this flurry of emotion into my glare.

"Roger, I'm going to have to call you back." Without waiting a beat, he ripped the earpiece from his ear and tossed it onto the seat beside him.

His eyes assessed me, his perfect lips pulling into a half smile. I was sure my hair was a mess and I had bags under my eyes, but he seemed pleased with what he saw.

"Noriko." His voice moving across my name was seductive like bassy jazz.

"Mr. Blackwell, I presume," I replied in English.

"Please, call me Drake."

"Drake," I repeated his name. It felt like power on my tongue. "How good of you to notice I'm here," I couldn't help adding.

His dark eyebrow raised in response. "I came to pick you up at the airport."

"Well, that certainly compensates for not being present at our *wedding ceremony*." My lips dripped with sarcasm.

"I had something important arise that I had to deal with personally."

"So you sent an assistant in your place to pretend to be you in front of the celebrant?"

He gave me an odd look, like he was trying to decipher me. I imagined that it wasn't often that he was met with such blatant disapproval. "My signature on the contracts are real, I can assure you."

I almost snorted. "Will you be sending an assistant to perform in your place on our wedding night?"

His lip twitched. Now I'd really pissed him off. "*That* will not be happening," he growled out between clenched teeth.

"Good to know that you will be present for *some* things."

"I'm a very busy and important man," he said as if he was telling me a truth, not bragging at all.

"And so humble, too."

"I'm just telling you how it is."

"I'm not surprised you think so. You seem to surround yourself with people who are all at your beck and call."

His lip lifted into a scowl. "Do you even know how much that telephone call that I *cut off for you* was making me? Do you even realize how much my time is worth?"

"I'm sure you're going to tell me," I muttered.

His eyes flared. Before I could react, he reached across the divide with his long arms, grabbing me by the wrist. His grip was firm, on the verge of hurting me, but not quite. He yanked me across to where he was sitting. I landed, sprawled across his lap. I let out a yelp and stiffened.

He was close. He radiated heat even through his suit; I felt my own body growing hot. He smelled heavenly, of expensive cologne, fresh and clean like a sea breeze.

His lips brushed my cheek sending tingles down through my body. *What the hell is this?*

"Forty thousand a minute," he said in a low voice, his deep tone vibrating through my cheekbone. "So the fact that I've taken time out of my evening to meet you at the airport and am choosing to sit here arguing with you, my dear wife, instead of on the phone with my CFO is a big fucking deal."

Forty thousand dollars a minute.

I didn't know what the equivalent was in yen so I had no idea what that meant.

He narrowed his eyes at me. "You don't seem impressed."

"Sorry, should I swoon or giggle insipidly at you?"

"I expected some sort of positive reaction, especially considering the conditions I pulled you out of."

I stiffened. *The conditions...?* As if my family lived in squalor. Okay, we were poor, but there was nothing that we wanted for. "Typical western man," I spat out, "you think money is the answer to all your problems."

He leaned in closer. I could feel the heat of his breath on my ear. "Money *is* the answer to all problems. Your father's problems were certainly solved with my money."

I sucked in a breath. He knew about my father? Of course he did. He probably had me researched before he picked me out. "Well," I said, "I hope you get your money's worth."

"I'm beginning to wonder about that," he muttered under his breath. "I thought you Japanese girls were supposed to be demure or something."

...you Japanese girls...

I should slap him.

But my stomach jumbled with fear, overriding my anger. *I thought you Japanese girls were supposed to be demure or something.*

I had almost given myself away. Mr. Blackwell thought he was getting a perfect little Japanese girl as a wife. Instead he got me. If I wasn't careful, Mr. Blackwell would annul the marriage and take back the money meant for my father.

I couldn't let that happen.

I forced myself to bow my head. "Mr. Blackwell, I do apologize. I didn't sleep on the plane. I'm delirious. I don't know what I'm saying."

"Lying to me already, dear wife?" His voice was a mixture of amusement and suspicion.

I tensed. Finally, I had the sense to remain silent. I'd already pushed my luck tonight. I knew I wasn't making a good impression on my new husband. I was surprised he didn't throw me out of the moving car. Damned if I was going to let him get away with treating me like another one of his staff.

"What?" He shot me a smug look. "Nothing snarky to say back?"

I shook my head slightly, remembering myself. I was here to be his good wife. In exchange for the money my father needed for his experimental treatment.

I caught him studying my features, my eyes, my cheekbones and finally my lips. "As least you are beautiful to look at."

I couldn't believe it. "Well done."

"For what?"

"You've managed to compliment me and insult me all in the same breath. You certainly are talented."

His stare grew intense and heated. Something shivered down my spine. "In so many ways, wife, as I'm sure you'll soon find out." He grabbed my hips, tugging me closer. I gasped when the sensitive place between my legs pressed up against the *hardness* in his pants.

Oh. My. God.

Suddenly I was all too conscious of how I was sitting, straddling his strong thighs. Suddenly I was all too aware of how a man and a woman fitted. A liquid heat began to pool in my lower half.

His head dipped to my neck. He nipped at my ear, sending a rush trickling down my body. "I could take you right here in this limo."

I flinched. He wouldn't, would he? "B-But you won't."

"Won't I?"

A shudder ran through me. I didn't know whether it was from fear or anticipation. Could it be…both?

Mr. Blackwell grasped my chin forcing me to look at him. This close I could see the flecks of lighter brown and amber in his chocolate eyes. "I own you, little girl. I can do what I like with you…" his fingers trailed down my neck, over one of my breasts, "…with this body."

Real fear gripped me. I couldn't move. He was right. I was alone in this new country. I knew no one. I had no money. My family could not help me. No one could.

Chapter Nine

Noriko

"Don't look so scared, little wife," Mr. Blackwell said with a smirk. "Whatever I plan to do to you, I guarantee you'll enjoy it."

I had never in my life met such an arrogant…impossible, frustrating man. A blatant, aggressive man. He was looking at me like…like he wanted to devour me. I couldn't look away. I couldn't move. His eyes roaming over my face, his fingers gripping my hips, he looked ready to lunge for me.

I wasn't sure I could stop him if he did.

The car halted. I blinked, the spell broken. "We're here. Home sweet home." I detected a hint of bitterness in his voice. "My plans for you must wait, I'm afraid." He slid me off his lap just before the driver opened the door.

"Oh." Underneath this rush of relief, I was… disappointed. Why the hell would I be disappointed?

As I sat there trying to figure out what was going on with me, Drake shuffled smoothly along the seat, picking up his earpiece as he went. He slid out of the car with all the grace of a panther.

I sat there like a mute.

Mr. Blackwell stuck his head back into the car. "You coming?"

Yes. Right.

I grabbed my bag and scrambled out of the car, tripping on the door edge. A hand grasped mine to steady me. It took me a second to realize it was Mr. Blackwell who stopped me from falling.

Our eyes met.

Something…strange went through me.

Something that felt very much like…hope.

He pulled his hand away and cleared his throat. I felt the ghost of his touch still on me.

"Welcome to Blackwell Manor."

I turned to get a look at my new home. And almost fell over.

The mansion was so large I had to turn my head from side to side and up and down to take it all in. The two projecting wings of the house disappeared out of view. Three stories of gray stone slabs with a dark, steeply pitched roof, spires and turrets, ornamental sculptures and gargoyles edging the thing like morbid cake decorations. It sat like an alien among the peaceful trees surrounding it.

Holy hell.

"You're gawking," Drake said in my ear.

I flinched away from him, snapping my mouth shut, angry at myself for losing my senses. "I am not."

"Try to keep up, will you, dear?" Drake strode up the steps to the front door, his long legs consuming the distance. I followed.

As we approached the entry door, it swung open. A woman, perhaps in her forties, her back board-straight and her chin held high, held the door open. A conservative black dress sat on her plump form and a pristine white apron circled her waist. I couldn't help wonder how she kept it so clean.

He motioned for me to enter first. At least he wasn't *entirely* devoid of manners.

"Oh, there she is. Master Drake," the woman said, "she's a beauty."

"Too bad about her attitude," I heard him mutter.

Scratch that. My new husband was utterly mannerless.

"Mrs. Blackwell," the woman said, her voice shaking with obvious pleasure. She took my hand in both of hers. I was treated to such an enthusiastic handshake that it rattled the teeth in my skull. "We are *so* pleased you've arrived."

"Thank you."

"I'm Loretta, the head housekeeper here. If you need anything, anything at all, or have any problems, come straight to me."

"I'm Noriko. Thank you. Again."

"Welcome home."

Home. This word echoed around in my head like a gong. *This isn't my home.* I didn't say my thoughts out aloud.

"You don't take your shoes off here," Mr. Blackwell said as I prepared to slip off my flats. "We don't do that here."

I blinked a few times, trying to let this different custom sink into my body. It felt so...*wrong* to walk inside with outside shoes on. So dirty. "Are you sure?"

"Are you questioning me again?"

I fought back an urge to roll my eyes.

My low-heeled shoes echoed as I stepped into the marble of the entryway. I had to hold back my gasp as I raised my eyes up.

Inside, the mansion was even more obscene. The entryway soared up all three stories, held in place by thick marble pillars, a gliding stairway wrapping around it, hallways branching out from it. The door clicked shut behind us, leaving me in the white-cold glare of the huge crystal chandelier hanging down like a wasp's nest.

"There's no need for you to come with us," Mr. Blackwell said, addressing Loretta. He turned towards me, a wolfish glint in his eye. "I can show Mrs. Blackwell to her room."

From the trap into the spider's lair.

He reached out. "Let me take your bag—"

"No," I snatched the bag out of Mr. Blackwell's reach.

His eyes narrowed imperceptibly at me.

Shit. If he opened my bag. If he looked inside…

I was screwed.

My father was dead.

"I mean," I fumbled, "that I wouldn't want to trouble you."

"It would be no trouble."

"Please," I said quietly, honesty making my voice quiver, "let me hang on to the one thing left that is mine."

After a pause, he nodded. "As you wish."

He led me up the staircase. I tried not to gape down the wide hallways that reached out like arms, solid walls lined with paintings or sculpture pieces. This place felt like a museum. Not a home. I was sure to get lost here.

I felt lost already.

"The top floor is reserved for our private suites," Mr. Blackwell said as we reached the top floor. "We're in the east wing." He stopped suddenly, turning to stare at me. "You are not to go in the west wing."

I glanced up the other hallway shrouded in darkness. Every other hallway had been lit except this one. I took a step towards it. "What's in the west wing?"

Mr. Blackwell snatched my arm, yanking me back. "I just told you never to step foot in there."

"Why—?"

"Never. Do you hear me?" A darkness glittered under the surface of his eyes.

He was hiding something in the west wing. Curiosity flared in my gut like embers catching on paper.

I could do nothing but nod.

He let go of me so suddenly I almost stumbled back, before turning and continuing on. I chanced a glance back at the dark hallway behind me before I followed him.

Chapter Ten

Noriko

We reached a western-style door that swung on the hinges rather than a sliding one like the ones we had at home, painted pale blue, trimmed with cream. It wasn't exactly the kind of bedroom door I imagined Mr. Blackwell would have.

He pushed it open for me. "After you, Mrs. Blackwell."

"It's surprising how you can be crude and yet, such a gentleman."

"Why? Because I'm holding the door open for you?" He smirked at me as I passed him. "I just want to check out your ass."

I gaped, my cheeks growing hot. If I wasn't so distracted by the monstrous room I'd walked into, I'd turn and glare at him.

The room was massive, the high ceilings making it seem cave-like, the walls painted cream and pale blue to match the door. Elegantly shaped yet uncomfortable-looking cream chairs were arranged in the center of the room around a low glass table. More tables were dotted about with large empty Japanese vases placed upon them.

In the center of the room I spun around, frowning. Something vital was missing. "Where's the bed?" I asked. I thought westerners slept on soft, high mattresses. Maybe I was wrong.

"This is your formal living area. Your bedroom is through your private living area." He walked to another door and pushed it open.

Another living area?

It turned out that his "bedroom" wasn't a room. It was a collection of several large rooms: two living areas, a guest bathroom, and a bedroom with a private en suite. His bedroom alone was bigger than the house that fit my parents and us three children. My stomach panged, craving to feel the warmth of my home again. Our house was barely big enough to contain us and our lives, but it was cozy and full of love.

One year. You just have to survive here for one year.

I stared at the giant bed in the middle of the bedroom sitting on a raised wooden frame, covered in sheets and pillows the same pale blue as the door. "Which side should I take?"

"Whichever side you want."

"Which side is yours?"

"I don't sleep here."

"You...don't?"

It hit me. This room was too feminine to be Mr. Blackwell's. There were no personal items anywhere, no photos, no books on the bedside table. My own husband wouldn't be sharing this room with me. I would be sleeping here alone. I didn't know whether to sag with relief or cry.

My parents shared a room. But they were also in love.

"Well, not *that* kind of sleeping..." Mr. Blackwell closed the distance between us, his eyes simmering with hunger.

I stepped back, evading him. "I'd like to call my father. To tell him I've arrived safely."

Mr. Blackwell frowned, obviously annoyed that I'd evaded his touch. "That won't be necessary. I'll have him alerted."

"*I* want to speak to him."

"I don't think that's a good idea, do you?"

"What? Why not?"

"It'll make you homesick."

"You would deny me to speak to my own father? My sisters?" Disbelief and horror welled up in me, damming up my voice box so it was hard to speak. Who did I marry? A beautiful yet cold monster.

"You're not theirs anymore. You're mine."

"*Yours?*" I hissed, my composure cracking. "You might have bought this body, Mr. Blackwell, but I will *never* be *yours*."

His eyes narrowed. "Your attitude will determine whether your life here is heaven or hell. I suggest you rethink it."

Anger seeped from me. He was right. I needed him on my side. I grabbed at his shirt, my desperation overruling me. "One call. Please."

"I'm not discussing this anymore." He peeled my hands off him. "The answer is no."

Something broke in me.

"You can't... You..." Before I could stop it, tears blurred my eyes. He let go of me. I sank to my knees on the plush carpet and sobbed as my heart finally fell apart. After holding it all in. Of trying to be strong.

In the edges of my grief, I heard him back away from me, across the carpet. The door opened and shut. Asshole. Here I was having a breakdown and he just…left.

The room felt swollen. The chasm yawned open all around me.

I was all alone. So very alone.

Chapter Eleven

Drake

Noriko was…crying.

I couldn't move from shock as she slid to the floor, rocking on her heels, her cries tearing through me. I wanted to make her stop. I wanted… I wanted her to stop hurting. I didn't know how…

My hands flinched at my sides, helplessness tearing through me.

Well done, Drake. You had her for less than an hour and you broke her. This is why you can't have nice things.

She sounded exactly like…Mama.

And you're just like him, a voice hissed in my head.

I… I stumbled back from the tiny sobbing creature on the floor. No. I'm not like him. I'm not…

Before I knew what I was doing, I was racing out of Noriko's bedroom. I didn't stop until I pushed my way out into the corridor, almost barreling over Loretta in the process.

"Oh, Mr. Blackwell I was coming to— What's wrong?"

I shook my head, guilt burning my lungs. Damn her. Damn Noriko. "I didn't do anything," I snapped. "She just started crying."

"Oh, poor thing." Loretta's face pulled into one of concern. She gazed past my shoulder to Noriko's door. "It's understandable. She's had to leave her family behind, now she's all alone in a foreign country. All these new people."

I stiffened. Perhaps I was a bit hard on her. No one ever thought to take it easy on *me*.

I waved at the mocking silent door. "Go in there and…" I had no damn idea what. I let out a growl. "Just make it better. Make *her* better."

I spun on my heel and strode away, ignoring the look of disapproval on Loretta's face. The knot that'd wound around my heart tightened, my complete ineffectiveness and helplessness like a noose around my throat.

For the first time in a long time, I felt totally and utterly out of my depths.

Chapter Twelve

Noriko

What had I done?

I'm sorry Papa, I don't think I can stay here.

I must. I could not live if my papa died. This experimental treatment was his only hope. I couldn't live with myself if I killed him.

My sacrifice ripped me apart. I gripped the carpet of my gilded prison as my heart spilled out onto the floor. I cried for my father who I could not reach, I cried for this unfair life, and I cried, selfishly, for myself. For marrying such a horrible, horrible man.

Between my cries, I heard the door open and shut. I felt soft, fleshy arms pulling me to my feet and motioning me towards the bed. "There you go, love." It was Loretta, her voice soothing. "Get into bed." She pulled the covers over me, clothes, bag and all.

She sat beside me and brushed my hair. I couldn't help but lean into her touch. She smelled like lavender and baby powder. It had been almost three years since I felt a gentle hand stroking my hair back. God, I miss Mama so much. If only she were here.

"There now," Loretta shushed softly at me. "Everything's going to be alright."

No, it's not. "I hate him."

"He's a good man. You'll see."

"He's a beast of a man," I sobbed.

"He's a bit rough around the edges, yes. A good wife will help smooth those edges out."

"He won't let me call my father."

Loretta sighed. "He's got his ways, Mr. Blackwell does. If he refused you to speak to him, it's only because he thinks it's best."

I gritted my teeth. Best for *who*? Best for him?

Loretta smiled. "You just need to give him a chance."

"He doesn't deserve it."

"Everyone deserves a chance."

I was running out of tears. They were drying on my cheeks. I folded my arms across my chest and stared off at one of the walls. Mr. Blackwell did not deserve anything from me.

She patted my arm. "You have a choice, dear, on who you want Drake Blackwell to be. I've seen him tear down his opponents without mercy like they were made of paper. But if you are loyal to him, if you stand by his side, he can give you the world."

"I don't want the world. I want my papa. I want my family."

"There comes a time in every girl's life when she needs to leave her family and start one of her own."

I clutched my bag closer to me. Loretta didn't know my plan. No one did. Mr. Blackwell would never be my family. I would never have his child. *Never*.

"When Mr. Blackwell told me he was going to take a wife, I was tickled pink. It's about time that man settled down and had a family of his own. Lord knows, he deserves it after…" She cleared her throat.

I sat up in bed. What was she about to say? After what?

"It'll be good to have children here again. It always cheers up the house when they're around." Loretta smiled, her face lighting up, her eyes going misty.

I sniffed and wiped my cheeks, my curiosity overriding my sadness for now. "How long have you been here?"

"Since Mr. Blackwell was born. I was his nanny. When he stopped needing a nanny, well, I suppose I never left."

I let out a snort. "I don't think he ever stopped needing a nanny."

Loretta laughed and rubbed my arms. "I'm glad you're here, Noriko. You're a breath of fresh air. I daresay, you might be the best thing to ever happen to him."

Not likely.

I said nothing. No need to burst Loretta's bubble or make her suspicious that my intention was to leave after one year.

She patted my arm. "You take tonight to be sad, girl. I'll have someone come up with some dinner."

"But, Mr. Blackwell…" It was our wedding night. The memory of his devilish eyes brimming with some kind of primal hunger sent a shiver through my spine.

"I'll handle him, don't you worry." She moved towards my bedroom door.

"Loretta?" I called before she disappeared out my door.

"Yes, dear?"

"Thank you."

She nodded before she left me alone with my swirling thoughts.

Chapter Thirteen

Drake

I paced my study, a mahogany and forest-green room off to the side of my bedroom.

Damn her. Purchasing a wife was supposed to be easy. Uncomplicated. Unemotional.

I ran my hands through my hair, my eyes falling to the nearly full bottle of 55-year-old Macallan scotch I kept in a glass cabinet for when I had guests. I never drank. Alcohol numbed my brain and I needed my brain to run my business properly. Tonight, the scotch seemed to call to me.

Just one drink wouldn't be so bad, would it?

Someone knocked on my door, breaking that line of thought. Loretta entered the room, shutting the door behind her.

"Well?" I demanded.

"She's calmed down. For now."

"About damn time."

"Mr. Blackwell…" From the tone of Loretta's voice, I could hear a lecture coming on.

I cut her off at the pass. "She's disrespectful."

"Good. Someone needs to stand up to you."

"She's obstinate."

"She's practically still a child."

"I should send her back."

Loretta sucked in a breath. "Your wife is not a manufactured good you can send back for a refund. She's a girl, a woman, a human being. Be kind to her."

"I am kind." I made her my wife, didn't I? I opened up my home to her. All her needs and whims would be forever taken care of. Women all over the country would kill to be in her position.

"You need to be gentle."

"I am gentle," I roared. The irony slapped me in the face. I let out a sigh and sank into an armchair. "I will try to be gentle."

"Good. Even though I'm sure you're eager to, um, get acquainted with her, I think it's best if you leave her be at least for tonight."

"*What?*" My dirty thoughts about *getting acquainted* with her that had been swimming around in my head since she tumbled into the limo all came back to me. Her slim body looked breakable. Her perky breasts looked like they'd fit in my mouth. And God, her lips did this pouty thing when she spoke back to me in that insolent tone that made me want to bend her over my knee and—

Hot desire coursed through my body. She was my wife. I *wanted* her. I wanted to possess her. I wanted her belly swollen with my child. With my heir.

She was mine. Her body was mine. There was no way I was leaving her alone for another second.

I stood and strode towards the door. Loretta blocked my path, jamming her fists onto her hips. "Drake Blackwell. I will not have you going in there and forcing yourself on that poor girl while she's in a vulnerable state."

I growled at Loretta, but I didn't push her aside. I muttered something about obstinate women under my breath. Loretta glared back at me, not a shred of fear in her eyes. It reminded me of another obstinate woman…

"You have one chance to get her to like you, perhaps even care about you. She could make you happy, Drake, if you let her."

She could make you happy. Loretta's words poked at something long lain dormant deep inside me.

"Are you listening to me?" she said. "Don't. Fuck. It up."

I lifted the corner of my lip. "Loretta, I'm shocked. Did you just swear?" I didn't think I'd heard her swear. Ever.

She straightened up, brushing down the front of her uniform, the one she insisted on wearing. "I don't remember saying anything of the sort." She gave me the eye. "Promise me that you'll let her be until she's ready."

I growled. Suddenly I felt like a teenager who'd been told by his mother that he couldn't have his girlfriend sleep over. Except that I was her boss, a fucking grown man, and the woman in question was my damn wife.

"Drake…" Loretta's voice was a warning.

I let out a sigh. "Fine. I won't *get acquainted* with her. Just for tonight."

"For the week."

The week? "Not a fucking chance."

"Language."

"Two nights."

"A week."

I gritted my teeth so hard my jaw ached. "Three nights and that's my final offer."

Loretta's eyes narrowed. "I'll agree to four nights. Only if you promise to use that time to get to know her."

What? "That wasn't part of the deal."

Loretta frowned. "You shouldn't have to be coerced into getting to know your wife better."

"There's one way I want to get to know her better but you've put a stop to that for four nights. You might as well have cut off my balls."

"Language, Drake Blackwell." Loretta's mouth pressed into a stern line. "You are not too old to set over my knee, you know?"

Dear God, I bet she would, too. I let out a huff, feeling beaten already. "What do you suggest I do with her, then?"

"What do you usually do with your dates?"

I raised an eyebrow at Loretta. *Come on, really?*

"Oh dear Lord." She shook her head, mumbling a small prayer under her breath. "Take her out somewhere nice. Have dinner with her. Talk to her."

"About what? I doubt she has a mind for business."

Loretta threw her hands up in the air. "There are a lot of things to talk about that are *not* work-related."

"Like what?"

"I'm sure you'll think of something."

Damn obstinate woman. "Fine. I'll take her somewhere. Nice. And talk…about something."

Loretta let out a long-suffering sigh. "You drive a hard bargain, Mr. Blackwell. Four nights it is and you'll get to know her *outside* the bedroom. She'll need a new dress to wear. Or ten. And shoes, women love shoes."

I blanched. "I know nothing about dresses or shoes."

She laughed. "Lord, no, Mr. Blackwell. You're not going to take the girl shopping. I am." She held out her hand. "Your credit card, please."

It was only after she'd snatched the card I'd somehow found myself holding out for her that I wondered how the hell I got here.

Loretta beamed at me, clearly pleased. Somehow, I'd been duped. I suspected this was her plan all along.

Chapter Fourteen

Noriko

True to Loretta's word, Mr. Blackwell did not darken my door that night. I spent my wedding night alone.

I slept fitfully. Partly because I was in a strange bed, in a strange room, in a strange house, but mostly because I spent the night in battle, fighting off the fierce pangs of homesickness that rose inside me. I missed the way Papa would say goodnight with a kiss to my forehead. I missed the sound of my sisters' deep breathing around me, the rustle of blankets as my sisters moved in their dreams.

I gave up on sleep early the next morning, drawn from my room in search of food. Mr. Blackwell had already left for work. My family and I always ate meals together. Didn't they do that here, too? Obviously not.

After the strangest breakfast I'd ever had—no rice, but eggs, bacon, bread and formed pieces of meat and spices called sausages—I was left to my own devices.

There was nothing left for me to do except to explore the mansion. I opened each door, peering around, listening for footsteps. I might live here for now, but this was not *my* house any more than I was a real wife.

There were an extraordinary number of guest bedrooms and sitting rooms, each one looking cluttered with all this elaborate furniture, fringed lamps, vases and fuss. I repressed a shudder as I peered into yet another large, overly dressed room. I missed the simplicity of my real home, the clean lines, the sparse furniture. How could Mr. Blackwell stand to live here?

There was also a library, a ballroom, a spa with treatment rooms and a sauna, and a twelve-seat cinema. Did Mr. Blackwell even use any of these rooms? When was he ever home to use any of it?

Finally, I built up the courage to explore my new husband's bedroom. You could tell a lot about a person from their bedroom and despite being determined to hate him, I couldn't help my curiosity.

Who was the man I married?

I'd casually asked Loretta at breakfast which room was his and she told me it was one door down from mine. I stood before it, a deep green door, and tested his door handle. Finding it unlocked, I slipped inside.

Mr. Blackwell's bedroom was palatial and deeply masculine, dominated by dark wood and black leather, each piece of furniture thick and boldly designed. As I walked deeper into his lair I smelled a hint of something spicy in the air.

In one corner were floor-to-ceiling bookcases and a huge green chair near the window. I ran my fingers across the titles as I peered at his library collection. His fiction collection was small: only a few works of Poe, Hemingway, and Steinbeck. It seemed he read mostly nonfiction: business books, of course, marketing, finance, economics. He also had a number of books on leadership.

He was obviously very good at what he did. He cared about his work. His success was hard-earned by the looks of all this self-education and obvious by his fine home, his private jet, all his staff. A thread of admiration weaved through me. I promptly got annoyed at myself and stuffed that admiration aside.

There were two doors that led off his bedroom. My bare feet sank into the rich blue carpet as I crossed his room. I tried the first door. It was his bathroom. The spicy scent I detected earlier must be an aftershave; I could smell it more strongly in here. There was a shower that could easily fit four people and a large built-in spa bath encased in marble.

The second door wouldn't open, even as I shook and rattled the handle. It was definitely locked. I stared at the simple door of polished wood, looking different from all the rest of the decorated doors. What was in there? Why was it locked?

Perhaps he kept a secret ex-wife in there?

The source of a magical curse?

A dead body?

Stop being so dramatic, Noriko.

I spun to face the room. For some reason, his king-sized bed, covered in a dark gray spread, beckoned to me. I walked right up to it and stared at the expanse. This was where my husband slept. I guessed the right side was his, a book sitting on the bedside table. I fingered the soft cotton and glanced at the door. Did I dare?

He was my husband. I would be well acquainted with this bed soon enough. Better get used to it.

I crawled into the middle of the mattress and lay down on the cool sheets, staring up at the ceiling. I got a flash of his chiseled, smirking face raised over me. I could almost feel the press of his hardness against me, again causing a heated shiver to run down my body. I sat upright, startled at the force of my body's reaction.

How…strange. I didn't even *like* my husband.

How was it possible for my body to react in one way while my mind revolted?

He had almost kissed me in the limo. I could see that he wanted to before we were interrupted. I found my fingers rising to press at my lips.

I'd been kissed before by a boy from school. He was handsome and I liked him well enough, but I had felt more curiosity when I allowed him to lean in and press his thin, cold lips against mine.

Mr. Blackwell's lips were perfectly formed, precisely defined, and plump with blood so that I couldn't imagine they'd ever be cold. *Just his heart, then.*

What would Mr. Blackwell's mouth feel like against mine? How would he kiss?

I brushed these thoughts aside, trying to calm my nerves. I would find out soon enough. Too soon. Not soon enough.

Something struck me about his room. I stared across to his bedside table, to the mantle above his fireplace, then to the other flat surfaces. That was odd. Where were his photos? In fact, I didn't remember seeing a single photo frame in any of the rooms so far.

The few surfaces of my family home were covered in photos of us all; my parents' wedding, the birth of all us children, and us three girls, in diapers, in school uniforms, dressed in costumes for school plays…

Where were the photos of him and his family? Where were the photos of his parents?

That night, I felt immense relief when Mr. Blackwell didn't arrive for dinner. I sat in the formal dining room in one of the high-backed gold and red cushioned chairs, the only person at the rectangular heavy wooden dining table that stretched across the entire room. The staff door swung open. I straightened up in my chair.

It wasn't Loretta. But another housemaid, a pretty girl of ebony skin, thick hair the color of ravens tied back at her neck into a prim bun. She kept her eyes on the crowded silver tray she was holding, a slight crease between her brows indicating her concentration. I fought the urge to get out of my chair and help her.

She set her silver tray down on the serving table at the side of the room. In front of me, she placed a silver platter domed with a silver lid. When she pulled the silver dome off, steam rushed up around me. The scent of vegetables and garlic filled my nose, clearing to reveal a bowl of thick vegetable soup garnished with a sprig of parsley. My stomach rumbled.

She set down a small plate of warm brown bread beside it.

"Hi," I said to her before she could move away again.

She blinked at me. "Are you speaking to me?"

As if there was anyone else to talk to. "Yes," I said, giving her a warm smile. "What's your name?"

She paused before she answered, folding her hands across her stomach. "It's Celeste, ma'am."

Ma'am. As if I was as old as her mother. I guessed she would be a few years older than *me*.

"How long have you worked here, Celeste?"

She flinched as if I'd slapped her. "Did I do something wrong?"

"What? No. Why would you think that?"

"All these questions…"

"I want to get to know you a little bit. I mean, we're both living here."

She gazed at me for a few moments, the whites showing around her inky irises, before she quickly lowered her lashes. "I'm sorry. I must get back to work." She snatched up her tray from the side table before hurrying out of the room.

"I just want to talk," I called out.

But Celeste was gone.

Back home, dinner would be a rowdy affair; steam and chatter would fill the warm kitchen as we all helped to chop the food and set the table. The four of us would eat elbow to elbow around our small, low table, laughing or sharing stories about our day.

In Blackwell Manor, I sat eating dinner with only the stiff-lipped portraits around the room for company, my spoon hitting the side of my soup bowl and echoing off the high ornate ceilings. I felt like an insignificant flake at the bottom of a bowl, my loneliness poised to swallow me up. I eyed the empty place at the head of the table to my right. Maybe eating with Mr. Blackwell wouldn't be so bad.

After dinner, I returned to my room, a restlessness itching under my skin. When I reached the top of the stairs, my eyes fell upon the darkened west wing. It was the only place in this mansion I hadn't explored. Curiosity tickled my insides. What could Mr. Blackwell possibly be hiding there?

"You are never to go in the west wing. Never. Do you hear me?"

Defiance flared in me. Who does he think he is dictating where I may go and who I might speak to? He refused to let me talk to my father, I refuse to obey his orders.

If he found out that I disobeyed his orders, he'd be furious.

He'd never find out. Who was around to tell him?

I took a confident step towards the darkened corridor.

My step faltered as I moved into the edge of the dim space. I remembered the flash of pain that went across his face when he eyed the west wing. Whatever secrets the west wing was hiding, they were painful for him. I chewed my lip, the defiance buried underneath a rising pity, a knowing curiosity. Perhaps if I understood him more...?

Would it hurt if I looked?

I glanced around again. I couldn't see anyone. I couldn't hear anyone coming.

Just one minute. Just one quick look. I let the darkness swallow me as I hurried farther into the dim hallway, my heart beating faster in my chest.

What would I find?

Discovering the first door was unlocked, I pushed it open and slipped inside.

Chapter Fifteen

Noriko

The room was large and dim, dust motes floating in the only strip of dying sunlight coming in from between the dark drapes drawn across the windows. I tried the light switch. Nothing happened. I waited a moment for my eyes to adjust. Slowly the darkness receded.

I was standing in a bedroom, the walls a pastel yellow and cream, the bed unmade, the sheets yellowing with age, a moth-eaten bathrobe draped across the back of a chair. Dust was everywhere, thick like a gray cloth on the furniture on the window sill.

I let out a long breath, almost laughing with relief. It was an unused bedroom. Why was Mr. Blackwell insistent that I never come here?

I walked over to the window and peered out. The view looked across the other side of the back gardens, across a thick carpet of trees and bushes.

I wandered over to the dresser where glass perfume atomizers sat among beads and lipsticks. This was a woman's bedroom. Mr. Blackwell's mother? His sister? A chill seemed to go through the air. Where was she now? Why isn't she living here?

I picked up a gold photo frame, so thick with dust I couldn't see the photo. I wiped a streak across the glass with my thumb, clumps of gray molting off. I revealed a boy, perhaps eleven or twelve, with dark hair and dark eyes. He had such a solemn look on his face as he stared at the camera, the weight of the world already bearing down on his shoulders.

This was Mr. Blackwell, I realized. This was him as a boy.

Oh, sweet boy. Why are you sad?
Who's in the photo with you?

I reached with my thumb again to—

Someone grabbed my arm and I let out a scream, dropping the frame with a clatter to the dresser.

"What are you doing here?" Mr. Blackwell was glaring at me, his grip so firm it bordered on pain. He must have just gotten home.

"Y-You're hurting me."

"I told you never to come here." His voice was cold. Hard as steel.

I gulped back my excuses. I disobeyed him because I wanted to get him back for refusing me any contact with my family. And because I was curious.

"Whose room is this?" I asked, trying to remain brave but failing.

His jaw twitched. "Get out."

"It's just a room. What's wrong with it?"

"What's wrong with it?" His voice rose in volume and pitch. "What's fucking wrong with it?" He grabbed the back of my neck and marched me to a spot near the bed. He forced my head down as if I was a naughty puppy who peed on the carpet. "You nosy girl. You want to know the truth?"

I was too terrified to move or say anything. I stared at the faded cream fibers, now gray with dust. I couldn't see anything different about this spot.

"Do you?"

I nodded my head as much as I could with his thick hand still wrapped around the back.

Mr. Blackwell leaned right in, his hot breath in my ear. "My mother died right here."

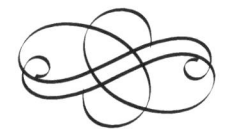

Chapter Sixteen

Drake

Noriko gasped. Her eyes snapped to mine. Bending over her like this, I realized in that second how close we were. I could smell her sweet, subtle scent of cherry blossoms.

Her eyes widened. "Oh, Drake…" Her voice swelled with sadness. I couldn't stand to hear it. I couldn't stand to see the pity in her eyes. It was like a blast of heat on this icebox of a heart in my chest, stinging as it thawed. I shoved her away from me. She almost tripped but managed to right herself.

"Get out," I growled. For a second she remained on the spot, her eyes still gouging me with pity. "Get the fuck out!" I roared.

She yelped as if I'd slapped her. She sprinted out of the room as I stood there shaking, chest heaving. The door slammed close behind her and some of the tension slid out of me.

I shouldn't have yelled at her. I was just so mad. She disobeyed me. Nobody disobeyed me. Nobody ever dared to.

"Mom?" I called as I knocked on her bedroom door. She didn't respond. I sighed. "Louisa?"

God.

This room.

So many ghosts here.

Why did Noriko have to come here? Why did she have to go stirring up old memories? I felt them clawing for me, trying to pull me under. The room swiveled around me.

I pushed open her door, slowly. In the gap of her bedroom door I saw part of a leg hanging off her bed. Her bare leg was skinny. Too skinny. I needed to get her to eat something. I pushed her door open wider and moved slowly to her side so as not to scare her. "Louisa?"

No movement.

I shook her.

She let out a small moan.

"You need to eat something. Please."

Her eyes fluttered open, revealing her startling blue eyes. For a moment she stared back at me with such clarity in her irises that I felt a surge of hope. Maybe she'd come back to me. "You're such a good boy, Drakey," she said, her voice cracked and her breath sour. The whites of her eyes were bloodshot and yellowed.

Stay.

Instead they unfocused and glossed over.

I rubbed my face, trying to shove *her* back down in my mind.

I let my ghosts chase me out of the room, slamming the door firmly behind me.

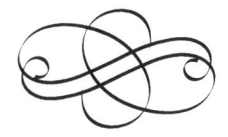

Chapter Seventeen

Noriko

All the next day I berated myself for going into the west wing. The way Mr. Blackwell's voice cracked, the slip of pain showing from under his façade. The memory stabbed me. I thought of the unloved and lonely state of his mother's bedroom, imagining this was what the inside of his heart looked like.

My cheeks burned with shame, my chest felt heavy with swollen pity. Thankfully, he never seemed to be around so I didn't have to face him. Maybe I could avoid him for the entire year?

When I entered the dining room that night, I found I wasn't the only one eating.

Mr. Blackwell was there, sitting at the head of the table, staring at his phone. He was actually home early enough for dinner.

My nerves began to jumble. Was he still angry? Should I say something? Should I apologize for what I did yesterday?

He looked up from his phone and our eyes met. His dark stare pinned me to the spot and I had to fight to breathe. My insides twisted into a bunch. I didn't want to fight with him. I didn't want him to hate me.

"Are you going to stand there all damn night?"

Well…that broke the spell. "As charming as usual, I see," I muttered.

I sat in the chair to his side feeling very underdressed in my cream linen pants and plain white blouse. Drake was still in his suit, albeit his jacket had been discarded and his sleeves rolled up. My eyes drew to his thick, tanned forearms. What would he feel like under my fingers? Shocked at my thought, I forced my eyes up.

He had slight bags under his eyes. Did he not sleep very well last night? His hair fell across his forehead. I found myself wanting to push it out of his beautiful eyes, his lashes so thick and dark, almost pretty, I found myself envious of them.

I licked my lips, which had gone dry. I wanted to tell him how sorry I was. For invading his privacy yesterday by going into the west wing. I wanted to reach out, place my fingers on the back of his large hand and tell him that I understood what it was like to lose a mother.

The words wouldn't come out.

"What?" he snapped.

I blinked. "What?"

"You're staring."

My cheeks burned. "No, I'm not."

His eyes narrowed. He didn't believe me.

Celeste entered to place our plates on the table, and we were forced into silence. After she set everything out, she bobbed and hurried out. Drake and I were left alone in this vast dining room.

Mr. Blackwell attacked his food with all the enthusiasm of a man who hadn't eaten in weeks. He cut his steak and vegetables into enormous pieces before they disappeared into his mouth. The silence, broken only by the clattering of cutlery, felt like it was swallowing both of us. How could I feel even lonelier with him here? I didn't know whether to laugh or cry. I was so desperate for some human interaction, I was prepared to overlook his coldness, to try to make the best of this marriage.

I cleared my throat. "So…how was your day?"

He looked up from his meal and swallowed. "Excuse me?"

"Well, we are married. We could try to be…civil to each other. Talk."

"About what?"

I sighed. "I don't know. How was work?"

He frowned. "Busy." He shoved a piece of meat into his mouth.

O-kay. "Are you working on anything in particular?" I suddenly realized that I had absolutely no idea what my husband actually did for work.

"Of course."

I repressed a groan. This was like pulling teeth. At home it was a fight to get a word in edgewise. "What are you working on exactly?"

He wiped his mouth with a napkin, his brows creased. "Why can't we just eat?"

I sagged into my chair, tears pricking at my eyes, loneliness suffocating me like a too-tight blanket. I didn't know why I thought that he and I could talk, to be civil at least? I was married—married—to a man who wanted nothing to do with me, whose staff were too terrified to speak to me. I was all alone on the other side of the world in this huge house with no one. I picked at my vegetables, leaving my steak. I wasn't used to eating so much meat. Besides, I'd lost my appetite.

I realized from the lack of cutlery noise that he hadn't resumed eating. I looked up to find him staring at me. A strange prickle of awareness skittered across my skin.

"What is it?" I asked, my voice a little too eager.

He didn't answer.

Hope sank like a stone inside me. I turned back to my plate, trying to ignore the sadness welling up inside me.

When I was younger, I wasn't sure I would ever get married. If I did, it'd have to be with someone…special. Blame my parents for setting a high standard with their deep, true love. I told myself I'd never settle for anything less than what my parents had. And now…

It's only for one year, Noriko. It's not a real marriage.

"I…" Mr. Blackwell began.

I glanced up.

"I'm not used to…" He waved his hand around.

"Being polite?"

He scowled. "Dinner."

I raised an eyebrow. "You're not used to having dinner?"

"Dinner *with* someone. Here. I mean."

"Oh."

"I spend so much time talking…at work…"

"Okay." I focused back on my plate.

He still didn't pick up his knife and fork again. "I don't know what you want me to say." He was still staring at me, confusion written across his face. I almost felt sorry for him.

I shrugged. "I don't know anything about you."

"I'm 34, CEO and majority shareholder of Blackwell Industries, worth billions, graduated summa cum laude from

Harvard Business School and with an MBA from Yale, third richest man in America. What else do you need to know?"

I laughed. "You forgot to tell me your driver's license number and shoe size."

He frowned. "Why do I get the feeling that you're mocking me?"

I shook my head and smiled. "What do you like to do when you're not working?"

His lips pressed into a line before he answered. "If I'm not working, I'm either sleeping or eating."

Was he serious? "That sounds…"

"Busy."

"I was going to say…sad."

His eyes widened in surprise before narrowing. "It's not sad."

"There's more to life than work."

His frown turned into a glare. He opened his perfectly formed mouth, most likely to argue with me again. Before he could, his phone began to ring. He snapped his mouth shut, staring at his phone screen before scowling. "Excuse me. I have to take this." He grabbed his phone as he stood. "I am not sad."

I said nothing.

He scowled and grunted *what?* into the phone, still glaring at me.

He left the room and I turned back to my dinner.

I didn't see him for the rest of the night.

Pity was quickly replacing the hatred in my heart. Drake Blackwell might have money, but he was the poorest man I'd ever met.

Chapter Eighteen

Noriko

I started out of my sleep by the sound of someone opening my bedroom door. I sat up with a gasp, clutching the blankets around me.

Mr. Blackwell was standing at the entrance to my bedroom, already dressed for work in yet another beautifully tailored suit, this time a dusty charcoal. For a second I thought he was a dream. Then I squinted at the curtains, the backs of my eyes feeling gritty as sandpaper. Dawn light trickled in. Enough so I could see him snapping his mouth shut and frowning at me.

"Why the fuck are you sleeping on the floor?"

I looked down. Oh, right. I threw the blankets down on the floor last night and made myself a makeshift futon. I lifted my chin and tried to look as dignified as possible while wearing Tweety Bird pajamas. "I'm not used to sleeping on a western mattress. It's too soft."

His frown deepened. "Why didn't you say something?"

"Oh. I didn't want to bother anyone."

He let out a noise that sounded halfway between a snort and a sigh. "Noriko, you are my wife. These people are being paid to see to your needs and wants."

I pouted. "I'm not comfortable with the idea of anyone waiting on me hand and foot."

"Get used to it," he snapped. "There's a charity auction tonight. You're coming with me."

"Please."

"What?" he barked.

"Generally, when you invite someone to come with you somewhere, you say please."

The crease between his brows deepened. "I'm not asking you, I'm telling you." He slammed the door shut behind him.

I rolled my eyes. "*I'm not asking you, I'm telling you,*" I repeated in a mocking tone. "Come here. Do that. Sit. Stay. Roll over."

The door opened again. He pushed his scowling face back in.

Shit. Did he hear me? I sank back, feeling guilty as hell at being caught.

"Be ready at eight." He disappeared again.

I poked my tongue out at the door.

He stuck his head back in through the door. "And Loretta will be taking you out today to find something suitable to wear." The door shut.

I grabbed my pillow and glared at the entrance to my bedroom, daring him to come in one more time.

Lucky for him, he didn't.

I hated this. My feet hurt. My stomach was growling. I didn't care about *tonight*.

Loretta and I were in the exclusive VIP section of a department store, a huge room filled with cream couches and soft lighting, a pretty set of screens in one corner to allow me some privacy as I changed. Loretta was sitting on the couch, as happy as could be, sipping on the champagne which our own personal shopper poured for us.

I hadn't been allowed to touch mine. I'd had to try on stupid dresses for what felt like weeks.

Before this, we spent hours in some fancy beauty salon with a team of strangers dying, snipping, plucking, waxing me, all in the name of beauty. All the while I grumbled away. Men didn't have to go through this crap. Why do we?

Beauty *sucks*.

In the VIP room of a fancy clothing store, I stepped out from behind the screen in a pale green flowing dress. Both Loretta and the sales lady, a stylish blond wearing too much pink for a girl over the age of ten, made the appropriate gushing and cooing noises.

"I think Mr. Blackwell will really like this one," the sales lady said.

"I think," I muttered under my breath, "Mr. Blackwell should shove this dress up his uptight ass—"

"Noriko!" A slight crease appeared between Loretta's brows, the only sign that she heard me. "Don't you think Mr. Blackwell will be impressed?"

"Why should I care about impressing him? He's *such* an ass."

The sales lady gasped. Loretta merely snorted. "Tell me something I don't already know, dear."

I crossed my arms over my chest. "I want to go home."

"We'll be on our way back as soon as we pick out the right dress for tonight."

"Not to Blackwell Manor." I squeezed my eyes shut as the backs of them prickled. "My real home."

Loretta let out a sigh. "Sarah," that must've been the sales lady's name, "can you leave us for the moment?"

Sarah's eyes widened. I saw a flash of disappointment flit across her face. She probably wanted more dirt on why the newlywed Mr. and Mrs. Blackwell were already fighting.

She slowly exited the room, sticking her head back in through the door to say, "I'll be out here if you need me."

I felt a stab of regret. I shouldn't be airing my dirty laundry in public. This was not the actions of a good wife. None of my actions so far had been those of a good wife. There was something about Mr. Drake Blackwell that made me so…so…damn frustrated.

Loretta placed her champagne on the table and walked towards me. "What's the matter? Mr. Blackwell has opened his beautiful home to you, he's been generous enough to bankroll today's shopping spree, which, mind you, most women would be grateful for."

Well, didn't I feel like a brat. "He's rude. He won't let me speak to my family. He hardly speaks to *me*. Unless he's yelling at me or ordering me around."

She sighed. "Mr. Blackwell has never had a wife before. He doesn't know how to treat you. His parents…" Loretta's mouth tugged down at the corners, "God bless their souls, were the worst example of married people to stain this earth."

The worst kind of parents…? Jesus, how bad were they? I chewed my lip. "What happened with his parents?"

Loretta inhaled deeply. "I suppose I wouldn't be telling you anything you can't find out from the gossip papers and the internet."

I hadn't even thought about looking Mr. Blackwell up. Perhaps I should? Not that I had access to a computer. I couldn't find one at the manor.

Loretta took my arm and we sat on the couch together. She glanced at the door before speaking in a low tone. "Drake's mother was only seventeen when she married Drake's father. He was fourteen years older than her. His family didn't approve. He had come from a long line of wealth, you see. She hadn't. He cut off his whole family for her. He loved her and, apparently, she loved his money."

I blanched. This story sounded too similar to Mr. Blackwell and *me*.

She continued, "She fell pregnant almost immediately. It was a difficult pregnancy. I don't think it helped that Mr. Blackwell moved to another bedroom during her pregnancy. He said that it was because she kept him up all night. Truth was, she became difficult to deal with, constantly needy and overly-emotional at everything.

"Soon after Drake was born Mrs. Blackwell began an affair...a torrid, passionate affair. One of her husband's business associates. They met at a party of her husband's. Ironic, really."

"Did Mr. Blackwell know?"

"Of course he did. Everyone knew. You couldn't be in the same room as Mrs. Blackwell and her lover without knowing something was going on. Mr. Blackwell couldn't stop her. He never really could control her. He loved her, so he wouldn't leave her."

"Why didn't she leave him?"

"Drake. She had a pre-nup. If she left him, she got nothing and she lost her son. Mr. Blackwell would get full custody. I heard him threaten her several times that if she left him, he would ruin her. Eventually Mrs. Blackwell and her lover ended things."

"What happened to him? The lover, I mean."

"He used to be a very wealthy man. Not as wealthy as Mr. Blackwell Senior, but he still controlled a company and had a small fortune. After Mr. Blackwell found out about the affair he made sure that no one would ever hire the man or do business with him in this country again. He went bankrupt, had to sell everything. Business-wise, he was finished. Rumor has it that he moved to Australia to start over, got himself an Australian wife, eventually had children of his own."

"How tragic."

"The real tragedy is how it affected Drake. He was a young boy by then. After her affair ended, Mrs. Blackwell became more and more distant towards Drake. She refused to spend time with him, refused to play with him. I think she blamed him for the loss of her lover and of the life she could have had. Although she loved him, he became another shackle on her ankle."

"And Mr. Blackwell Senior?"

"He started drinking. He would fly into the most furious rage. He'd start yelling at her, breaking furniture. Eventually, he hit her. His drinking got worse. He began to beat her regularly."

"Oh God." My heart twisted.

"Her affair turned into affairs and packets of white powder to escape from him."

"What a horrible, horrible man."

"She became as bad as he was. Drake was a young teen when their relationship became violent. She would pull Drake right into the middle of all their fights, trying to manipulate him against his father. Sometimes she would use Drake as a shield, hiding behind him when Mr. Blackwell was violent. Mr. Blackwell would get so drunk he couldn't tell who he was hitting."

Oh God. My heart ached. How could a mother do that to her son? How could a father?

"They were a perfect and terrible example of a violent, destructive cycle," Loretta said quietly.

I began to understand a little more about the man I'd married. No wonder he felt that it was safer to "buy" a wife than to risk falling in love. Look at the examples his parents made of themselves. No wonder he was guarded and distant with me. He thought marriage was a game of power.

I thought back to the photo of a young Drake that I found in his mother's room yesterday with a new understanding.

The armor around my heart began to loosen, the muscle swelling with empathy and sorrow. *Oh, Drake, you poor thing.*

"Noriko," Loretta said, "I can see you're homesick. But for whatever reasons, you agreed to marry him. You agreed to be his for life."

I flinched as I remembered my promise to my father. I wasn't here for life, just for one year.

"Please, give him a chance. Show him another way. Don't leave him cursed by his past."

"I—"

"The ones who push love away the hardest are the ones who need it the most. You're the only one who has a chance to get through to him." Loretta gripped my hands, her eyes boring into mine, begging me to save her master. A man, I realized, she saw like a son.

I remembered the flash of deep pain Drake let slip through his eyes when he caught me in his mother's room.

I lost my mother. I could at least understand that pain.

I nodded, my throat in a knot. "You're right. I will try." I really vowed to.

At least, for the year that I was here.

I walked behind the screen again and slipped out of the dress I was wearing. I fingered through the rack of dresses back there, grabbing one that stood out to me, before pulling it over my head and zipping it up.

I smoothed it down and stepped out from behind the screen. "What do you think?"

Loretta sucked in a gasp. "Oh, Noriko." She clasped her hands to her chest. "Yes, this is the one."

Chapter Nineteen

Drake

"Where is she?" I paced the marble foyer in front of the front door.

The limo had been waiting outside for almost twenty minutes. I had been waiting for ten. I couldn't remember the last time I had to *wait* for anyone.

"Give her a few more minutes," Loretta said. "Be patient."

I let out a frustrated growl. "If she's not down in two minutes—" I cut off as Noriko appeared at the top of the stairs.

Oh my God.

She took my breath away. Literally.

Her hair was up in an artful bun, exposing her slender neck. Her dress was a sumptuous red, the color of ripe cherries, with sheer lace sleeves to the wrist, hugging her body in all the right places, making her breasts look fuller, cinching in her tiny waist and skimming over her hips to stop mid-thigh, revealing lean and shapely legs. Her mouth had been painted in the same deep red color as the dress, those piercing eyes darkened.

I tugged at my collar—damn thing's too tight—and stared as she stepped down the staircase, as graceful as a swan, to stand before me. She was wearing heels, I realized, when the top of her head came up to my mouth.

"Oh, Noriko, you look lovely," Loretta exclaimed beside me. She smacked my arm with the back of hers. "Doesn't she look lovely?"

"I…um, yes," I mumbled. Mumbled? Drake Blackwell didn't mumble. What the hell had happened to my voice?

"Thank you," Noriko said. She was watching me with suspicion, a small frown between her brows.

I slapped myself internally and cleared my throat. "I'm afraid Loretta is wrong. You are *beyond* lovely, Noriko. You're an absolute vision." There, better. I didn't know where the charming and suave Drake Blackwell went for those few seconds but he was back now.

Her features relaxed. She granted me a smile, a wide, genuine smile that reached the corners of her exotic eyes. Something kicked inside my chest. I found myself smiling back.

This was my wife.

My wife.

My chest filled with pride. "Shall we?" I held open the door for her.

She walked past me. I choked on my tongue. Holy shit. Her dress was backless.

Backless.

It looked decent from the front. But the back—Jesus Christ, *the back*—was open all the way from the base of her neck, dropping in a low scoop to the top of her ass. I could see the beginning of those curves and the hint of her... Was she even wearing panties?

"You can't go out like that," I spluttered.

Noriko spun to face me.

"Drake Blackwell," Loretta admonished. "Don't be stupid."

"She's practically naked," I ground out between my teeth.

Loretta let out a snort.

Noriko glared at me. "If you'd prefer I can go and change. I think I have something that would be suitable for a nun to wear."

"That would be preferable."

"Noriko, you will do no such thing," Loretta exclaimed. "Mr. Blackwell, you are being ridiculous. She looks stunning, you said it yourself."

Noriko and I stood there glaring at each other. Neither of us prepared to budge. Neither of us prepared to speak over Loretta either.

"Go on, you two. You're going to be late for your function." Loretta practically shoved Noriko out the front door and into the waiting limo.

Before I could climb in after her, Loretta grabbed my arm. "You behave yourself, Drake Blackwell," she hissed under her breath. "Don't you dare say anything more about that dress. Don't make me ashamed of you."

"Yes, ma'am," I muttered, as I wondered exactly which one of us was the boss.

Chapter Twenty

Noriko

In the limo I sat, legs crossed and arms across my body, as Mr. Blackwell sat on the other side of the limo from me.

I was absolutely fuming.

And totally confused.

When I reached the top of the stairs and my eyes met his, I swear I saw awe. There was a look upon his face. *That look.* The way that Papa used to look at Mama like she was the most beautiful creature to ever grace this Earth. I felt, for the first time in my life, like a woman. Like a beautiful, cherished woman.

He had to go ruin it all by snapping at me over the dress. I shifted in my seat. What the hell was wrong with this dress anyway? I thought it looked good on me. So did Loretta. Didn't he think so?

Why did I care what he thought?

I don't care.

Mr. Blackwell cleared his throat. "I may have…possibly…maybe…overreacted. Back there. About the dress, I mean."

I glanced over to him. He looked so uncomfortable, tugging at his collar, fidgeting with his diamond cufflinks, I almost laughed. "Go on."

"You do look…nice. The dress is…fine."

I raised an eyebrow. "Are you apologizing?"

He let out a huff. "It appears so."

"Haven't done it in a while, have you?"

"No," slid out between his teeth.

I softened my voice. "People usually use the words 'I'm' and 'sorry' when they're apologizing."

He glared at me.

I smiled at him, batting my lashes.

He sighed. "Fine. I'm…sorry." He almost sounded like he was in pain.

"Apology accepted." I uncrossed my arms and smoothed down my dress over my thighs. It wasn't lost on me that his eyes followed my hands, a hungry glint growing in them. Suddenly it felt very, very hot in here.

It didn't help that I suddenly heard the limo doors locking. The partition between us and Felipe was fully raised. It was just me and Mr. Blackwell here in this limo cabin that felt like it was getting smaller and smaller by the second.

Jeez, it was…stuffy in here.

The gates of the manor opened. Under the flood of spotlights, I spotted a crowd of people on the other side, some of them with placards. I could hear chanting muffled through the windows but I couldn't make out what they were saying. Who were these people?

We drove through the gates, the security guards coming out of their box and walking behind us, I assumed to make sure these people didn't get into the grounds. I gasped and sank back into the seat as the crowd swarmed us, their faces and hands banging on the car, pressing against the glass. They looked angry.

Mr. Blackwell slid into the seat beside me, startling me as he wrapped an arm around my shoulders. "Don't worry," he said softly in my ear. "They can't get in."

I released the breath I didn't realize I was holding. His presence was like a hot balm against my side. His nearness calmed me. God, he smelled good. A fresh cologne like a sea breeze. I couldn't help but press closer.

The driver proceeded slowly until we broke away from the crowd. I looked back at them through the window, their chanting fading. I noticed that Mr. Blackwell had not loosened his hold on me. Even stranger, I didn't seem to mind it. "Who are those people?"

"They're protesters."

I shot Drake a look. "Really? I couldn't figure that one out for myself. What are they protesting against?"

"Me."

"Against *you*? I can't see how *you* could anger anyone enough to garner protesters." My words were sarcastic but my tone was light.

"You looking to join them, wife?"

"Join them? Heavens, no." I grinned. "I thought I should lead them."

He rewarded me with a laugh. There you go. I made the beast laugh. Perhaps there's hope for him yet. "They're not protesting me, per se. Well, I suppose they are in a way. They're really protesting what I'm doing."

"Cutting down the rainforest? Dropping trash into the oceans? Eating little children?"

He clasped his chest with his free hand. "It hurts to see how little you think of me."

I laughed. "Go on. What did you do that is worth protesting?"

He paused, unable to meet my gaze. He obviously didn't want to say.

"Don't worry," I said lightly. "I can't possibly think any worse of you."

He snorted. "That's one small mercy."

I nudged him. "Come on, Drake. I'm supposed to be your wife. If you can't talk to me, who can you talk to?"

He let out a huff. "Fine. I set up and funded a country-wide charity for women who were raped and need emergency abortions."

It was like he'd slapped me.

I couldn't even speak. Had I completely misjudged him? Could this beast actually have some good in him? Did he possess warmth underneath his cold façade?

I finally found my voice. "That's a wonderful thing you did."

He turned his head to look out the window. "Not everyone thinks so."

I stared at his profile, his jaw twitching as he ground his teeth together. His bad reputation hurt him, despite what he told himself.

I weighed up the many sides of this man that I'd seen these last few days. He refused to let me call my father. But he looked at me sometimes like I was the very moon in the sky. He was rude, crass, and a terrible workaholic. But he was generous and he actually *did* things to make this world a better place.

I got this inexplicable urge to brush aside the hair that had fallen over his forehead. It was like he was two different men. Which one was the truth? *Who are you really, Drake Blackwell?*

Chapter Twenty - One

Noriko

I stared around the cavernous gallery, stark walls painted white to showcase each piece. There were dozens of other people here but we all had our space. "Why are we here, exactly?"

Drake handed me a flute of champagne. "To support the charity." He mentioned earlier that twenty percent of the proceeds of this auction would go to fund heart health research. "Mostly because I want to buy some art."

I fought not to roll my eyes. "I was just thinking that the walls at home are so bare."

Drake let out a laugh. Two for two tonight. I was on a roll. "Come and help me spend my money, dear wife." He placed the tips of his fingers on my bare back and led me through the gallery, pointing out the paintings for auction. I began to relax, enjoying his hypnotic voice as he made his commentary on each piece.

Finally, he directed me to a large painting of lilies on a lake. "And this is a—"

"A Monet." I gasped. "Oh my God. It's a real Monet."

He nodded. "One of his best works, in my opinion. Unfortunately, this painting is only on loan to the gallery and not actually for sale."

I let out a sigh as I took in the smudges of color and dappled light. There was nothing like seeing a Monet in person. It looked like the artist had figured out how to mix sunlight into his paints and danced it across the canvas.

I felt Drake's eyes on me. "You like it?"

"I love Monet's work. Especially the pieces he painted when he was living in Giverny. See," I pointed, "how he focuses on light and color as opposed to shape and lines."

"It truly is exquisite."

I glanced over to him, only to find that he was looking at me. I dropped my arm and folded my hands together in front of me. "You're not looking."

"Yes, I am. Perhaps harder than ever."

I felt myself flushing under his gaze.

"You know about art," he said. "It's refreshing."

I mock gasped. "Why, husband, is that actually a compliment?"

He laughed again, the crinkle around his eyes endearing. "Don't get used to them."

"You know a lot about art as well."

"I'd like to think I'm a connoisseur of beautiful things." The way he was looking at me made me feel like he'd given me another compliment. I blushed and look away. "Did you study art in Japan?" he asked.

"No."

Drake tilted his head. "But that's what you wanted to do."

I nodded, sighing. "I enrolled in international business instead."

"Why?"

I shrugged.

"I see," he said solemnly.

"Do you?"

"As the eldest, especially without any brothers, you are expected to be responsible for your family."

I gaped at him. "I didn't say that."

"You didn't have to." He nodded across the room to someone he must have recognized. "I do business in Japan often, Noriko. I understand the pressures that must have been on you."

It wasn't often I found myself so…easily read. Even stranger, that this rude, cold, arrogant man had been able to do it.

"As my wife, you do not need to do anything you don't want anymore," he said, startling me with his accented Japanese, still managing to make it sound like a melody from his lips.

"You speak Japanese?" I replied. To use my native tongue felt like a gift.

"Only enough to butcher it thoroughly," he said with a smile.

I smiled back. *"I think you speak very well."*

"You're just being kind. Tell me," he said, switching back to English, "why do you love Monet so much?"

I chewed on my lip, wondering how much I should reveal. "I like to think that he can teach us a lot of life through how he views his art."

Drake's stare grew even more intense, like he was studying me. "What, exactly, do you mean by that?"

"Well," I turned to face the painting, feeling like if I held his gaze any longer I might forget how to breathe. "You know he painted the same scenes over and over again, including this one, during different times of day and different seasons. He never got bored of the same scene, because he understood that the difference can be appreciated in even the slightest change of light. He understood that we don't always need *more* or *new*, but to view the same thing with new eyes."

Drake was silent for a pause. "How...insightful."

My eyes couldn't help but draw to him again. He seemed to be searching my face, looking harder than anyone ever has before. I felt naked, raw. Like I had unwrapped my soul and laid it out for him. Before I could change the subject, before I could tear my eyes away, he spoke. "When I'm stuck in a problem," he said, "I like to remember Monet."

I frowned. "How so?"

He walked behind me and placed his hands around my hips. I sucked in a breath as heat radiated through my body from where he touched me.

"What are you doing?"

"Just...go with it." After a pause, he added, "Please?"

He actually *asked* for once. I nodded. I let him gently push me forward until I was inches away from the painting. He stepped in close behind me until his front was flush against my back and his hands slid around my waist.

Oh God, he was so close. So everywhere. His heat, his scent, his presence like fire.

His touch was causing all sorts of strange twists and sparks in my body. What was happening to me?

"What do you see?" he whispered in my ear. Heat cascaded down my body, pooling into a hot cauldron between my legs. My knees trembled. I was glad he was holding me up.

Focus, Noriko.

I took in a shaky breath. "I see..." thick splotches of paint, violent slashes of color, smears, ridges, swipes, dabs. I sucked in a breath as his lips grazed my neck. "Chaos."

Drake lifted me suddenly like I weighed nothing, my heels rising up off the floor. I let out a small yelp and struggled, even as a part of me reveled at being so helpless in his thick arms, thrilled at his obvious strength. He strode back, back, back...until—

"And now?"

I saw...the whole picture.

Drake set me down gently. I could feel the eyes of the patrons around us, some in amusement, others in disapproval. For the first time in my life, I didn't care what anyone else thought.

I slowly turned to face him, my soul light and aching from this realization. Almost toe to toe, I came up to his lips in these heels. I had to tilt my head to look at him. He seemed more stunning than the last time I looked at him. So beautiful it was almost inhuman. "That's brilliant," I said. *You're brilliant.*

Who would have thought that this cold, workaholic bastard could be such a deep thinker. And to love art... Something squeezed in my chest.

His hand came up, his fingers brushing my cheekbones. That one touch had me leaning into his palm. He flinched and his gaze darted to his hand as if he only just realized what he was doing. "You...um, you had an eyelash."

"Sure." I tilted up my chin, offering him...I wasn't sure what.

His fingers grew surer, sliding around to the back of my neck. I held my breath as his eyes dropped to my lips. He leaned in and—

"Drake." A male voice caused us to jolt apart.

A rush of heat rose to my cheeks. If we hadn't been interrupted… My stomach twisted up in knots.

Underneath it, there was a cold trickle of relief.

Don't get too close to your husband, Noriko. You're only his wife for one year.

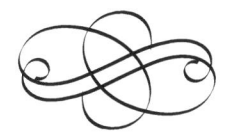

Chapter Twenty - Two

Drake

"Drake." My name broke through my haze.

Noriko jumped back, her cheeks coloring pink. I had been about to lunge for her, her dark eyes, sparkling with life and intelligence, drawing me in. As did her perfect pink mouth like a soft strawberry. I had a feeling that once I tasted her, I was going to end up dragging her back to the house and doing every single dirty thing to her body I'd wanted to do since I set my eyes on her.

Remember your promise to Loretta. You have to give Noriko three more days to settle in before you attack her.

Loretta would have my balls on a plate if I broke my promise. Then she'd serve them to me for dinner. Maybe it was a blessing that I was interrupted.

The periphery around my gaze opened up and the rest

of the world rushed in. I tore my eyes away from my wife and turned to face the intruder. My hackles rose when I saw the smug bastard standing in front of me.

"Jared Wright," I said, biting back my hatred. In so many ways he was my antithesis. Blonde with pale blue eyes, he was an all-American jock if I ever saw one. Even in college he never failed to rub his perfect family and their perfect business in my face.

He was a good-looking fellow, I supposed. If you were into smarmy, arrogant assholes.

Did Noriko think so?

My eyes darted back to her. She was looking at this newcomer with open eyes and a smile on her face. The logical part of my brain reasoned that of course she's smiling, she assumed Jared was my friend. She was being a good wife. The rest of me wanted to kiss that smile off her face. To kiss her so hard that she'd never have smiles for anyone but me.

"Drake Blackwell," Wright said in the same biting tone as mine.

I turned back to Wright, noting how I instinctively moved forward to place myself slightly between him and Noriko. "You have the timing and grace of a plague. Swift, sudden and completely unwanted."

Wright laughed, amusement twinkling in his eyes, my insult rolling off him. "Guilty as charged. I couldn't go a single second longer without meeting this ravishing angel you've somehow managed to convince to come here with you tonight." He turned to Noriko. "Tell me the truth. How much is he paying you?" He laughed out loud at his own lame joke.

I flinched as his words hit home. There was too much truth in what he just said. Noriko was only here because I paid her to be. She was here because she needed money to save her father. Not because she wanted to be. If she looked like she wanted me to kiss her earlier, it was because I was paying her to.

Noriko recovered faster than I did. Her smile broadened but it didn't reach her eyes. "You are a funny man. Did the gallery hire you to entertain us?"

I caught a flash of insult on Wright's face. He didn't like being mistaken for the help. It disappeared behind a charming smile. "Good heavens, you mustn't be from around here if you don't know who I am. Allow me to introduce myself. I'm Jared Henry Wright."

I bit back a growl. Wright was flirting with her.

"Noriko." She held out a slender wrist.

He took her hand. Bending, he put his lips to the back of her hand.

He had his lips on my wife.

My blood sizzled. Outwardly I remained calm.

Jared didn't pull away. In fact, he sniffed her. He *sniffed* her. "My," he said, looking up at her through his lashes, "that's an intoxicating perfume you're wearing."

"Alright, that's enough." I snatched Noriko's hand away from his mouth and pulled her firmly to my side, wrapping my left arm around her shoulders. My right hand gripped into a fisted ball by my side.

Wright chuckled as he straightened. "Very touchy, Drake. You've never been this way around any woman before."

"This isn't *any* woman," I spat out between my teeth, "this is my *wife*."

His eyes widened. He glanced between Noriko and me, a gleam in his eye. I wished to hell I'd said nothing. "So the rumors are true," he said. "America's most wanted bachelor is finally tied down."

"America's most wanted bachelor?" Noriko asked, all innocence.

"Now I *know* you're not from around here," Wright's eyes narrowed. "Japan?"

"Yes."

"How did you two meet?"

Shit. My mind drew a blank. Noriko and I hadn't worked out a "story" for our arranged marriage. We hadn't done anything except argue until tonight.

"Darling, there you are," a female voice called.

I was grateful for the reprieve. Until I saw who it was.

Fuck. My. Life.

Kristie, the one who thought Jackson Pollock was an actor, strutted up to Wright and faced me. As always, her blonde hair was blown out around her face. Her clingy black dress plunged so low I could practically see her belly button. She was the very last woman I dated before Noriko.

"Drake," she said, an edge to her tone, her chin held high. She slid her arm through Wright's elbow and pressed to his side. Trust her to jump straight into the next billionaire's bed.

I nodded but I didn't offer my hand. "Nice to see you again, Kristie."

She managed to make her smile look like a scowl. "I wish I could say the same for you."

Noriko gasped beside me. Japanese culture was endlessly polite, this catty game we played here would be totally foreign to her. I ignored Kristie and turned to address Wright. "Sniffing around my leftovers, I see."

Kristie bristled. I paid her no notice. I had been prepared to be pleasant with her before she threw the first blow.

Noriko tensed at my side. Ah, shit. If only I'd had time to warn her that she'd be facing my ex tonight.

Wright merely laughed, a sly look in his eye. "Lucky me, you always manage to piss off your ex-lovers. Which makes it so easy for me to swoop in and take your secrets.

How did you think I found out that you were working the Mercer deal?"

I bristled. The bastard.

I turned to Kristie, ready to berate her for selling me out. She didn't even have the decency to look guilty. She was glaring at Noriko. "And *who* is this?"

"Get this, Kristie," Wright chuckled as if he was gearing up to tell a joke, "she is Drake's new *wife*."

Kristie's eyes almost popped out of her head. "You're married?"

I sighed. Here we go. "Yes."

Her eyes searched Noriko's hands and found…the ring. A simple white gold wedding band. I never bought Noriko an engagement ring.

Kristie's eyes narrowed, fixing on Noriko. "When did you get married? When did you even meet?" Her eyes swung to me, I could see the calculations going off in her head. It'd only been six weeks since I told her I didn't think it was going to work. I groaned internally. I could see exactly where her mind was going. "You cheated on me?" she practically shrieked.

I could feel Noriko's eyes on me, questioning, wondering.

Dear God, can this night get any worse?
No, wait, don't answer that.

"Excuse me?" A chirpy voice said. It belonged to a rather keen-looking woman, thick red hair tied back in a ponytail, dressed well in a slightly crinkled black pantsuit. I could tell by the off-the-rack fit that she wasn't a guest. "Can I take your picture? It's for the gallery press release." She lifted a huge black camera.

Goddamn it.

"Yes," Wright said.

"No," I growled out at the same time.

"Come on, Drake." Wright said with a jovial laugh. He leaned into the photographer. "Forgive him. He gets grumpy when he hasn't taken his meds."

Before I could protest further he planted himself on Noriko's other side, between her and Kristie, sliding an arm around Noriko's waist.

"Get your hands off my wife."

"It's for the press, Drake. Relax."

"It's okay, Drake," Noriko said.

"Smile!" A flash went off in the corner of my eyes. "Um, maybe we can do that one again. Mr. Blackwell, can you face the camera, please?"

I was still glaring at Wright. He grinned at me over Noriko's head, daring me to make a scene in front of the press.

Damn him. As much as I wanted to rip his arm off by its socket and shove it up his ass, I couldn't. Part of my success was based on my reputation. I couldn't be seen brawling with a fellow businessman. At a charity auction, no less.

The quicker I faked a smile, the quicker the photo would be taken, and his slimy paws would come off my wife.

I faced forward and forced a smile, tugging Noriko closer to me. I heard Wright chuckle.

The flash went off again and the photographer thanked us.

I yanked Noriko away from Wright. I was ready to leave, but I had to make one last thing clear.

I glared at Kristie. "I never cheated on you. We were never exclusive. I made that explicit."

She sniffed. "You did not."

I sighed. I gave up. "As much as I am dying to stand around all night trading pleasantries, we really must be going."

"Drake, my boy, they're about to call the first painting," Wright said. "The Renoir that I noticed you were paying particular attention to. I was looking forward to snatching it right out from under you."

"Noriko has a headache."

"She didn't say anything about a headache."

"She doesn't have to. I can tell by the tension in her... er, forehead. That's what happens when you find the one you're meant to be with—you can just tell things about each other. Good night." I spun, taking Noriko with me, and charged for the door.

"Drake," Noriko hissed. "Slow down."

"Not until we are out of this tiger's den," I muttered. *And safely in the limo.*

"I thought you wanted to buy some art?"

I growled, as I dragged her beside me. "I changed my mind."

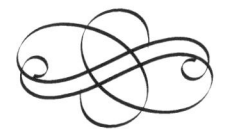

Chapter Twenty - Three

Noriko

Drake and I sat facing each other in the limo even though he'd sat next to me on the ride here. Strangely, I missed his warm presence beside me. The leather seat was much too cold.

He was staring out the window, not even looking at me.

Was he thinking about that blonde? She was pretty and buxom. She seemed more like the kind of woman that a billionaire like Drake Blackwell would be with.

Curiosity tumbled around my insides like a pinball machine until I couldn't keep it in anymore. "She was your ex," I blurted out.

He looked over to me for the first time since he climbed in and sighed. "Hardly."

"She seemed to think so."

He rolled his eyes. "Kristie and I went on four dates, maybe five."

Kristie definitely seemed more…hurt by Drake than a four-date relationship. "Did you…" Oh God, I didn't want to know. Shit, yes, I did. I needed to know. "Did you sleep with her?" I asked, my voice coming out all strangled.

Drake pressed his lips together and turned his head.

Shit. That means yes.

Drake was a beautiful man in his thirties. Of course, I could see how he must have been sexually active before me. The thought of that woman's hands on Drake made me want to claw something. Preferably her eyes out of her head.

Since when was I a violent person… especially over someone like Drake?

Shit. When did I start thinking of him as Drake and not Mr. Blackwell?

Oh God.

I was jealous.

Over *my husband*.

What a disaster.

I changed the subject. "And you and Mr. Wright…?"

He growled at the name. Actually growled. "What about that fu—" Drake cleared his throat, "that guy?" He stopped himself from swearing around me. How cute.

"What's his story?"

Drake's lip lifted. "You stay away from him."

I was planning to. There was something about the tall blond I didn't like. But being ordered around just made me combative. I crossed my arms over my chest. "I'm your wife, not your slave."

"Oh, for fuck's sake." And now we're back to swearing. "Jared Wright is the sneakiest, dirtiest, most self-interested snake you'll ever meet."

I flicked through my impressions of Wright. Arrogant, without a doubt. Sleazy, to a point. But a snake? "He seemed…well-mannered enough."

I could almost hear the sizzle of Drake's blood. "If he's nice to you it's because he wants to take you from me. If the bastard thinks he can swipe you out from under my nose like you're some Goddamn painting I will fucking kill him with my bare…" he spluttered before slamming his mouth shut, tearing his eyes away from me to glare out the window.

Oh…wow.

Drake was jealous. *Over me.*

A warmth bubbled up inside me. *Silly girl.* I was an intelligent, modern woman. I shouldn't be condoning such caveman sentiments. I shouldn't be happy that my husband is feeling possessive over me.

Still… Feelings were funny things that often didn't make any damn sense. Besides, no one had to know what *I* was feeling.

"What are you smiling about?" Drake asked in a gruff voice.

"Nothing." I beamed at him, causing him to scowl.

At the manor, Drake placed his hand on the small of my back as we walked up the stairs. My stomach jumbled. Oh shit. We're going to the bedroom. He wanted…

Sex.

The mere thought sent a rush of heat through me, making my cheeks burn. At the same time, an anxiousness knotted in my stomach. What if I was no good? What if he saw me naked and he didn't like it?

Every step towards my bedroom felt like my feet were getting heavier, my head dizzier.

My first time.

My stomach did an elegant little loop and promptly tied itself into knots.

"Are you okay?" he asked.

"Yes," I squeaked out. "Yes," I tried again. "Fine."

He peered at me. "You look a little pale."

I shook my head.

By the time we reached my bedroom door, I had to fight to keep breathing properly.

"Well," he said, facing me.

Oh my God, this was it.

"Well…" I wiped my palms as inconspicuously as I could on my thighs.

He smiled, that *look* in his eyes. I want to cry at how beautiful he appeared right at this second. "I had a wonderful time tonight, Noriko." He paused. "At least, until Wright showed up. Even then, it was bearable because you were on my side."

"Of course. Me too." My voice came out all breathy. I found myself tilting my face up to him, my lips parting, my fingers itching to run through his hair.

His eyes dropped to my lips, hunger flashing in his eyes as it did earlier. This time, there is no Wright to stop us. No Kristie, no photographer. He slowly leaned in and…

Stopped.

He dragged his eyes away, suddenly finding the door over my head really interesting. He cleared his throat. "Well. Good night, then." He turned on his heel and walked down the hall, disappearing inside his bedroom.

I sagged against my door. What just happened? Why didn't my husband kiss me?

Did he not want me? Rejection burned in my veins as I tried to sort through my jumble of thoughts.

I should be happy he doesn't want me. This made it easier for me to avoid getting pregnant.

Still, I was burning with disappointment. Why was I so disappointed?

Oh God, I might actually *like* my husband. I might actually want him. I wanted him to want me.

Why didn't he want me? Was it Kristie?

No. If he wanted Kristie, he could've had her. She wasn't over him, that much I was sure of.

I moved through my rooms, pushed open my bedroom door and flicked on the light. I froze in the doorway. My high wooden bed had been removed. Drake must have had it done while we were out. In its place was a double-sized futon. Just like the one my parents used to share.

I remembered our conversation this morning when he barged into my room to find me sleeping on the floor.

He had a futon put in here for me.

Despite my confusion over tonight, my heart warmed.

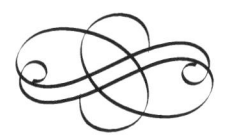

Chapter Twenty - Four

Drake

Standing outside her room last night I almost lost control. I *never* lose control.

I had wanted to kiss her so badly, I found myself rocking forward on my toes, drawn to her. I could almost taste her lips: she would have been sweet with a hint of the champagne she'd had earlier. The way she lifted her face towards me like a flower facing the sun…

She wanted me to kiss her.

She parted her perfect lips. I got a glimpse of her pink tongue as it swiped across her bottom lip. I had hardened instantly at the thought of those lips around me.

I *wanted* my wife.

But I had made a promise.

Now her four-night reprieve was over.

Tonight she was mine.

Mine.

Heat flooded my body as images of her naked body under mine, her head thrown back, my tongue exploring her sweet untouched folds, her cries—

"Drake?"

I glanced up. Samantha was standing behind my desk, tapping her pen on her notepad. Ah, shit. I pulled myself farther under the desk to hide my raging erection. The last thing I wanted was for my assistant to think it was inspired by her.

Her blue eyes narrowed at me. "Are you okay, Drake? You seem distracted."

"Fine," I said automatically.

I could go home. Right now. Noriko was at home waiting for me. My body screamed, *fuck, yes*.

But all this work... I glanced over the files and papers on my desk. More reports to read, more papers to sign, financials to review... There was always more work that needed doing. It was never-ending.

Right now, I couldn't think of anything I wanted to do less.

Noriko's voice rang in my head. *"There's more to life than work."*

What did it matter if I took off early for once? The world wasn't going to stop turning. What was the point in being the boss if I couldn't make the fucking rules?

"Actually, I have to go," I said, standing and grabbing my jacket from the stand behind my desk.

"Go?" Sam shuffled through her papers, then looked up. "You don't have any meetings on your calendar."

"I'm not going to a meeting. I'm going home." To my wife. To my sexy, combative wife. I was glad my button-up jacket hid my obvious excitement over this prospect.

"But…" Sam blinked rapidly at me as I grabbed my wallet and phone from the desk, "…it's quarter past five."

"Don't people usually finish work at this time?"

"Yes, but…*not you*."

"Go home, Sam. There's more to life than work."

Her mouth dropped open and she stared at me. "Who are you and what have you done with Drake Blackwell?"

I laughed softly as I strolled past her, still frozen to the spot. My steps felt light. "Go home, Sam. That's an order."

As soon as I got home, I instructed Loretta to let Noriko know that I would be coming to her. As much as I was dying to go straight to her, I wanted to make myself presentable first. I had to…calm myself. In the shower, I palmed my aching cock in my hands, coming against the tiles to the thought of her.

I fussed around with shirts and pants for far too long. *What the hell is this?* I was like a teenager going on his first date. I growled and yanked on a plain white shirt. These clothes weren't staying on for long. A quick brush of my damp hair, a spray of cologne and I was striding down the short distance to her suite.

I paused outside her bedroom.

I could hear movement beyond the door. I lifted my fist to knock, finding I had to clear a tiny knot in my throat. Was I…nervous?

Ridiculous. Mr. Blackwell, CEO of Blackwell Industries, did not get nervous.

"Come in," her sweet voice called.

I slipped inside her room and shut the door behind me.

She stood in front of her futon, her fragile body precarious in a pair of towering heels, a black dress hugging her tiny waist and skimming over her slim hips. Her dark, long hair framed her sweetheart face, her lips a vibrant red.

Damn.

She was a siren cloaked in innocence, that perfect blend of girl and woman, built to lure men to their doom.

Mrs. Blackwell.

My wife.

Mine.

Satisfaction and lust pooled in my lower belly, causing my lip to tug up and my dick to swell again. This was turning out to be an extremely worthwhile investment.

Her eyes met mine, widening before her gaze dropped to the floor. For the first time since I met her, Noriko appeared nervous. Unsure.

I frowned. I wanted her to be comfortable. I wasn't sure how to do that. I knew that striding over there and tearing her clothes off with my teeth was not going to make her relax.

"Noriko."

"Mr. Blackwell," she said, her voice as soft as falling snow.

"Please, call me Drake."

What now?

Right. She likes to talk. Like she did at dinner the other night. I remembered some questions she asked me. "Did you have a good day?" I echoed her.

Her eyes lifted to mine in surprise before she lowered her lashes again. "Yes, thank you."

"Good. Very good." I cleared my throat. What now? "What did you do?"

"I...read."

She liked to read.

"What book?"

She shuffled a little. "Sun Tzu's *The Art of War*. I...took it from your library. I hope you don't mind."

The Art of War. From my library. I didn't mind. In fact, a tug of respect went through me. Perhaps…perhaps she'd like to discuss it after she was done reading it. "Of course not. This home is yours, too. You can do what you like. Go where you like."

"Except call my father. Or go into the west wing," she blurted out. "Sir," she added quietly, seemingly remembering herself.

I couldn't help a laugh. *There she is.*

When she raised her chin this time, there was a glare on her face. "What's funny?"

"You are." I closed the gap between us in several long strides, causing her throat to bob and her eyes to widen. "You acting all unsure and nervous. Almost like you're scared of me."

She blinked at me before looking away. Her onyx eyes, wide and pointed at the corners, reminded me of a cat's. Her mouth was a tightly closed rosebud. I almost groaned when I imagined her lips making a vivid red circle around my cock.

"Usually you are not so scared of me."

"I'm not scared *of* you…"

I understood. "You're scared about what I'm going to do to you."

She folded her bottom lip in between her teeth.

"*Don't be afraid,*" I said in my clunky Japanese. "*I won't hurt you. Will never hurt you, understand?*" Not unless you ask me to. But I didn't say that. Not yet.

She nodded, her shoulders relaxing a little. Her eyes drew to mine. They caught me, drawing me in, tugging me, urging me to lose myself in her. The effect was even more startling than when I was gazing at her photo. She was here. She was real. A beautiful wife of my own. An odd, satisfied feeling warmed my chest.

I lifted my finger to her cheek to feel her skin. Damn. She was softer than anything I had ever touched. A blush deepened under her pale skin. God, I bet she was this soft *everywhere*.

I traced down her neck and to her shoulder, where I flicked off one shoulder strap, then I trailed across her collarbone, enjoying her shivering, before I flicked off the other. My fingers were surprisingly steady, unlike the erratic raging of the beast inside my body. I'd been aching for her for four days, the pressure built up; it felt like my lust had its own heartbeat. This creature inside me wanted to tear her apart. Perhaps if I was younger I'd lose control like that.

"Turn around."

She obeyed. I caught a whiff of her smell, fresh clean soap, uncluttered by expensive perfumes that women usually wore like a cloud around them. Just a hint of cherry blossoms. Her shampoo, perhaps. I wanted to press my nose into her hair to make sure. I restrained myself. I didn't want to scare her any more than necessary.

I brushed her long, straight raven hair—so damn soft—aside to access the opening of her dress. My cock hardened at the sound her zipper made as I drew it down. I let go. Her dress slid down over her hips, obediently to the floor. She was slender and tiny. Something about her made me want to…protect her. To take care of her.

I tugged down her panties, reveling in the way she shuddered as my fingers trailed down the sides of her thighs. They fell around her heels in a swirl of lace.

I walked around her and took her all in: slim waist, pale slender legs, her budding breasts, tiny brown nipples tipped with pink. I was filled with the urge to pinch them between my fingers and watch her mouth part. My cock throbbed, straining against my slacks. I haven't wanted a woman like this in…in a long time.

My self-control was going to be tested. I knew this for sure.

Her eyes remained down, her tiny fists at her sides.

I'd never had a woman remain so still for me.

The minute a woman wanted to dominate me in bed she lost me. If I wanted to fuck someone with balls, I'd fuck a man. I wanted something soft and…breakable. But I didn't want her to shatter if I barked too loudly.

She was fire and silk. Bite and fragile beauty.

She was…perfect.

I held her chin, tilting up her face. "You're a virgin."

It wasn't a question. She answered anyway. "Yes," she whispered.

A thrill shot down my spine. I'd never had a virgin.

Even expensive toys weren't this exclusive. Take my Bugatti Veyron, two-toned in black and silver. I paid $1.7 million and change for it. There were only three others in America. But there was only *one* of this exquisite treasure. Nobody else had touched her. Nobody else would have her…except for me.

She was mine.

Soon she would be carrying my child.

My fingers trailed down her neck, to her small, perky breasts. My hands took their fill of her soft, natural flesh, rolling those nipples between my fingers, which hardened into pebbles and caused her to whimper. That sound was delicious.

As I explored her body my own began to relax, my mind began to unclutter itself of the day's burdens, the coils in my muscles unwinding. My focus drew solely on her, her reaction to my fingers against her clit, her breathing deepening, her body tightening, the wetness marking her entrance.

I wanted more. I wanted to be inside her. Where no man had touched before. I slipped a finger into her soft heat. God help me, she was warm and wet. My cock ached from jealousy. I slid my finger in and out, at the same time rubbing my thumb over her clit. I was rewarded by her little gasps, noises she was trying hard not to make, her sweet little pussy growing wetter and wetter.

Chapter Twenty - Five

Noriko

What the hell was he *doing* to me?

His fingers playing with my sex, slipping in and out of my womanhood, his thumb swirling against that sensitive button, his other hand running across my naked skin, making my flesh tighten and tingle. I was going to lose my mind.

At the GW Agency they'd told me about sex. I understood the mechanics, I wasn't ignorant. They had said that it was something I would likely have to endure.

This, I never wanted to stop.

Never in my dreams had I imagined it would feel like this… Was this some kind of voodoo? Were these feelings—so intense, threatening to consume me—normal?

I was making noises. Oh God, I was moaning and gasping and—

I pressed my lips together trying to keep them all in.

He ran his thumb across my lips. "Don't hold it in. I want to hear what I'm doing to you."

I released a long pent-up moan. His thumb slipped just inside my mouth. Without knowing why, I closed my lips around it and suckled it. I wanted to take him all into my mouth, into my body.

He let out a curse. I released his thumb. Did I do something wrong?

"You," he said in a gruff voice that tickled the base of my body, his eyes glistening with hunger, "are going to make me certifiable."

He pulled away, making me whimper. "Lie on the bed."

My knees were weak. I half-fell, half-collapsed onto the futon. There was no grace in that movement. None. I forgot to take off my heels. I bent over to undo the strap—

"Leave them on."

I looked up in surprise at Drake standing over me, unbuttoning his shirt. "You want me to leave my shoes on? In bed? But they're…shoes."

He let out a groan. "Is there ever a time when you won't argue with me, woman? Leave. Them. On." The fire in his eyes was wild, almost feral.

He liked it—me in bed, naked except for these heels on. A rush of power lit up my veins. He yanked his unbuttoned shirt out of his slacks and let it drop off his shoulders.

Oh my.

Drake had lightly tanned skin with rounded shoulders and a wide chest smattered with dark hair. *A real man*. I followed the waves of his rippled stomach down. Who would have thought that my husband could look like *that* underneath his suit?

He draped his shirt over the back of a chair. As he slipped off his shoes and socks my curiosity burned hotter. I wanted to yell at him to undress faster, but I didn't have enough breath to do so, it kept catching in my lungs. He slipped out of his pants, revealing strong thighs. Finally—dear God, finally—he pushed down his dark gray Armani boxer briefs, his erection springing free. It was the first time I'd ever seen a man naked. I couldn't help but stare.

He was beautiful.

So beautiful he'd give Michelangelo's David a run for his money. A statue of raw power, of masculine confidence. No wonder he was damn arrogant.

He kneeled before me on the edge of the futon, his eyes locking onto mine. The intensity burned right through me. Right—it seemed—into my very soul. He slid his hands over my feet, still in heels, up my ankles and my calves, his touch tender and reverent. I felt like a goddess. Like I was being worshiped. I didn't even protest when his hands slid between my knees, making me shiver. He spread open my legs. My sex, my body, my lungs, they all burned from his eyes on the most private part of me. I was totally exposed. He made a strangled sort of noise in his throat as he stared at me. Did this mean he liked what he saw?

My body flushed—but not from shame. No. I didn't feel shame or embarrassment; how could I when he gazed upon me with such awe? I flushed from the intimacy of his stare. From…want. From need.

I *wanted* my husband.

Don't enjoy this too much, a voice said inside me. *You're only his wife for one year, remember? One year.*

Before I could react, he bent forward, like he was praying, and pressed his mouth to my core.

Oh my God. I nearly tore out of my skin. The pleasure lashing through my body unlike anything I'd ever felt before. Unlike anything I could have ever dreamed could be possible on this Earth. My body jerked, trying to rise up from the futon. His hands held my hips down as he groaned against me. "Sweet Jesus, you taste like…like cherries."

His wet tongue dragged across my slit, teasing my entrance, swirling at the top where this foreign pleasure radiated from. His lips sucked and teased, his stubble scraping against the insides of my thighs. It was magic. As violent as a snowstorm. God, I wanted his mouth everywhere.

I looked down and found he was looking up at me from between my legs.

It was the single sexiest thing I had ever seen in my life.

Just when I thought it couldn't get any better, he slid a finger into me and curled it to hit a sensitive part I didn't even know I had. He rubbed that spot, and licked and sucked, the pressure inside of me building up to breaking point.

Oh my God.

Literally, God. I thought I saw him.

My world turned into pure light and I broke apart, my body shuddering as wave after wave of pleasure and fire crashed over me. My hands fisted into the sheets. My back arched off the futon, even as Drake continued to pin my hips down.

I blinked as I came to, the plasterwork on the ceiling coming into focus.

What in the hell was *that*?

I was suddenly aware that Drake was moving his way up my body, up, up, up until his face aligned with mine and his hips settled between my legs, his erection pressing at my soaking entrance. I clung onto his thick muscled sides. This was it. A shiver of anticipation went through me.

"Are you cold?"

"No." He had the most beautiful lips, wide and full, an elegantly defined shape.

"Look at me, Noriko."

I lifted my lashes and was caught in his gaze. There was a concerned look on his face, a flash of fear going through his eyes. Somehow that made me feel better, less…alone in this new experience.

"I made sure you're ready," he said, "but this still might hurt a little."

I tensed.

He breathed in my ear, sending another shiver down my spine. "Relax."

"So demanding," I muttered.

He inched the tip of his cock inside me and paused. I could feel his eyes on me as he pulled back to look at me. "Are you okay?"

I nodded, my teeth biting against my bottom lip.

Slowly he pushed in, a slight flash of pain as he slid to the hilt. He sat foreign, low in my belly.

He groaned. "Oh, Jesus, sweet Mother of Mercy."

"Are you okay?" I asked.

"I should be asking you that." He pulled back to look at me. "You feel…you feel like…"

I couldn't help but smile. "Blasphemy-worthy, apparently."

The corner of his lip quirked up. "That sounds about right."

He began to move, slowly at first, his thrusts shallow. All the while he watched me. I hid my eyes under my lashes because it felt too intense, something clenching and tumbling in my belly. The discomfort faded. To my surprise, that sweet, sweet pressure started to build again.

My breathing deepened, a moan escaped me.

Before I could demand he move faster, he did just that, sensing my urgency in the way I tilted up my hips to meet him. I didn't have to be taught, I was *feeling* my way through this experience, losing all rational thought as I succumbed to the pleasure.

He rose up on his arms, his breath heavy and hot between us, pulling one of my knees up so he could penetrate deeper.

Oh God. That spot. He'd found it again.

His hand slid down between us. He vibrated the pad of his thumb against my sensitive button. I gasped and cried and my hips met him with violence and it seemed my body was completely out of my control.

If I could paint what I was feeling, it would be vibrant reds and bright purples, whirls and wild splashes of paint flung about the canvas, stars of the brightest white sparkling like snowflakes through the crimson storm.

I felt my grip on my control slipping. My fingers started clawing at his back as he slammed into me.

Oh my God. Am I going to…

Again?

Was that even possible?

"Come, Noriko," he demanded. "Do it now."

For once I obeyed without question. My body shuddered with pleasure, my nails digging into his skin. I heard him growl his own release and felt him pulse inside me.

Our breaths were in time, our hearts beating at each other from where our chests met. We stared at each other, a slightly stunned look on his face, mirroring mine.

He collapsed, rolling off me to the futon to lie beside me, just our shoulders and sides of our fingers touching. His beautiful chest, rising and falling, was shiny with perspiration, making his chest look all the more defined. I wanted to touch him, to run my fingers against the hair on his chest. I repressed the urge.

"Well…" I said, my voice all croaky.

"Well."

I cleared my throat. "It is always like that?"

He looked over to me, a spark of surprise in his eyes. His throat bobbed as he swallowed. "No," he said quietly, "it is not."

Chapter Twenty - Six

Noriko

This moment—our gazes locked, the mixture of our sex in the air, the slight touch of our naked, sated bodies—it felt like it had gravity, something winding around between us like ribbons on a maypole.

He tore his eyes away from me, rolling up to his feet. Instantly I felt the loss of his shoulder, of our pinkies kissing.

I sat up, clutching the sheets over me. I didn't know why I was suddenly self-conscious. He'd seen everything.

Excuse me, had his *tongue* in everything.

"Where are you going?" I asked, wincing internally. I didn't mean to sound so…needy.

"I'll be right back." Drake walked naked to the bathroom and returned with a damp hand towel. "Open your legs."

I sighed and lay back. "You managed to stop being bossy for all of two minutes. It must be a record."

He snorted. "You actually obeyed me without arguing. Twice. Looks like we're both breaking records."

My cheeks heated as I realized what he was referring to. *Come, Noriko. Do it now.* And dear God, did I obey.

He wiped between my legs, folding the towel over. I caught a glimpse of blood on the pristine white.

It hit me. I had sex. I was no longer a virgin. The girl in me had died. This was what was left.

He placed the towel in the laundry basket and gathered his clothes from the chair by my futon. I heard the click of the bathroom lock and the sink began to run.

When he exited the bathroom, he was fully dressed. I was still sitting up on the mattress. He walked to my side and bent over, placing a kiss on my forehead. "Good night."

"Why aren't you staying?" I asked, my voice high and tight.

He frowned. "I have my own bedroom."

"I don't like sleeping alone," I admitted. Back home I slept between my sisters. Their warm limbs and soft snores wrapped me up with the feeling of belonging, of comfort. I wanted desperately to feel it again.

"I like my bed," he said.

I started to climb out of my futon. "I can come with—"

"No!" He cleared his throat. "I don't sleep well with someone else next to me." He didn't meet my eyes. "Besides, I have an early start tomorrow. Good night."

He disappeared out my door, shutting it behind him, leaving me alone, with only a tender spot between my legs and a girlhood lost to remind me he had ever been here.

I remained stunned for a moment, half expecting that he would come back, one leg out of bed, blankets pushed partly back, before it became clear that he wouldn't.

Did my husband like me? He wanted me, that much was clear, but did he *like* me?

I thought we shared something tonight. Until I asked him to stay and his cold mask crashed down. There was something so broken inside this man, so shut off.

Could he love me? My heart did a flip.

Really, Noriko, you don't care whether he could love you or not. One year, remember?

I turned off the side light placed on a low table beside the futon and curled myself into a ball, pulling the covers over me. I tried to ignore the tiny sting of tears at my jaw.

I missed my family, the ones who loved me. I missed them which such a fierceness, I thought I might shatter from the inside out. In the darkness of my foreign bedroom, this giant house loomed around me like the walls of a canyon. I lay deep in the bitter depths of it, feeling lost and very alone.

Chapter Twenty - Seven

Noriko

The next morning when I woke, a dull soreness reminded me of the loss of my virginity. Now more than ever I needed to keep to my plan.

I leapt out of bed, glancing at my bedroom door. I hurried over to my closet where I stashed the bag that I brought with me. I took out the secret contraceptive pills that I'd been reaching for every morning.

I was sure Drake had the "unproductive wife" clause written into our contract to ensure he could get out of the marriage if it turned out that I *couldn't* deliver him a son or daughter. It meant that I would get nothing further from him except for his initial upfront payment, the payment that had gone solely to my father's experimental treatment.

But this clause also meant that I could keep my promise to my father and return home after one year.

I was doing the right thing. I belonged with my family.

So why did guilt weave its way through me as I pushed the tiny pill out of its packet and placed it into my mouth, tasting the bitter sweetness of the coating before I swallowed it dry?

My head was whirring as I replaced my secret into its hiding place and pulled on some clothes to go to breakfast alone as I did every morning since I arrived.

I'd been taking the pill for weeks now. Why was I suddenly conflicted over it?

My mind slipped images to me like stolen gems—Drake tugging me into his side as the limo drove through the protesters, Drake and the Monet painting, the way he moved inside me yesterday, touching such a deep part of me that I knew my soul would never be the same shape again.

I knew why I was conflicted, why guilt crawled in my underbelly like blind worms. Because I'd seen a side to Drake that he rarely showed. He wasn't a cold stranger, easily overlooked. He was a man of flesh and blood, with a bleeding heart and a bruised soul. I wanted nothing more than to unravel all his secrets so I could care for them all.

Be careful, Noriko. Don't get any closer to him. Don't let him in any further.

Don't forget your promise to your father.

I flung open my bedroom door, starting at the figure standing there. The very man who was taking up my thoughts was now taking up my vision, one hand poised to knock.

Those guilt worms gave out a wriggle. Surprise swept my breath into my throat. *Does he know? Could he hear my plotting?*

Don't be ridiculous, Noriko, he can't hear your thoughts.

I forced a smile, clasping my hands in front of me as if it would be enough to shield me. "Drake," I bowed, "Good morning. I thought you had gone to work already."

He looked incredible in a light gray tailored suit that hung across his wide shoulders like armor, a stunning crimson silk tie knotted at his thick throat. He hadn't shaved this morning, his jaw dark, stubble sharpening his strong jaw, making him look gruff and brutish. I got a flash of that beautiful face between my legs, felt the ghostly scrape of his facial hair along the insides of my thighs. A shiver ran through me.

He lowered his hand. "I'm about to leave for work."

I waited for him to explain why he was here. Drake just looked at me with a slight crease between his brows.

I chewed my lip. "I'm on my way to breakfast." As if to punctuate my statement, my stomach let out another growl.

"Right. Of course. You're hungry. I won't keep you." He stepped aside to let me through.

That was it? He didn't have anything more to say? He showed up at my door to say…nothing?

I stepped into the gap. At the same time, he stepped in again and we bumped together. "Oh," I let out, as he grabbed my upper arm to steady me, "sorry, I—"

He leaned in, his heated presence rolling around me like a blanket, causing me to cut off as I sucked in a breath. He brushed his lips against mine. They were oh-so soft and warm. For a second I couldn't move. A heat bloomed in my chest. I reached for him, opening my mouth instinctively to turn this into a real kiss…

He straightened, clearing his throat. My chest fluttered at the loss of him.

For a second we stared at each other, my arm heating underneath his palm, a flush rising to my neck.

Lean into him. Steal a kiss back off him.

Don't you dare, Noriko. Show no such affection. It'll make it harder on you, on him, when you leave.

As if he could sense the conflict inside me, he let go of me as if I burned him. "Well, then. Have a good day," he said. He strode down the hallway, his long legs propelling him to the end before I could make myself move.

What the hell was that?

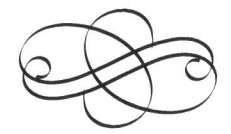

Chapter Twenty - Eight

Drake

What the hell was that?

I sat alone in the back of my limo, buttoning and unbuttoning my suit jacket, trying to make sense of this strange morning. I hadn't slept well at all last night after I had left Noriko and returned to my own bedroom. I had tossed and turned until almost four in the morning.

This morning I was like a zombie, moving through my morning routine like the air was made of honey. I even forgot to shave, I realized when I buttoned up my collar and found my fingers scraping against stubble.

From my bedroom, I had to pass Noriko's room to get to the main stairs. Instead of walking right past it like I had done every damn morning, I'd found myself in front of her door, fist held up to knock. I froze, wondering what the hell was my intention in knocking.

After a long pause, I realized with a start that I just wanted to see her before I left. After all, that was what good husbands did, right?

I'd told myself not to be stupid, that she was probably still asleep, even though it was later, much later, than I usually left for work.

Before I could walk away, she had opened the door. As if she'd heard my thoughts, as if I had breathed life into my silent desires. I had kissed her.

Jesus Christ, I had *kissed* my wife.

Her lips were so damn soft and perfect, I almost gave in and sucked her bottom lip into my mouth.

But she hadn't moved.

She didn't *want* my kiss. How could she? She was a woman I had paid to be my wife. I pulled away before I could embarrass myself any further and practically ran away from her like a shaking dog.

I shook my head, trying to clear it. The limo was silent even as we entered the highway towards the city, cars rushing around us. Usually I spent the time alone during my commute to make calls and reply to emails. Today, my head contained only steel wool. I pressed the button that drew down the divider to the front cab. Felipe's dark head, covered in his usual black cap, appeared in my view.

"Felipe."

"Yes, sir?" he replied, his slight accent giving his voice a music tone.

"Do we...do we have any music or anything?"

"Music? Sir?" He sounded totally confused.

"Yes, music. You know, when instruments are played and sometimes someone sings?"

"I know what music is, you've just never—" He cleared his throat. "Any particular type of music?"

"Something…upbeat." I sank back into my seat as Latin music danced from the speakers. This was a totally inefficient use of my time. Lord help me, I couldn't help but tap along to it.

Chapter Twenty - Nine

Noriko

"Even though Sun Tzu's philosophies are over two thousand years old, they still apply today," Drake said, his hand skimming up my inner thigh. "Because the fundamentals of human nature haven't changed."

"I agree," I said, sucking in a breath as he brushed the scrap of moist lace between my legs with his fingertips.

He paused and raised an eyebrow. "You, dear wife, agreeing with me?"

I shot him a dirty look. "I can agree with you."

"Only you choose not to." He returned to his exploration of me, his touch like sparks to dry grass.

"I only disagree with you when you're wrong." His hands were magic all over me, painting a starry, starry night across my body, kicking up ash and embers in a swirl of muggy heat.

He hummed against my neck. "The supreme art of war is to subdue the enemy without fighting."

"Is this what you're trying to do?" I asked, indicating the way he was palming my breasts, freed from the top of my crumpled shirt, and cupping my sex, weaving taut, silken threads between both. "Subdue me?"

"You are certainly the most beautiful enemy I've ever had to battle with." He pushed my underwear aside, finding my wet heat with his demanding fingertips. "Perhaps the most dangerous."

"Dangerous?" I let out a moan as he slipped two fingers deep inside me. "Why dangerous?" I breathed.

"You are sharpness and intellect encased in a fragile, innocent-looking package. What is more dangerous than someone who is underestimated?"

"Appear weak when you are strong," *more, I need more*, "and strong when you are weak," I mumbled as I ground my hips against his hand.

I whimpered as he stole his hand out from under my skirt. Palming my ass, he lifted me onto the dresser, my skirt falling apart over the tops of my thighs, revealing my lacy white underwear.

"You are so fucking sexy when you quote Sun Tzu to me." Before I could speak, he tore away my underwear—*ripped it*—right from my body. "Do it again."

I let out a cry which turned into a moan as he thrust his freed erection into me. "Oh God, that's good," I cried, my head thrown back, my inhibitions dissolving, as he moved in and out of me.

He stopped—goddamn him—he stopped moving and I wanted to hurt him. "I don't remember Sun Tzu ever saying that."

I glared at him and ground my core against him. "Shut up and fuck me, husband."

He grinned. "That I will submit to."

Chapter Thirty

Drake

My skin buzzed as I pushed through the front door to my home. Home. When had I started thinking of it as *home*, rather than simply a place to sleep and store my clothes?

"Good evening, Drake," Loretta said. As usual, she was standing inside the door, ready to take my jacket and to update me on the household if needed. She studied me. "You look happy. Very happy."

"No more than usual."

She frowned at me. "You're *smiling*."

Damn. So I was.

"Good day, then?" Loretta asked, a hint of curiosity in her voice.

It had been a good day. It had been a good week, actually. I felt reinvigorated at work in a way I hadn't felt in a long time. I was full of energy, my chest swollen with purpose all day. Both Sam and Roger had commented on it.

"A great day." It was about to get even better. "Where's my beautiful wife?"

"In her room, I believe."

A strange surge of warmth filled my chest. For the last few days I'd been coming home to Noriko, waiting for me, her body open and with another one of my books to discuss. I didn't think it was possible to find such a perfect combination of sexual chemistry and intellectual tussle in one woman, but I had. Somehow, I'd found her. Or she found me. I had half a mind to send Isabelle Taylor a gift to thank her.

A gift.

I halted, struck by a sudden urge. "I want to buy something for Noriko…something nice."

Loretta lifted her eyebrow. "You're asking me for advice?"

"No, I'm asking the butler. Yes, you."

Loretta folded her hands over her apron. "Well, sir. I'm flattered you'd *ask* for my advice. For once."

"Don't make me regret it."

"Get her something thoughtful," she said quickly.

"Right. Of course." I spun on my heel and stopped. I frowned, turning back to Loretta. "What does that mean, exactly?"

She sighed and muttered something under her breath that sounded a lot like *"utterly hopeless."*

"Think about what Noriko has told you she likes," she said, "things that she's interested in, that she enjoys. Has she mentioned any hobbies of hers in particular?"

Things she likes… Hobbies…

An idea stirred.

Chapter Thirty - One

Noriko

It was a Sunday. Drake had insisted on taking me for a drive in his car, something called an Aston Martin Vanquish. It was a very nice car. Pretty to look at. Hell if I know what went on under the hood. I didn't even know how to drive.

As the car wound through the streets, I tried talking to Drake. He replied with monosyllabic answers. I soon gave up and stared out the window as the city passed by us. He was silent, even as I studied his profile, a crease between his brows. Something was worrying him. But there was no point in pushing with Drake. If he wanted to tell me what was bothering him, he would in his own time.

As soon as we returned home, I made a beeline for the kitchen. Drake had initially been so enthused about this drive that he'd rushed us through breakfast. I hadn't eaten as much as I had wanted to. My stomach had been growling for the last twenty miles home.

Drake grabbed my hand and tugged back. "Where are you going?"

Now he wants to talk? "Kitchen. Food. Hungry."

He directed me towards the stairs. "No, we have to go to your room first."

I gawked at him. He dragged me out for a drive where he completely ignored me and now he wants to have sex? "Drake, I'm starving."

"Room first. Two minutes."

I huffed. Drake never only took two minutes.

He strong-armed me up the stairs and down our corridor. I glanced at him as we reached my private apartment. Now he seemed jittery, nervous, almost. "Drake, what is going on?"

"Just two minutes, I promise. Then I'll feed you anything you want."

I repressed my argument. When Drake got in this mood, there was no way in hell that anyone, not even me, could convince him to change his mind. Shifting Mt. Fuji with my bare hands would be easier.

He opened my bedroom door, practically shoving me inside.

I spun to face him, my hands fisting at my hips. "Okay, alright, I'm here. What do—?"

My eyes locked onto the unfamiliar painting on the wall behind Drake.

Oh. My. God.

My mouth dropped open. *The Japanese Bridge*. The lake. The lilies.

"Do you like it?"

I could do nothing but stare at the whirls of color, the dappling of light on the painting, shimmering as if it were alive.

It was the Monet from the charity auction. The one we had almost kissed in front of.

"I wanted to do something…nice for you," he said, his voice hesitant. "If you don't like it, I can—"

Something caught between a laugh and a sob came out of my mouth. I slapped my hand against my lips. Then spoke through my fingers. "For me?"

Drake brushed a lock of my hair behind my ear. I leaned into his touch. "Just for you, Noriko."

I pressed a hand to my chest where I felt swollen and raw. What had he done? He'd slipped his fingers into the cracks of my guarded heart and pulled it open.

"I can't believe… Is…is it real?" My voice squeezed out of my throat. I walked slowly up to the painting as if it were a mythical beast that might fly away if I moved too fast.

"You really think that I would buy you a fake?"

Of course not.

Drake bought me a Monet. A Mo-fucking-net.

This was why he wanted to take me out for a drive. He wanted me out of the house so he could have this painting installed in my room. He wasn't ignoring me in the car, he was anxious about giving me this gift. This incredible gift.

Do you think he'll let you take it with you when you leave him?

Like a crane caught in violent wind, I dropped from my soaring high and crashed into the ground. My stomach felt like it had been dashed across the rocks.

Drake was watching me with a growing frown on his face. He'd noticed the blood draining from my cheeks. He'd seen the outward signs of my wretched guilty soul.

"I…I thought it wasn't for sale," I said weakly, trying to explain away my inner turmoil.

"It wasn't."

"How did you…?"

He was serious when he spoke. "There's a price for everything."

Oh God, wasn't that the truth.

Chapter Thirty - Two

Drake

Relief filled me, releasing the tension I'd been carrying all morning.

Noriko loved the painting.

I could see the way she clutched at her heart, the way her eyes rimmed like a dam before overflow.

Then something happened. Something broke the shell of her joy, seeped out like poison, stealing the blood from her cheeks.

Before I could interrogate her, she walked up to me, her steps like a ballerina's, pulling off her clothes with her dainty fingers. Her silent plea was written across her flushed body, her hardened nipples like Morse code, her pretty cunt, already wet, was calligraphy in ink.

"I thought you were hungry," I choked out, my decency

trying to fight against the hot chains of lust wrapping around every inch of my body.

"I'm starving. For you."

How, tell me how, could a man say no to that?

Afterwards, we lay on her mattress, sated, still naked, a half-eaten platter of food I'd had sent up earlier, set aside.

"I love it, Drake. I still can't believe you bullied out a Monet for me."

"I didn't bully…" She raised an eyebrow. I let out a huff. "Alright, then, maybe there was a little bullying."

She laughed and crawled into the space beside me, her head nudging into the crook of my arm. We were like two puzzle pieces. Like she had been carved from my side by the ultimate sculptor.

"I wish I could tell my sisters about what you did for me. They'd giggle and swoon over you like they do their anime boyfriends."

I tensed, my defenses rising. Was she trying to manipulate me into letting her call her family? Was she trying to guilt me?

"Sorry," she said quietly, "I know you don't like me talking about them."

I looked down upon her face and saw no signs of an alternative intent. When I picked apart the subtext of her words, I could uncover no ulterior motive.

"Tell me about them. Your sisters, I mean," I said without thinking.

She glanced at me. "Really?"

I nodded, surprised to find that I meant it. I wanted to know more about where she had come from, about her life before me. I coveted everything about her, as if every piece of gifted knowledge and stolen secrets would make her all the more mine.

A smile lit her face, as radiant and full of light as the very painting I had given her. She was my Monet, I realized.

My chaos made sense, my dappled sunlight. She was the same scene I yearned to capture at all times of day, in all seasons, and never grow tired of.

"I have two sisters," she began, "Tatsuko is fifteen. She's obsessed with your singer Gwen Stefani."

"My singer?"

"You know," she flapped her hand, "you Westerners. She wants to be Gwen when she grows up. My youngest sister, Emi, is thirteen and gaga over fashion. She tried to beg and guilt my father into buying her this designer *randoseru*—"

"What's that?"

"It's the leather backpacks that all grade schoolers take to school. They're expensive enough already without having to buy a glamour one."

She continued to regale me with stories of her sisters. My chest warmed as I let her sweet voice wash over me.

I could get used to this.

Even as I had that thought, a flash of fear went through me. *It's dangerous to get too used to this.*

Chapter Thirty - Three

Drake

A few nights later I slammed open my front door before Loretta could open it for me.

Her crinkled eyes widened before drawing to concern. "Drake, are you alright?"

No. I wasn't fucking alright. My head felt swollen. It buzzed as if someone had thrown in a whole hive of bees. My gut churned with hunger. I ignored it, a greater need overriding it. "Where is she?"

"In her bedroom." Loretta knew I meant Noriko. "What's wrong?"

I strode past Loretta without another word. A tiny part of me chastised myself for being curt with the woman who practically raised me. But I could barely think through the poison in my blood.

I needed Noriko. I needed her *now*.

I shoved open her bedroom door, causing her to jolt from her chair and the book in her hand to fall to the floor. My periphery narrowed on her as I advanced. She would make things better. She would make this noise in my head stop. I needed her. My drug. My Valium.

Her mouth moved but I didn't hear what she was saying.

I grabbed her, my body surging with adrenaline, all of the pent-up anger from today crashing around inside me, rattling around like steel balls.

Her face. She was near tears and terrified. I couldn't stand to see her looking at me like that. I just…I needed this. I needed her. Then it would all be okay.

I needed to be inside her. Now.

I tore at her clothes, her wretched clothes preventing me from feeling the warmth of her body on mine. My fingers were shaking from frustration. I couldn't get the buttons running up the front of this yellow dress undone. "Fucking things." I grabbed the material and tore it apart, buttons scattering like scared ladybugs. I'd buy her another one. Fuck it. I'd buy her a dozen. One in each color.

I pushed the ruined dress off her slim shoulders.

"Drake."

"Don't talk." I gripped her as tightly as I could, despite her feeble attempts to push me away. I picked her up and pulled her legs around my waist, almost losing my mind when her warm core pressed up against my hardness. Her ass felt firm and tight under my hands as I carried her to the thin mattress on her floor.

I kneeled, dropping her down on it, grabbed her ankle and flipped her onto her front so she was on all fours. I tugged her underwear down, revealing her beautiful pink entrance. The sweet-musky smell of her sex hit my nose. I swear to God, I salivated. Holding her hips I pushed into her tight little body.

Oh damn. So wet. So warm. My little refuge.

As I poured my aggression into her, she tightened around me, and in turn I began to soften. My mind began to let go, the knots inside my gut untwisting. She was like warm balm on a screaming burn.

Inside of this beautiful woman, I was free. No pressure, no requirement to achieve anything. There was no end-of-year financial, no shareholders' report to justify my every action. With her, right now, I was unburdened, unshackled by anyone else's expectations.

I tried to hold back as I thrust into her. I could barely maintain grip on myself, on reality. She pushed back with her hips, urging me to speed up, her breath coming out in short bursts as I slammed against her body, fragile like a vase. I felt the pressure building quickly inside me. I tried to hold off. I tried.

Noriko cried out, shuddering underneath me. Thank fuck. My orgasm surged through my body, my fingers clawing into her bucking hips.

Just as quickly, the energy seeped out of my limbs. I half-fell on top of her.

She was a drug. My drug.

I rolled to her side so I didn't crush her. My breathing had calmed down and my tension slipped to a bearable level.

She remained still, limp.

Dear God. I broke her. You fucking animal.

"Noriko?" My fingers touched her hair and her bare shoulder. I wanted to roll her towards me but I was terrified of what I might find on her face.

"Did I hurt you?" *Please tell me I didn't hurt you.* "I don't know what came over me." What the fuck was wrong with me?

You're turning into him, a dark voice whispered.

I almost shoved her away in horror. Her soft voice cut through. "You didn't hurt me. I was scared at first…"

I stiffened.

"…because I didn't know what you were going to do. But…I liked it. More than liked it." She turned towards me, her eyes hooded, cheeks flushed from sex, a smile playing at her cherry lips.

I exhaled. Thank God.

I should go. I still had business to take care of, phone calls to make…

I couldn't bring myself to leave. I didn't want to yet.

I pulled her against my chest and wrapped my arms around her, making sure her hair wasn't caught under my arm or that I wasn't putting too much pressure on any part of her.

After a few moments I felt her relax, and I too, settled.

This was fucking blissful, having this gorgeous creature in my arms, sated, in our own cocoon. I could get used to this.

I suddenly became aware of how much this woman seemed to affect me. No one had affected me like this. Ever.

I didn't like that. I should go. I shouldn't stay… The longer I stayed like this the more complicated things would get.

She pulled back and her gaze locked on mine. The reasons why I had to leave were relegated to a blurry spot in the back of my mind.

She patted my arm. "Sit up."

"What?"

"Sit up facing away from me."

Did she give *me* an order? "Why?"

She rolled her eyes. "You're not very good at taking orders, are you?"

"That's because I give the orders."

She nudged me. "Just do it. Please?" she added with a smile. That smile. That Mona Lisa smile. I'd do anything for that smile.

I did as she asked, partly wondering if I would regret it. Perhaps she would stab me in my back now that I had it turned to her.

She kneaded my shoulders, pleasurable pain spreading out from her hands. God, they're stiff. So much tension in them.

I let out a low growl. "Oh God, that's exactly what I need."

"You've had a very bad day at work."

I didn't reply. *She's too perceptive.* Perhaps I should have guessed that by the sharp intensity of her eyes, those very eyes that first drew me in. I felt myself relaxing as her fingers worked my muscles.

When she finished I grabbed her arm and pulled her down to sit next to me. Her shoulder was pressed against mine, this small touch comforting me. "You're right," I admitted. "It was a very bad day."

"Tell me about it."

"You don't want to hear about it."

"I want to hear about the things that trouble you."

I wanted to tell her. I wanted to unload my day to her. Perhaps in sharing it with her, I could share the burden. "You really want to know?"

She nodded.

"Okay." The knot of guilt still sat deep in my belly, a poisoned tree in a cursed garden. "I recently bought a company. It's been a...challenging task. They're more inefficient with their resources than I first thought. There's a lot of 'dead wood' I have to get rid of."

Mick O'Connor's crumpled face flashed in my mind. He had been the first that I had personally let go.

"Mr. Blackwell, I've been with this company for twenty years. I don't know anything else. Please, don't do this."

I had done it anyway. I had done it with an icy façade, showing no hesitancy, no regret, knowing if I showed any weakness, they would attack it. I remained like marble as I reduced grown men to tears.

Noriko squeezed my hand, pulling my mind back to the bedroom with her.

"Today I had to fire some people." I rubbed my tired eyes. "Two hundred employees lost their jobs today because of me. Two hundred families..." All their faces flashed in front of my mind, all still haunting me. I couldn't get them to stop looking at me with their pleading, accusing eyes.

"You said the company you bought was inefficient with resources?"

"They would have gone under in less than six months if we hadn't bought them out."

"How many employees are in that company?"

"After the two hundred I let go today, only around two hundred left."

"So perhaps it's not that you took away two hundred jobs today, but that you *saved* two hundred. You yourself said that the entire company would have gone under if you hadn't bought them out."

I stared at her, feeling like she had flicked on a light switch, chasing these ghosts away. *I didn't ruin two hundred lives. I...* "Saved two hundred... Do you really believe that?"

"I do. But it's more important that *you* believe it."

Something inside me shifted. Perhaps it wasn't a shifting as much as it was an opening. Something inside me opened, just a crack.

I brushed my fingers across her cheek and tucked a stray lock of her hair behind her ears. "You are...so much more than I expected."

She raised an eyebrow. "What did you expect?"

A demure, obliging bride. Now the mere idea made me uncomfortable. A nervous laugh escaped me. "I'm afraid to say."

"Afraid to say because you…think I might be insulted?"

Dear God. I can't hide from her.

"Yes," she had me admitting.

Once again, I was filled with the need to be inside her. I grabbed her, pulling her across me to straddle my lap. I rocked my erection against her wetness. "You've seen through me again. How do you do that?"

"You are easy to see."

I let out a curt laugh. "I should hope not," I muttered.

She smiled as she slid her tight, wet pussy down onto me with a small moan. "Drake, I *like* what I see."

Do you? Really? I wanted to ask. Her words filled my lungs with something lighter than air.

We fuck again as we were, her straddled across me, her fingers alternating between grabbing my hair or gripping my shoulders like talons. For the first time in a long time I let a woman take control.

She wasn't just any woman.

She was my wife.

I let her find her rhythm. I let her control the pace. Let her slide her hips up and down my length as I leaned back on my hands, gripping the sheets so I wouldn't grab her and force her movements.

I fucking loved it.

This time, as she moved me to orgasm, I didn't possess her. She possessed me.

Afterwards, she lay against my side, our skin damp, bodies like puzzle pieces, Noriko tracing my chest with her dainty finger. We didn't speak. We didn't have to. The sated silence was enough.

I couldn't believe I always left right after sex. This… this was even better. Well, maybe not better. Sex with her was fucking incredible. But this, lying with her like this, made my body loosen, my muscles relax. My mind slowed and something akin to bliss seeped into my bones.

Slow down. Spend time with someone you love. This was what Dr. Tao had meant.

I flinched.

Spend time with someone you love.

Of course, Noriko noticed. "What is it?"

I stared at her, her delicate eyebrows pulling down over her almond eyes, those spear-tipped irises that went straight through me and saw everything. Did she know what I had realized?

That I loved her.

Holy fuck. I loved my wife.

"I love you," I blurted out before I could stop it, those words like wild horses, desperate to run free.

Shit. Had I really let those words out of my mouth? I was so new at this, I was like a bumbling fool. I had no shields, no strategies. I wasn't prepared for *her*.

She started, shock flashing across her face.

Shock.

"I…" her voice was quiet, "I don't know what to say."

I shoved her away and leapt to my feet, grabbing my clothes and tugging them on.

She sat up. I could feel her eyes following me around her room. "Drake, please don't—"

"I just remembered something. Important. Work." I couldn't even look at her. I practically ran out of her bedroom, shirt hanging over my arm, slamming the door shut behind me.

I sagged against it. I couldn't breathe.

She didn't say it back.

She *didn't* say it back.

She didn't love me.

Panic clawed at my throat. Fix it. I had to fix it. How would I fix it?

For the first time in my life, I don't fucking know.

Late that night, I was in my home office. I couldn't sleep. I was trying to distract my whirring mind by looking over management reports, the black text blurring so I couldn't read any of it.

I heard a knock at my door. Loretta appeared with a small tray of steaming tea. "You weren't in your bedroom. I assumed you were in here."

"Thanks, Loretta."

She walked in and placed the tray at my side. "You're working late."

Trying to work. Trying to ignore the hole ripped across my heart that made it hard to breathe. I inhaled and exhaled. "Yes."

"Is...is everything alright?"

Of course Loretta would notice. She practically raised me.

I shrugged.

She let out a sigh. "Oh, my dear boy, you work so hard. Try not to stay up too late, okay?" She patted my shoulder and turned to leave.

"What does it mean, to love someone?"

She turned back towards me and I caught the fleeting surprise in her eyes. "To...love someone?"

"How do you love someone?"

"Well," she spoke slowly, her head tilting as she weighed up her words, "love is selfless. It means that their happiness means more to you than your own."

I frowned. "No, I mean, how do you make—" I stopped, cleared my throat, a knot suddenly developing. "Never mind." I turned back to my desk, effectively dismissing her. "Forget I said anything."

She didn't move.

"You can go now," I snapped.

"You don't have to go through everything alone, you know?"

"Did you not hear me? Get out." I glared at the innocent papers in front of me because I couldn't stand to meet Loretta's eyes. I didn't want to see the pity on her face that was so clear in her tone. I didn't want her to see the turmoil inside me that I wasn't sure I could hide.

By the grace of God, she left, the door clicking shut behind her.

I sank into my chair, already berating myself for how I had treated her.

What had I been about to ask?

How do you make a woman love you?

Chapter Thirty - Four

Noriko

Drake loved me.

Every time I thought of it, happiness bubbled up inside me.

Until it burst and soured because underneath it was rotten guilt and bad seeds. Because he loved me and I would eventually have to leave him.

When I did, it would destroy him.

Dear God, how my heart ached at the thought. I didn't want to hurt him; if only I could absorb the pain meant for him into my body. If only I could make him love me less…

I couldn't stay. I promised my papa. My papa needs me.

So does Drake.

I had hated him on sight. I cared nothing for what he thought. As a consequence, he was the first person I'd ever truly been myself in front of.

If I had only been more vigilant. If I had given less of myself. Held back.

But Drake was a magician. He had removed my shields with deft fingers, distracted me with his enchanted words, drawing all this *feeling* out of me like a line of vibrant handkerchiefs.

I had to talk to him.

And say what? I had no idea.

A day went by and I didn't see Drake. Not at dinner. Not afterwards. I stayed awake longer than usual, my ears pricked for his footsteps. But he never came home.

Maybe he had a work emergency? Maybe he had a work trip he forgot to tell me about? He couldn't be avoiding me, could he?

Two nights and three days went by and he didn't darken my door.

"Loretta?" I asked her at breakfast the next morning. "Has Drake been away these last three days?"

She looked a little confused. "No."

"Oh."

"He's been coming home and taking dinner in his office down on the second floor. It's probably a bad time at work."

"Right. Of course." I couldn't shake the feeling that it wasn't about work. I couldn't shake the feeling that it had to do with the words that he said. And the words that I didn't.

I was still thinking about it that afternoon as I sat in a chair, staring out the window.

The door banged open, making me jolt.

Drake was standing in the doorway looking as beautiful as ever. An aching washed over me, making my stomach wring out warm pain. Now he was here and I had no idea what to say.

He glared at me. "You're coming out with me. You have ten minutes to change into something smart but comfortable."

I placed down my paintbrush. "Where are we going?"

He didn't answer. He spun on his heel and disappeared out the door. I hurried to my room to throw on a crisp knee-length skirt and a soft sleeveless blouse, sliding my feet into ballet flats.

I hurried to the front of the house and found a limo waiting.

I slid in—still not having gotten the hang of it—and Felipe shut the door behind me. Drake was already waiting in the limo. He sat opposite me against the far window, his elbow on the arm rest, staring with stormy eyes out the window.

He didn't look at me. Not even as the limo set off. Not even as I cleared my throat.

"I haven't seen you in a few days," I tried.

He said nothing. Only the deepening of his frown told me that he'd heard me.

"Where have you been?"

"Working."

Working. Right.

"Is everything okay?"

"Fine."

Apparently one-word answers were all I was going to get out of him. I sank into my seat with a huff. We drove for what felt like forever, Drake staring out the window, me staring at Drake, oscillating between wanting to smack him for being so damn obstinate and feeling wretched because I knew that he was only acting this way because I'd hurt him.

Finally we stopped and Felipe opened the door again. At that point I was fuming. I pulled myself out of the car first without looking back.

I froze.

We were at a private runway at a smaller airport, his private jet sitting there on the tarmac, a TSA official ready to stamp my passport which Drake, now out of the limo, pulled out of his pocket and handed over.

Oh my God.

He was sending me back.

He wasn't even going to wait the full year. He was sending me home.

The bottom of my stomach dropped down to my feet.

I should be happy that he was ending our contract. I'd get to keep the money for my father and return home a full eleven months early. Why did I feel like I was going to throw up? Why were my guts twisting into hollow, brittle vines?

Drake led me by the elbow to the plane. I was so stunned at this turn of events, at my obvious dismissal, I didn't protest.

I didn't even pack anything.

Stupid girl, did you think he would let you take anything with you when he sent you away?

I didn't get to say goodbye to Loretta.

"Get in," he said, pushing me up the flight of steps.

My shoe clanked against the first step and I thought I might faint, my breathing growing short and shallow. I couldn't let him send me away. I turned towards him, my fingers clutching at his jacket lapels. "Drake, I'm sorry. Please, don't send me away."

He frowned. "What are you talking about?"

I blinked up at him, hope filling my chest. "You're not sending me away?"

His distant behavior. His coldness in the limo. We lived in the same house and I hadn't seen him in three damn days. He'd been avoiding me, I was sure of it.

He let out a snort. "Get in the plane, Noriko," he said in a softer voice. He still managed to make it sound like a command.

I was too confused to do anything else, so I obeyed.

I stumbled up the stairs and found myself sitting in the same white leather chair that I sat in on my way here from Japan. Drake sat beside me and buckled himself in before reaching over me and buckling my belt around my waist. His fingers brushing at my legs, our first touch in days, sent waves of aching through me. I hadn't just missed his touch. I'd missed…him.

If he was coming with me, then…he couldn't be sending me away. Right?

"Where are we going?" I asked as the plane took off.

Drake glanced over to me. "Breakfast."

We ate a silent dinner on the plane. At some point, I fell asleep in the huge bed at the back cabin of the plane after exhausting myself over trying to get any information out of Drake. He was a steel trap. No amount of chiding, begging, or probing would get him to reveal where we were going for "breakfast".

In my dreams, I sensed his eyes on me, watching over me. I felt his fingertips brushing my hair back off my face. I felt myself being lifted up by strong hands. I smelled Drake's fresh cologne and I could have cried with happiness as I pushed my face into his chest, squeezing my eyes against the light. I felt us descend stairs and I was placed gently on a leather couch in the darkness of what I guessed to be another limo. Drake lifted my head and allowed me to use his thigh as a pillow. I mumbled happily and clutched his leg and let myself drift back to sleep.

"Noriko," Drake's voice broke through my sleep. "We're here."

I groaned and stretched before sitting up in the limo and rubbing my eyes. "You damn billionaires." We'd been flying all night. We couldn't be in the States anymore. "This is a long way to go for breakfast. It better be worth it."

"I'm sure you'll find it was worth it."

Drake got out of the car first and held out his hand for me. I stepped out after him, blinking as my eyes adjusted to the light. Wherever we were, it was morning. Glancing around, I saw a stone house and a beautiful garden. It all looked familiar. Except it couldn't be. I'd never been here before.

I heard the limo driving off and it was just Drake and me now.

"Where are we?" I took a step towards the start of a garden path. The place seemed painted in light and magic, drawing me in with its quaintness and too-vibrant colors.

Drake didn't answer. He held his arm out as if to say, *after you.*

The garden was in full bloom, growing around a stone house covered in ivy, green shutters flung open. Along the paths grew roses, tulips, lavender and many other flowers I couldn't name, their fragrances perfuming the air and lifting my heart. It was gorgeous, just like a painting.

Oh shit.

It looked like a painting because *it was* one.

This was Monet's house. His fucking house. His garden. There was the lake and the water lilies and the Japanese bridge that he painted. We were in Giverny, France.

Oh my God.

I grabbed Drake's arm, trying to speak but failing. He had stolen my voice. My head was spinning so hard, I thought I might pass out.

"It's usually open to the public," Drake said. "I convinced the trust to let me book it out privately for the day."

He did this *for me*.

Suddenly his awkwardness in the car shone under a different light. He wasn't being distant. He was nervous.

Emotions bubbled up inside me and I clasped my hand to my mouth to try to hold them in. To no avail. Sobs tore from my lungs.

"Noriko," Drake cried out in alarm, "what did I do?" He cupped his hands on my face, urging me to look at him. He peered at me with such concern, I could only cry harder.

"Oh, Drake," I said between sobs. "No one has ever, *ever*, done anything so wonderful for me." It had always been *me* doing for others. Me putting my needs and wants aside for everyone else.

Drake blinked at me. "But...but you're crying."

I started to laugh through my tears, shaking my head. Tumbling and fluttering inside me like I was a cage full of birds. More tears and more laughing. Until I let out a scream. "Monet's house! I can't fucking believe this," I yelled to the sky, giddiness overwhelming me.

Claude Monet's house. His garden. Holy shit.

"Did you just swear?"

I turned to him. "You... You, Drake Blackwell, are the most wonderful man."

He shifted his weight. "Not everyone will agree with you." How was it that a man so confident it bordered on arrogance, could be uncomfortable with my compliment?

"Whoever doesn't, can't see what I see."

He stiffened. "I'm not perfect, Noriko. Far from it. Just, please...remember this moment when…" he trailed off. *When I fuck up*, I finished for him in my head.

I took his hand and we walked through Monet's garden. He led me to a table set up with breakfast goodies like croissants and jam and scones.

I laughed as he pulled out my seat. "What, no waiter?"

"No waiters. No one else is here. I wanted you all to myself." He flicked out the napkin and laid it across my lap.

I mock-gasped. "Drake Blackwell, how much shall I tip you?"

"Careful, Noriko. My price might be too much for your body to handle." The glint in his eye had me squirming in my seat.

When we finished breakfast, Drake took me by the hand and pulled me to my feet. "And now…you must work for your breakfast."

He led me to the lake's edge where a picnic blanket waited for us. Beside it was a large suitcase and a large bag.

I stood on the water's edge and let out a sigh. I remembered this exact view from several of Monet's paintings. He stood right here. Looked over the lake as I did. Tilted his face up to the same sun. Filled his lungs up with the same air. "He painted right here."

"And so will you."

Drake opened the suitcase, actually a painter's suitcase filled with tubes of paint and paintbrushes. From the bag, he pulled out a small framed canvas and handed it to me.

This was all too much. I half-sat, half-collapsed on the blanket.

Was I really here? In Monet's garden about to paint my own version of his Japanese bridge? Or was this a dream?

Drake lay himself across the grass and flung his arm over his head with a flourish. "Paint me like one of your

French girls."

I let out a snort. "Perhaps you should leave that to Kate Winslet."

He smirked at me. For this moment, I forgot about the secret I was keeping from him. That I would one day betray him. I forgot that I could never return his love.

I tried to focus on my canvas, each stroke of paint done with equal bliss and anxiety. How could I ever compare to the Man himself? How did I even deserve to be here? Drake kept staring at me, drawing my attention to him like a magnet, making it even harder to paint.

I didn't notice his hand reaching out for a paintbrush until he'd drawn a wet blue line on my knee.

I shot him a glare.

"What?" he asked, his voice all innocence.

"Stop that."

"Stop what?" He made another mark, and another. Until he'd written *Drake4eva* on my leg. "I think blue suits you." He smirked at his "artwork."

I could only stare at him. Could this playful, lighthearted man be the same cold, arrogant brute I'd met four weeks ago?

Before I could think it through, I'd dabbed a spot of green on his nose. "What do you know? Green suits you."

His eyes narrowed. "You, Noriko Blackwell, will pay for that."

He lunged for me and I let out a squeal. We ended up rolling in the grass, laughing, smearing paint on each other.

Somehow the mood turned heated. Our clothes were discarded and our bodies came together, streaked wet with paint, sweat and desire, until we were both crowing each other's names to the sun.

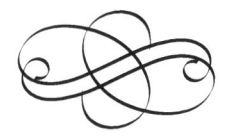

Chapter Thirty - Five

Drake

Much later, Noriko resumed painting wearing only my shirt, looking so sexy I almost lunged for her again, her skin marked by dried streaks of paint and flecks in her hair where we rolled across her pallet. The grass was streaked with paint too. Whoops.

We needed a shower but not right now. Neither of us wanted to leave this beautiful garden.

I sat in my briefs—it was warm enough to be almost naked—reading papers I brought along with me. It was still a workday after all.

"Is that work?"

I looked up from my papers to find that Noriko had abandoned her painting. She was watching me instead. I gave her a wry look. "It's always work."

"What are you reading?"

"Contracts."

"For the company you just bought?"

I shook my head. "It's a big government contract we're thinking of applying for. I'm reading through the job terms and conditions now."

"Sounds interesting."

I snorted. "Not really. Contracts are always overwritten drivel by a bunch of stuffy-suited lawyers trying to cover their asses while using big words to show off how smart they are."

"Oh."

"Luckily I have my own group of stuffy-suited lawyers. I still like to read through the contracts. I am the one signing them, after all."

She nibbled her lip, and I knew she wanted to ask something. "Drake, do you…like what you do?"

"Do I like…?" What a simple question. What a beautifully simple question and yet…I began to laugh.

She frowned. "What's funny?"

I shook my head as my laughter faded. "You know, in all my years, all the hundreds of interviews I've done, no one has *ever* asked me that question. They all want to know what the secret is to my success or how I feel about my success. They want to know what my tips are for other business owners or what my plans for expansion are… No one has ever asked me if I *like* what I do."

"So, do you?"

"I…" I felt like I'd been slapped. "I don't know."

She made a humming noise. "If it was your father's company and it was handed to you when he died, I guess you felt you had no choice but to continue."

There it was. The reason I fell in love with her to begin with. The thing I saw in her when she was just X, the girl with the Mona Lisa smile, the thing that made her stand out to me even from the beginning.

She *saw* me.

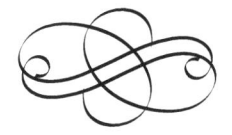

Chapter Thirty - Six

Noriko

"You see me so effortlessly, don't you?" he said.

I shrugged, suddenly feeling hot under the intensity of his stare. "You're easy to see."

"No, I'm not. I'm rude, arrogant, I piss more people off than not. The only ones who care about me are paid to."

"You're more than that!"

He was right. I did see him. I saw the rude armor that he wore, the arrogance he carried like a shield, his inability to act the "right" and "proper" way when he tried to express something meaningful to him. They were all lies. I saw past them as if they were children's games, as if they were mere sheets of rice paper, right into the broken, scared boy inside of him that screamed, *love me! Love me, because no one ever has.*

Something surged up inside of me. A need. An all-consuming need.

I crawled to him and straddled his legs, pushing his papers aside. He didn't protest. He only watched me with a hunger and underneath, a kind of weariness. His cock, already hard, pressed against my core. I whimpered. I wanted him. I wanted *that*. But there was something else I wanted more. A need more than physical. More than sex.

I leaned in, cupping my hand on his cheek.

He frowned. "What are you—?"

"Shhh."

"But—"

"Are you going to argue with me about everything?" I asked lightly, repeating words he once said to me.

He didn't reply. I didn't give him a chance to. I closed my lips on his. He tasted like champagne and croissants with jam, his cologne wafting around me like a fresh breeze.

For a moment he didn't move, and it was just me, brushing my lips against his, surprisingly soft, taking in his taste, his smell, giving myself to him, taking as much.

He started to move, slowly, as if he was unsure.

Perhaps he was.

Perhaps he'd never kissed anyone before. *Really* kissed someone. With his heart and his soul and the strength of all his hopes and dreams.

His lips grew firmer, exponentially surer. His tongue explored my mouth, dancing with my tongue. I slid my fingers through his silky strands and he weaved his fingers into my body.

Our first real kiss.

It was glorious. I never wanted it to end.

Our kisses grew hungry, needy. Desperate. Suddenly these scant clothes were like steel walls between us. I needed to feel him. All of him. With my hands between us, I pulled his shirt off me and his briefs off him. I pressed my breasts against his chest, our two hearts beating like drums against each other, both keeping the same glorious time. My arms wrapped around his neck, his palms flat against my back crushing me against his hard body.

Unthinking, we shifted, me sliding up his body, him guiding me up with his hands until his erection slipped between my legs. Slowly, achingly slowly, I slid down to take him—all of him—willingly into my wet, open body.

He moaned into my mouth, I breathed it in and groaned back into his lungs. We were a single being of soul and breath. Of tongues and wet lips. Of hearts and hands.

Neither of us moved, not yet. We were mindless and dizzy and drunk from our kisses, sucking every drop of champagne out of each other's mouths.

I broke away from his mouth and pressed my forehead against his for just one breathless second. Before we started to move.

When we moved, dear God, when we moved, I didn't want it to stop. Every pull and drag and push piled fire upon fire in my body. My heart began to fill and kept on filling. I feared I might burst.

He whispered to me in Japanese. *"Your tight, wet pussy will be the end of me. I can feel your warm honey sliding down over me, dripping onto my thighs. I want to suck up each drop up but I can't let you go. I will die if you leave. What did I do to deserve you, Noriko? Tell me?"*

Each sweet, dirty word was another added flame. My fingers dug into his back and I ground on him harder and he pushed up into me like he couldn't get deep enough. And he pushed and I pulled and he rocked and we rocked and my hands and his hands and our lips and everything and nothing and all the pieces of our bodies became stars, all tightening and compressing and burning until…

Everything exploded in waves so intense, I saw galaxies.

My world became a space as vast and as infinite as the universe. Drake and I hung there like swirling pieces of stardust. Until the pieces of us fell back down towards the Earth.

And when I hit the ground—oh, God, when I hit the ground—my eyes opened with a gasp as two swords of exhilaration and terror ripped through my insides.

Oh my God.

How could I let this happen?

I was totally and completely in love with my husband.

I had to leave him in less than eleven months.

Suddenly, what had been my prison sentence has twisted, turning into a ticking clock.

Chapter Thirty - Seven

Noriko

I was a paper butterfly torn in two.

I was Noriko Blackwell, a woman who was desperately in love with this beautiful, complicated man. Drake was the first thing on my mind when I woke, my body rushing alive with anticipation to catch him before he left for work, me leaning into the open window of his limo, us kissing like teenagers until he was late. When he returned home and folded me into his arms, I was free.

I was a woman who was tumbling and spinning, like autumn leaves caught in a breeze, deeper and deeper in love.

Then I was Noriko Akiyama, a daughter who made a promise to her sick father that she would come home after one year. A girl whose husband wouldn't let her speak to the family she left behind. A girl who still slept alone, whose husband still left in the dead of the night. Who woke up every morning in a cold marriage bed. And a wife carrying a secret as to why she was still not pregnant.

The wife and the daughter were two separate people living in one body. It was the only way that we could live with ourselves. But this careful separation was fragile, the division was thin and tenuous. The daughter was growing to despise the wife, to hate her for loving her husband who kept her from her father.

The wife was beginning to hate the daughter for reminding her that her love had an ending because of a promise she made to her father. The wife hated the daughter for continuing to take those secret pills so that the family she wanted would never come to be.

The daughter and the wife were two different people, but they were both prisoners. As the weeks went by, the call for freedom grew louder and more desperate.

"Drake," I asked, one evening while laying in bed, "I want to take a painting class."

He paused his tracing on my stomach. "But you paint so beautifully."

I rolled my eyes. "You're my husband. You're supposed to think the world of me. It's an actual requirement, you know."

"I think that because you are truly talented."

"There's always room for improvement. I found a painting class in town that I'd really like to go to on Mondays, Wednesdays and Fridays."

He paused, a frown growing between his brows. "Aren't

you happy here?"

"Of course I am, Drake. But I'm bored. I need something to do with my days."

"I'll get the teacher to come here, the best one money can buy, every day of the week if you like."

I let out a frustrated huff and tried to keep my voice steady. "I want to be in a class. With other people. I only get to see you, Drake." The staff here always seemed too busy to talk to me.

"And I'm not enough?" His voice was chips of ice.

"Of course you are. I still want friends."

He stiffened. "*Male* friends?"

I shook my head. "Male. Female. What does it matter?"

He rolled aside, getting to his feet. "I am not letting you go gallivanting around some art school where there are opportunistic vultures sniffing around you."

I sat up. "Don't be ridiculous."

"Oh?" He began to pace. "You don't think the whole of LA is obsessed with you now as the wife of the third richest man in America. Trust me, Noriko, this city is full of sharks who won't think twice about using you."

"Drake—"

"I just want to protect you. I'll get you your own private painting teacher. That's final."

I rolled over, my back to him, squeezing my eyes shut against the waves of frustration crashing over me.

I was a prisoner here. He wouldn't let me leave. He wouldn't let me have friends. He wanted me to have only him. To sit at home and do nothing but wait for him. He loved me so much he was suffocating me.

I loved him. But I hated that he was like this.

This is why you have to get out when the year is up, the daughter in me screamed. *If you fall pregnant he will* never ever *let you leave.*

For once, the wife was silent.

I found myself growing restless during the day. I'd explored the entire mansion, I'd wandered the gardens and the grounds. I'd even made my way into the servants' quarters today just to find someone to talk to, and was promptly chased out by Loretta.

I was bored.

I felt like all I did was lie around reading, waiting for Drake to come home. For him to sit beside me at dinner. For him to come to my room afterwards and strip me and make love to me. For me to lose myself in his touch, in his beautiful body.

He still went to his room after we were done. I still slept alone.

I felt like I was only alive for three or four hours a day, a translucent cloth thrown over the remaining hours so they were muted and muffled.

That night, Drake appeared in my room later than usual. I was sitting with my legs up on my window seat, despondency making my head heavy, resting my chin on my knees. Today, for once, I had allowed myself to *feel* the bars that held me. Feel the chill radiating from the cage that seemed to close even tighter and tighter around me.

"I have something for you," I heard him say from my doorway.

"Great." I didn't turn my head towards him. There was a bird sitting on the branch outside, small and brown with round, alert eyes. She might have nothing except the wings on her back, but she was free. She had purpose.

"Noriko?" I heard Drake's footsteps as he crossed my bedroom towards me. He took my hands and pulled me up to my feet. Only then did I look up at him. "What's wrong?"

I wanted to yell at him. Like all of this was his fault. Even though *I* chose this marriage. I accepted this sacrifice.

"I missed," *my father, my family, my freedom,* "...you at dinner tonight." I wasn't completely lying. His company had become the one light in my purgatory. The one thing I looked forward to. I hated him for it. I hated him and I needed him just as much.

"I have something for you," he said again. "I think it will cheer you up. Come." He led me from the bedroom and we walked in silence down the corridor.

He brushed his fingers against my arm and found my hand, pushing his fingers into mine. I stared down at our hands, my pale bird-like one, and his tanned, large, immaculately manicured one, dotted with a plain platinum wedding band set with a tasteful row of tiny diamonds. I never noticed his wedding ring until now. I didn't remember him having one when we first met.

We stopped at a door farther down the east wing on the same floor as our bedrooms. I remembered looking inside this room. It was another stuffy sitting room. He squeezed my hand before he pushed open the door for me. Was he… nervous?

I stepped inside.

My mouth dropped open. Oh my God.

The entire room had been gutted, the floors stripped of carpet and replaced with polished wooden flooring. There was a huge table in the center, easels in all corners, stacks of framed blank canvases leaning against one wall next to a huge sink, another wall of shelves filled with paints and pots and brushes and rolls and rolls of paper—all kinds of paper, all colors and thicknesses.

That was what the workmen were doing these last few days. Loretta told me there had been a leak in one of the rooms and not to go in there. I had believed her. She had been in on this.

"Do you like it?" The hopeful look on Drake's face softened my sadness. He was trying to be a good husband. He was trying so hard to please me.

"I...I can't believe you did this for me," I said, my voice trembling. "It's wonderful."

His smile grew until it crinkled the corners of his warm brown eyes. "Good. Great."

I turned and surveyed the room again—*my* studio.

My studio for less than one year.

Guilt shot through me as I thought of my hidden pills. Maybe I should give Drake a chance? Maybe I could stay...?

No. Remember your promise. Your father needs you.

I couldn't accept this.

"Drake, it's wonderful, but it's too much. I can't—"

"Nothing is too much for you."

He dipped his face into my neck and inhaled, sliding his arms around me. He groaned against my ear, sending shivers down my spine. "You smell incredible, Noriko, I—" He cut off, grabbing the hem of my shirt and pushing it up to expose my breasts. "So beautiful," he muttered, before he swooped in and covered one nipple with his wet mouth.

I let out a cry, my head falling back as pleasure made my body tighten and ache. His tongue was magic. His touch like the caress of angels and the devil all at once.

His hands slid up the back of my thighs, picking me up and wrapping my legs around his waist. He strode to the table in the center of the room and laid me down on it like I was something precious. The way he was looking at me made me *feel* precious.

Don't get used to this, Noriko, the voice inside me said. *You're only his wife for one year, remember?*

I ignored that stupid voice. For the next few hours, I

forgot. I forgot about my promise. I forgot about my cage. I forgot everything except for the beautiful man here with me.

Drake and I had been getting along incredibly well for the past week. I thought it might be a good time to push an issue we didn't see eye to eye on. I had to pick my timing.

I studied Drake as we sat together for dinner that night. He seemed in a good mood. I waited until he'd eaten most of his meal before I decided to brave it.

"Drake?"

"Hmm?"

"I was thinking about my father today. How his treatment's going. And my sisters. Wondering how they are…"

He didn't speak. Something dark flashed across his eyes.

Unease tumbled around inside me. I barreled on anyway. "It would make me so happy if I could call—"

His jaw tightened. "We've already spoken about this, Noriko. Several times, in fact."

"I don't even know how he is. How his treatment is going."

"Your father's fine. They're all fine."

"If I could speak to him—"

"Do you think I'd be so cruel that I wouldn't tell you if something happened to him?"

"You're *keeping tabs* on them?" This revelation left me cold.

"Of course I am. What is important to you is important to me." His voice went all soft. "Your home is here now, with me. Any contact with them is going to make you homesick. I'm doing this for you, darling." He reached out to pat my hand, a patronizing move that made me want to punch him straight in the mouth.

I snatched my hand out from under his and crossed my arms over my chest. "I want to speak to my father. Don't you love me?"

"Don't you dare question my love for you." His fist slammed down on the table, his eyes glittering with rage. "You are all I think about. You are all I do anything for."

"Then why won't you—"

"I've just told you why."

"But, I—"

"No. Noriko, that is final. I know you think I'm being cruel. Trust me, it's for the best." He picked up his fork and resumed eating.

White-hot rage swirled inside me, forming and taking shape.

See, the daughter inside me wailed. *He doesn't love you. Only Papa and your sisters do. You must keep your promise.*

No, the wife cried. *He's only acting this way because he doesn't know any better. I can teach him…*

Chapter Thirty - Eight

Drake

I loved her.

I loved my wife.

And even though she hadn't said it, she must love me too, right? I mean, I gave her her own artist studio, I took her to Monet's garden in France. She had everything a woman wants, designer clothes, expensive jewelry...

So why did I get the creeping sensation that it wasn't enough?

Why does this fear grip me late at night? That I would lose her. I couldn't lose her.

I had to hold on tighter.

I felt like I was going out of my mind. I could barely think of anything else at work and people were starting to notice. I'd been postponing my business trips because I was terrified of leaving her alone.

Why did love have to be so beautiful and terrible all at once? Sometimes it felt like a fairy-tale, at other times like war, a tempest on my soul, a siege against my heart.

Tonight when I reached for Noriko, she pushed back. "Not tonight, Drake. I have my period."

"Your period?"

"I just said that."

"Which means you're not pregnant."

I slipped a hand on her flat stomach and felt her stiffen.

I was struck with the overwhelming urge to see her belly swollen with my child—our child. It had nothing to do with wanting an heir. I wanted a family. With her.

A baby would keep us together. A baby would tie her to me forever.

"I can't wait until you're pregnant."

She said nothing.

I slipped my fingers underneath the hem of her shirt and skimmed the skin of her belly, praying for a life that wasn't there yet. "Maybe we should go see a doctor."

"What? Why?"

"I want to make sure everything is…working."

She spluttered. "It's only been two months."

"I can't wait any longer."

She let out a huff. "These things can't be rushed."

"They have options. To get pregnant faster."

The look on her face betrayed her horror. "No, Drake. No doctors. No injections. No test tubes." She shoved my hand off her stomach and turned away, rolling onto her other side on her bed.

My fingers, still outstretched, felt empty. I curled them into a fist before retracting my hand, a bitterness flooding into my mouth.

Did she know how much her rejection stabbed me like a blunt knife? The dullness in her eyes like needles in my face? Did she know how wretched I felt when I had to take every kiss from her, my mouth filling not with her love, but with her sighs? I felt like she was punishing me for a crime I hadn't committed.

I wanted my Noriko back. My Mona Lisa with those piercing dark eyes. The woman who stirred laughter from my lungs, who tested me, pushed me, parried with me. Who knew how to peel back my masks and reveal myself even to me.

How do I make you happy? I yearned to ask her. *How do I make you smile at me again? How do I make you love me? What do I have to buy you?*

"Sure." I tried to keep my voice even, not to betray all of the tumbling, confusing mess inside my body. "We can wait."

How could I wait when I felt her slipping through my fingers like ash? The more I needed her, the more it seemed she pulled away.

I settled closer behind her, spooning her, tucking my knees in behind hers and propping my head up with my hand. She tensed and chewed her lip, her eyes on the far wall. I wanted to stroke her side, to touch her face. I couldn't deal with it if she rejected me again so I left my hand on my side, gripping at my thigh.

"So...what did you do today?" I tried.

Her tiny shoulder shrugged. "Read."

"What book?"

"*Rebecca* by Daphne du Maurier."

"What's it about?"

There was a pause. "A wife who's not sure who her husband is." I could hear the accusation in her voice.

I'm trying, Noriko. You're the one who isn't trying.

"You read a lot."

"There's not much else to do here." Bitterness poisoned her voice.

"Do you need a bigger library? A better studio? I can build you one."

She turned sharply towards me, guilt flashing momentarily in her eyes. "No. I don't need a library. I already have a studio."

I frowned. "Then what do you need?" *What do you need from me to fix this rift between us?*

She lay her head back on the pillow, facing away from me. "Nothing."

There had to be something. Anything, Noriko, you only have to ask. "Are you happy with this room?"

"Of course."

"If you weren't happy with any aspect of it—wrong color, wrong shape, wrong furniture—I could change it."

I would change anything you didn't like. I'd make this room a perfect paradise for you, just say the word.

"You don't have to do that."

"I would. If you wanted it."

She said nothing.

Panic shortened my breath, steel chains tightening around my lungs. I was losing her. Even as I held onto her tighter and tighter, she was turning to sand, slipping through my fingers.

This was how my poor father felt, loving my mother.

Disgust made my mouth taste sour. I didn't want to feel this empathy for him. I didn't want to *understand* him. I wasn't him. I would never be like him. And Noriko wasn't a whore like my...

My blood went cold. Could Noriko be cheating on me? Could she be saving her smiles and fire for someone else? I felt a choking sensation, fear clawing around my neck as I let this thought dwell.

I shoved it away. No, she couldn't. I'd kept her away from all of the socialite parties and the shallow pack of well-dressed wolves that was LA society. I had kept her safe from anyone who might try to take her from me. I had kept her safe.

I needed to fix my image in her eyes. "I landed a huge contract today."

"That's great…"

She'd always liked it before when I spoke about work. I spoke about the deal in detail. "It added another half a billion worth of value to the Blackwell shares." I paused, waiting for her gasp of awe.

Nothing. Her breathing had evened out. She had fallen asleep. I didn't want her to sleep yet. I brushed hair from her cheek, watching her eyes in case it was enough to wake her.

She didn't move and her breathing stayed the same. I felt myself floundering, alone, adrift, the emptiness of my life before Noriko gripping my ankles, threatening to drag me back into those cold, dark depths.

I couldn't go back to the emptiness of my life before her.

But she was keeping my happiness from me, making me work harder and harder to have it again. I would have it again. I just needed to find a way to fix us.

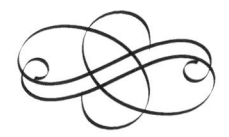

Chapter Thirty - Nine

Noriko

Dear God, Drake wanted a baby. I could see the joy in his eyes as he admitted it to me, as his fingers caressed my belly, the root of my betrayal.

Unbidden images of us as a family stole into my head like thieves. I tried to keep them out. I tried to protect myself from them. Still they found their way in, branding themselves on my heart. How could this be so pure and yet so wretched? It felt like love but it hurt like hate.

I had to turn away from Drake. How could I look him in the face when I held such a secret? How could I kiss him and mean it when I knew I would only end him? How could I keep absorbing him into my body when I'd have to purge him?

If only I could take away all the pain I would cause him. I didn't know how.

I had to make him stop loving me. It was the only way to save him.

Even as I considered this prospect, my own heart felt like I was tearing it in two.

How do you rid yourself of someone who was in your blood, in your cells? How do you cut someone out when your souls were like the weave of a tapestry?

Drake kept trying to talk to me. How could I reply when my words were lies? He curled around me, trying to love me, and all I felt was crowded, suffocated, my guts churning with poisoned sickness.

I couldn't do this to him. I had to tell him.

You can't. It will destroy him.

I'd destroy him anyway.

Drake was in London for a business trip. I was with him. He promised me that he'd have plenty of time to take me to as many galleries as I wanted.

I shouldn't have said yes. I should have kept my distance. But how could I say no to the London National Gallery? Or the Serpentine Galleries? Or the Tate Britain? The West End theatre which I'd always wanted to visit?

"I'm sorry, Noriko. I can't take today off like we planned."

I pressed my lips together and yanked my bathrobe even tighter around my body. "Okay…" The tone of my voice said it was definitely *not* okay. "You can't expect me to stay in here all day. Again." We'd been in London two days and all I had seen was the inside of this enormous suite. He wouldn't let me go anywhere without him. Even here I was a prisoner.

It was days like these that made it easy to justify pulling away.

Drake let out a huff and ran his hand through his hair. "Of course not." He was already dressed in a stylish navy pinstriped suit that made him look so delicious it hurt. "Franco will look after you." He indicated the giant hulking man who stepped into the suite. He was almost bursting out of his suit, standing by the doorway as straight as a soldier, sunglasses on even though we were inside. "He'll go with you wherever you need."

I crossed my arms over my chest, my anger overriding the guilt I wore like a coat. "I get a babysitter now?"

"He's a bodyguard."

I eyed Franco, the Silent Giant. "And what are you expecting that he will guard me from? Overzealous doormen? Dangerous pigeons? Obstinate Tube turnstiles?"

Drake looked horrified. "You are *not* riding the Tube."

I threw my hands up in the air. "You can't come to London and *not* ride the Tube. It's part of the experience."

Drake grabbed his wallet and keys. "I've been to London a hundred times and I've never ridden the Tube."

"Yes, well, you live on a different planet from the rest of us."

Drake sighed and walked over to me, slipping between my legs as I sat on the edge of the bed. He cupped my face and tilted it, forcing me to look right at him. "Please, don't argue with me. I will lose my mind if I don't know you're safe and being taken care of."

My anger softened, just a little, enough to let guilt stab me again.

He leaned in and kissed me hard on my mouth. I fought myself from kissing him back the way my soul wanted to.

My lips barely moved, my mouth barely opened for him, even as my fingers clawed at his shirt as if I were trying to crawl back into his heart.

He pulled away. Yet again, his confusion, his pain, over my conflicted behavior flashed in his eyes. God, Drake, I'm sorry. I'm sorry for everything but I don't know how to fix it.

"I have a car already waiting for you."

I didn't have strength to argue anymore. I was exhausted from fighting with him, with fate, with my own damn self. "Fine, I'll go with my babysitter and take your stupid car to the gallery."

He nodded, the closest thing to a thank you as I would get. He strode to the exit and paused to give Franco an assessing look. "Look after her. She is the most important thing in the world to me."

Knife. Heart. You don't know, do you, Drake? You kill me with your kindness. You choke me with your love.

Franco nodded. Drake left, shooting me one last ache-filled look.

I wanted to shake all of my turmoil off, if only for a few hours. I was in London, for God's sake. "So, it's just you and me, Franco. You ready for a fun-filled day?"

He didn't answer me.

I sighed. Today was going to be a riot, I could tell.

I promised Drake I would take his stupid car. I *did not* promise that I wouldn't give Franco the slip once we got to the National Gallery in London's Trafalgar Square. It was easy. In one entrance of the ladies' washroom and slip out the other.

I didn't want anyone following me around like a shadow. I just wanted a few minutes without Drake's presence reminding me of the mess I was making. I knew Franco would catch up with me soon. I wanted to enjoy the gallery in peace for a little while.

I stood in front of a gorgeous painting of the nude back of a woman by Velázquez, admiring the fine brushstrokes of his hand, when I felt a presence standing much too close to my side. I sighed internally as I turned. "Found me already, Fra—"

It wasn't Franco.

Jared Wright, the man I met at that charity auction, was appraising me with his cat-like eyes, looking too sure of himself in a tailored dark gray suit. "Noriko Blackwell, how wonderful to see you again."

I composed myself and forced a weak smile. "Mr. Wright, what a surprise."

"Please call me Jared." He leaned in and kissed me on the cheek before I could protest.

I stepped back to maintain some distance between us. "What are you doing here?"

"I imagine, the same as you. Admiring beautiful things." His eyes flashed. Before I could figure out the meaning behind it, he turned and waved at the painting. "Do you enjoy Velázquez's works?"

I nodded. "Drake took me to see the recreation paintings that Bacon, Dali and Picasso did as a tribute to him. I was curious to see his work in person. I heard he even influenced Manet."

"What did you think of the tribute pieces?"

"My favorite was *Infanta Margarita*. So whimsical, like a dream."

Jared pressed his palm to his chest. "A woman after my own heart." He grabbed my elbow. "Come, let me show you something really, really special."

"I don't think that's—"

"It's the new Italian Impressionists collection. It's not open to the public yet. But I'm a VIP member here." His eyes twinkled. "You can't miss it, Noriko. I promise you, you'll kick yourself if you do."

Damn him. I was a sucker for Italian Impressionists. I couldn't say no.

Not even if the snake was offering it to you?

I shoved this thought aside. I wasn't doing anything wrong by looking at paintings. It was a gallery, for God's sake.

I glanced around me. Franco still wasn't in sight. Maybe if I just had a peek?

"Two minutes," I said firmly.

Jared grinned, looking incredibly boyish. "Come."

He led me into a large curtained-off room. I stepped into the dim, hoping I hadn't made a terrible mistake. He flicked on the light and revealed the largest collection of Impressionist paintings I could ever hope to see.

I walked around in a daze, trying to imprint each beautiful piece on my brain. Three months ago, I was a student in a tiny town in Japan. Today I was standing among art's greatest. I was walking among history. How the hell did I get here?

Jared kept a respectful distance as he walked beside me, occasionally punctuating my awed silence with comments about the artist or the piece, but otherwise giving me space to admire each one.

I was quietly impressed. Perhaps Jared wasn't so bad, after all.

"So, why isn't good old Drakey boy here with you? Has he lost you already?" Jared let out a boisterous laugh that echoed around the large room, reminding me that I was here alone with a man who was not my husband.

The polite smile faded from my lips. "Enjoy the rest of your day." I turned to walk away.

He slid in front of my path, his hands raised in surrender. "Oh, come, now, Noriko, I was playing around."

"Of course you were."

"Noriko."

"It's Mrs. Blackwell to you."

He chuckled. "Mrs. Blackwell, I want us to be friends."

"I don't think that's wise."

"Why? Because of your husband? Doesn't he want you to have any friends?"

I flinched. He was too on the mark.

I shook his words off and lifted my chin. "I can have friends."

"Really?" Jared leaned in. "I've always known Drake to be such a controlling, possessive sort."

"You don't know the first thing about him."

"I've known him since we were boys." He let out a sigh and ran his hands through his hair, a gesture that reminded me so painfully of Drake when he was anxious. "Noriko, I think that you're the one who has been blinded."

"Excuse me. I need to get back to my escort." I spotted the door back to the main gallery over Jared's shoulder. If only I could get past him. I was determined to find Franco and stick by his side for the rest of the day.

"You know he killed his father?"

I froze. *What?*

I eyed Jared's face, remembering Drake's words, *Jared Wright is the sneakiest, dirtiest, most self-interested snake you'll ever meet.* "You're lying."

He shrugged. "It was deemed a suicide. Surprising how there was no note."

I shook my head, this possibility rattling around my brain like shards of metal. "Drake wouldn't murder anyone."

"Wouldn't he? Even to get revenge for the murder of his mother?"

I sucked in a gasp. Was it true? Did Drake's father kill his mother? A chill overtook me and I fought back the shiver. Was this why Drake avoided the west wing as if it were cursed?

"They say that Drake looks more like his mother." Jared spoke in a lower voice. "If there's one thing Drake has inherited from his father, it's his temper."

No. I wouldn't believe it. "That's just terrible gossip. Shame on you for repeating it."

I tried to shove past him. He grabbed my upper arm, stopping me from passing, pulling me too close to him. I could smell the sharp, spicy scent of his cologne, so different from Drake's clean, fresh smell.

"You might need a friend soon, Noriko. You might need someone to...help you." He pushed a business card into my palm. "When you do, call me at Wright & Sons."

I stiffened. Even if I did want to call him, I didn't have a phone.

Jared frowned at me. "What? What is it?"

"Nothing," I said, a little too quickly.

His frown deepened. "You're right. Drake can't find my card on you. Give me your phone and I'll save my number in there."

I swallowed, debating my reaction.

"Noriko? Where's your phone?"

"I left it at the hotel."

"You left it? Give me your number," he pulled out his phone, a slim, black smartphone, "I'll store it in mine."

"I don't remember my number."

His eyes narrowed. I could see his mind working over all of my protests. "You don't have one, do you?"

"I...do."

Jared shook his head. "He doesn't even let you have a phone. Here," he pressed his phone into my hand. "Have mine."

"I can't—"

"Yes, you can. I am serious, Noriko, about wanting to be your friend. If you ever need help. Use the phone. Call me. Just don't let your husband find it."

"Are you okay, Noriko?"

I flinched as Drake's hand came down on my arm on the leather plane seat. Drake and I were in his private plane again two days later, this time on our way back to Los Angeles.

"Fine," I croaked out, my throat having gone dry. Jared's phone was burning a hole wrapped in my underwear in the bottom of my bag.

"I'm sorry how this trip turned out," he said, apologizing for the fiftieth time.

I gave him a one-shouldered shrug. "It's fine."

"No, it's not," Drake's voice was so vehement it caused me to start. He gripped my chin in his hand. "Tell me what I can do to make it up to you. Do you want diamonds? More clothes? Shoes?"

I shook my head. "No, Drake. I don't need any of that stuff." He'd already sent me shopping yesterday at Harrods, London's most famous department store, hired a personal shopper to aid me with a budget that was worth more than my father's yearly salary.

"Then what do you want?"

I paused. I was still conflicted over what Jared had revealed to me. I wanted to hear my husband tell me the truth. "Tell me about your parents."

He sank back into his leather seat. "What?"

"I want to know about them. About your father, who he was... Why...why I'm not allowed in the west wing."

Drake's eyes widened. He looked at me as if I'd asked him to murder a puppy. The flash of honest feeling was quickly covered up by his cold façade. "I don't want to talk about them."

The distance between us widened, the space between us becoming more hollow. "Not now…or ever?"

Drake's jaw twitched as he ground his teeth together. "You can have anything else, Noriko. I can give you the world if you ask for it. Just don't ask for that."

I drew back into my chair, studying my husband. He suddenly appeared so foreign. Like a stranger.

Why wouldn't you tell me about your parents? Were you hiding something, Drake? You were controlling and possessive, but…were you a murderer?

Back in my bedroom I unpacked my bag, glancing at my door before I took out my hidden phone and slid it into the toe of a pair of boots in the back of my closet where I also kept my pills.

Another secret.

Another source of guilt.

But I wasn't going to refuse Jared's phone. Now I had a way to contact my father.

I waited until the next afternoon, after lunch. Drake was long gone and the staff had already cleaned our bedrooms and were now busy in other parts of the house. I would be mostly left alone until dinnertime.

I locked myself in the bathroom so I wouldn't be disturbed.

It was three o'clock in California. Japan was sixteen hours ahead of us. It would be seven o'clock in the morning at home. They should be awake by now.

My hands shook as I dialed the number of my family home, numbers that would forever be etched across my heart. My body thrummed with anxious energy as the ringtone sounded in my ear.

I heard a click. "*Moshi moshi.*" My father's warm voice in my mother tongue filled my ear. Instantly my eyes flooded with tears, blurring my vision. I didn't need sight. I clung onto his voice as if it were all my senses.

"*Papa? It's me*," I said in Japanese, trying to keep the sobs out of my voice.

"*Hime?*"

My father called for my auntie and they squabbled as they tried to share the phone receiver. There was a speaker button on their phone but they hadn't learned how to work that yet. I wasn't there to show them. My auntie had come to stay with them to look after the girls while my father was in and out of hospital.

They told me that everyone was fine and that my father had started chemotherapy and radiation. His second surgery was scheduled in a few days.

"Where are you?" my father asked.

"I can't answer that." It was part of my contract that I couldn't tell anyone from my old life where I was living now. They only knew *America.*

"Just tell me...are you okay?" He couldn't hide the worry in his voice.

"I'm okay."

"When are you coming home?" Auntie asked.

"At the end of the year. Like I promised."

"Hime," my father's voice broke, "come home. What you did for all this money, it doesn't matter to me. I love you."

"But your treatments. Your surgery."

"I'd give up these treatments, surgery, everything. Just come home."

"I have to go," I said, trying to keep the sadness from tearing at my voice. I didn't want to get off the phone. I wanted to listen to my papa's voice all day. But I couldn't take his begging for me to return earlier, my insides were already raw from guilt. "I promise I'll try to call again soon."

I asked my father to give each of my sisters a kiss and cuddle for me. I didn't ask to speak to my sisters because I knew that this phone conversation would last an age, each sister wanting to give me a full update and get one in return. I was conscious that the longer I spent on this phone call, the more expensive it would be for Jared. I knew he had the money to pay for long distance. I didn't want to take advantage of his kindness. I didn't want him to have any reason to cut off the phone's service.

"I love you," I said into the phone.

"To the stars and back, *Hime*."

Then I hung up.

I sank to the edge of the huge bathtub and pushed my face into my hand, a torrent of emotions I'd been repressing for months thundering over me. Had it been almost four months since I left them? It felt like forever ago, and yet it felt like yesterday.

I wanted to go home, I desperately wanted to see my father and my sisters again.

But Drake had become so precious to me over the last two months, this broken, confusing beast who just needed me to love him.

I sucked in a breath as realization struck me.

This was a smartphone.

It had internet.

I could look up Drake's parents.

I wiped the last of my tears from my eyes and opened an internet browser on the phone. I typed in: *Louisa Blackwell*, the name of Drake's mother.

The search results populated instantly. As I read over the headlines, my limbs grew colder and colder.

Wife of Millionaire Found Dead

Louisa Blackwell (nee Hamilton), wife of millionaire Pierson Blackwell, owner and founder of Blackwell Industries, was found dead today in her bedroom. Coroner has ruled it an accidental overdose of heroin.

Her son, Drake Blackwell, discovered her body late this morning. He is sixteen.

Oh my God. Poor Drake. My stomach twisted as I imagined him as a teenager, barely a man, finding his mother's body in her room. No wonder he didn't want anyone entering the west wing. He'd never gotten over his mother's death. He'd buried his pain underneath his work, driving him to become an obsessive workaholic, making him the outwardly successful yet broken man he was today.

I found more articles, cruel articles, outlining the breakdown of her marriage to Pierson, their many public fights, Louisa's many affairs and the number of suspected incidents of domestic abuse, thanks to the bruises that appeared on her body that she tried to cover up.

My throat grew tighter and tighter.

I found articles on Drake's father next.

Millionaire Found Dead. Suicide or Murder?

Less than six months after his wife's death, millionaire Pierson Blackwell was found dead of a gunshot wound in his home. Mr. Blackwell was discovered by his son, Drake Blackwell, seventeen, his sole heir who stands to inherit the entire Blackwell fortune, worth just over a billion dollars. The coroner has ruled it a suicide but sources close to the family say they heard father and son arguing only minutes before the gun went off. Was this truly a suicide? Or something more sinister?

Fear gripped my throat. I could not believe that my husband could be a murderer. I could not. He was only seventeen, for Christ's sake.

"You know he killed his father? It was deemed a suicide. Surprising how there was no note."

"Drake wouldn't murder anyone."

"Wouldn't he? Even to get revenge for the murder of his mother?"

"They say that Drake looks more like his mother. If there's one thing Drake has inherited from his father, it's his temper."

Chapter Forty

Drake

Thanks to that photo at the charity auction, and no doubt Wright helped supply them the details, the press had discovered the name of Mrs. Blackwell. They hadn't gotten any details about her. Yet. It'd stay that way if I protected her from this city's vultures.

Something my father could never do.

It seemed to me that Noriko didn't appreciate my protection. She was like an insolent child trying to make things worse, demanding that she attend a public art class, wanting to make friends with people who wouldn't think twice about selling her out to a reporter, giving Franco the slip in London and wandering the goddamn public gallery alone. My hands curled into fists when I thought of it. Thank God nothing had happened to her. This time.

She didn't know what people were truly like. She hadn't been burned enough. She continued to be obstinate, glaring at me as if *I* was trying to repress her. I was keeping her safe. Everything I did was for her own good. Couldn't she see that?

No. Apparently she couldn't.

She had to fucking test me.

That evening, Sam stuck her head into my office, even though I threatened to cut off the balls of anyone who dared disturb me. I'd been in tense board meetings all morning and barely had time to check my damn emails, let alone have lunch.

"Somebody better be dead or dying for you to risk coming in here," I snapped.

She said nothing. The thin press of her lips told me something was very wrong.

She slid the newspaper in front of me and backed away.

My vision bled in from the corners. Here it was, my worst fucking nightmare.

I slammed open the doors to the dining room. My eyes zeroed in on Noriko sitting at the end of table. She leapt to her feet, almost knocking back her chair.

"What's wrong?" her voice sounded fuzzy over the throbbing of blood through my skull.

What's wrong? What's fucking wrong? Her face grew pale as I approached her, newspaper crushed inside my fist. "I'd like for you to tell me why the fuck I'm looking at this." I slammed the paper down on the table. I didn't take my eyes off her. I didn't need to see the photo of her betrayal again. It was burned into my retinas: Noriko standing in an intimate huddle with Jared fucking Wright at the London

National Gallery, his lips near her face.

The headline, in large black font, screamed across the page the question that was on everybody's wagging tongue right now, the question my office had already begun to field from a thousand sticky-beaked reporters:

Mrs. Blackwell's Lover?

It has only been four months since the secret wedding of one of America's most eligible bachelors, billionaire Drake Blackwell, to a mysterious beauty known only as Noriko. Our sources say that Mrs. Blackwell is already seeking comfort and companionship outside her suffocating marriage. Here she is, caught in a tender embrace with none other than Blackwell's most fierce competitor, Jared Wright, billionaire and CEO of Wright and Sons. This reporter has to ask, is history repeating itself?

The whites appeared around Noriko's irises, her mouth making an O as she lifted her face to me again. "Drake, it's not what you—"

"Are you fucking him?"

She gasped so hard it sounded like she was choking. "How could you ask—?"

"*Are you fucking him?*"

"No. I didn't even know he'd be there."

Despite the chattering in my brain—*whore, whore, slut, just like your mother*—I believed her. Or maybe I just needed to believe her.

Noriko was too innocent, too naïve to have contrived a plan like this on purpose. How could she have even made contact with Jared to make plans to meet him; she had no phone.

She continued to ramble, "I tried to get away from him, I swear, Drake. He wouldn't—"

"I told you it wasn't safe," I roared. This all could have

been avoided if she had *listened* to me. "I told you to stay with Franco. But you deliberately went against my orders." Frustration unleashed from me as I stomped towards her.

She backed away. "I didn't know there'd be reporters—"

"It doesn't have to be a fucking reporter. Anyone with a fucking camera phone can sell pictures of you. Anyone can twist anything you say into a story. I fucking told you they're all vultures. Now they know. Now they have a juicy story to run with. Now they've got somewhere to dig. Oh yes, and dig, dig, dig they will, those little worms. They'll dig and they'll use whatever they find to try to tear me down."

My private life was already fodder for the fucking papers, juicy morsels of my flesh to dress their bare-boned, pallid lives. Now her precious life had become carcass for those hyenas and *I* failed to protect her from it.

I could barely think as rage surrounded me. I didn't even realize I'd grabbed her dinner plate and hurled it, smashing against the far wall. Noriko cowered away from the noise and the explosion of china, a scream coming out of her.

"Master Blackwell?" One of the staff, a younger, dark-skinned girl named Celeste, pushed through the dining room door. "Is everything alright?"

"You." I turned my focus on Celeste, anger making my periphery fuzzy and dark. "Leave us. Tell everyone else to leave us."

She just stood there like a fucking mute, looking at me, then at the remnants of the plate, then at Noriko, a story building behind her eyes.

"Get. OUT!"

She yelped as if I'd hit her and disappeared out the door.

"As for you..." I swung my body to face Noriko again. The mere sight of her made the black and white newspaper image superimpose across her face, Jared leaning into her space, his eyes hungry, his hand possessively on her arm. The whole image flickered like a broken cinema screen.

Noriko shrank back against the wall as I approached, her fear turning up the flame under my boiling rage.

She was my wife. She was supposed to be the one fucking person who'd trust me. The one fucking person who would respect my decisions because she knew I was doing it *for* her. Not because she feared me.

Was this what it'd take to make her obey me? Did I have to make her fear me like my staff feared me? Like my employees feared me? Did she need to fear me to obey me?

I rushed towards her, power surging through my body as I crowded her into the wall. I grabbed her, wanting to shake some sense into her.

"Don't!" she cried, her voice pleading, so full of raw fear, shredding at my insides, dislodging a memory of my mother's voice.

"Don't, Pierson! Please."

I stared at my monstrous hand, somehow now gripping her slender wrist, veins surging with blood under my skin. It didn't look like my hand.

It looked…like *his* hand. Like my father's hand.

Only then did I feel how fragile her bones were. Only then did I realize how hard I was gripping her. I could have crushed her forearm like a little mouse in my claws. The blood drained from my body.

"Noriko," slipped from my mouth. My fingers stretched open, stiff as an unoiled hinge. She curled away from me, cradling her arm with her hand.

Shit. Shit, shit, shit.

"Look at me."

She wouldn't.

My eyes kept drawing to the glimpse of my red finger marks between her pale fingers, a glowing accusation around her wrist.

This wasn't my fault. It wasn't. I had to make her understand. I was trying to protect her. I failed. That's why I was angry.

I wrapped my arms around her, grabbing at her even as she slipped through my fingers like a wraith. "Noriko, please, I would never hurt you. I love you." She had to believe me. Of course she believed me. "I'm not like my…" I caught sight of my reflection in one of the dining room mirrors. His face, Pierson Blackwell, flashed in front of mine, making me wince. I buried my face in her hair, smelling fresh like the sea and sweet like hibiscus. I tugged her wrist from her chest and pressed gentle kisses over the fading mark. See, all better. All better. "I'm not like that. You believe me, don't you?"

"Of course I believe you," she said, but her voice was quiet.

My hands traveled over her tiny body. So fragile. So breakable. If I could make love to her, she'd be close to me again. I needed to be close to her again.

My fingers slipped up under her skirt and I felt her flinch. It cut me right into my heart that she would react that way to my fingers.

"I need you." I tilted her face to look at me and pleaded with her silently. Let me love you. Let me show your body all the sorry I couldn't seem to make myself say.

She pressed her lips to mine in submission. Behind it I felt her flickering like a candle about to expire.

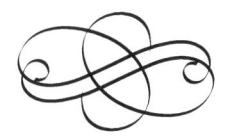

Chapter Forty - One

Noriko

Drake was a lonely rock in his very own sea of pain. And I didn't know how to reach him.

The mark on my arm had already faded by the time I got ready for bed that night. But I could still see his hand there. I traced my wrist with the fingertips of my other hand.

I remembered the fear that rushed through my body as his rage exploded around us like thunder and lightning, lush as a storm, his pain sourced from a well as deep as the ocean.

When his eyes glazed over and he lifted his hand to wrap around my wrist, I wondered who he was seeing in my face. His mother? His father? Or both?

He didn't hurt me. Even through his wild fury, his hand knew not to grip too tightly. I didn't fear him, not truly. How could I when pity tore through my fear like water through paper? How could I when I understood *why* he was the way he was? My heart ached for the little boy inside of Drake that was still drowning in pain. I ached more because he wouldn't deal with it. He wouldn't even talk about it. Even though I kept trying.

Drake Blackwell was a broken man. I wanted to heal him. I didn't know how.

"Papa?" I whispered into the phone.

"You sound sad, hime," he said. "What's wrong?"

I sighed and pulled my knees up to my chest. I was sitting in my locked bathroom in my huge bathtub, cradling the phone between my ear and my shoulder. I didn't think I'd be calling my father again so soon after our conversation yesterday. I needed to hear his voice. It anchored me. I felt adrift, confused.

"Nothing," I lied. "I just miss you."

My father paused. "Your new husband…is he…a good man?"

"Yes, Papa. He's has such a big heart. He appears gruff and jagged on the outside but he's kind and thoughtful. He's a scared little boy on the inside."

"You care about him."

"I do," I admitted, my voice almost a whisper. "I didn't mean to but I do." Despite myself, I smiled as thoughts of Drake weaved through my mind. "Oh, Papa, you'd like him a lot. He's incredibly smart, like you. Even though I'm stubborn—don't pretend like you don't think I'm stubborn—he manages to get under my skin, to make me soften."

"You love him, don't you?"

Trust my father to always know what was in my heart without me breathing a word of it. The smile on my face broke apart as guilt clawed at me. I was failing everyone. Ruining everything. "I'm sorry, Papa. I didn't mean to love him," I said, ashamed that I could let another man take up so much space in my heart. "I still love you more, I swear!"

"Oh, my darling girl." He let out a wistful sigh. "I cannot call you a girl anymore. You are a woman with her own family and her own life."

"I'm coming back. I promised I would. *You* are my family."

"Yes, Noriko, and we will always be your family. Part of our job as a family is to know when to let go of you so you can make your own."

I squeezed my eyes shut, hot liquid slipping out from the corners. "What are you saying?"

"You don't have to come back after a year, Noriko. Or come back just to visit."

"But—"

"You love your husband."

"Yes."

"Then make a life with him. Be there with him. Don't tear yourself in half and be half here, half there and really be nowhere. This old man has had his life. You need to live yours."

"Papa, don't say that!"

"Don't dismiss love, my child. Don't waste time. Or you'll find they are gone all too soon." His voice grew quiet and I knew he was thinking about Mama. They loved each other with the strength of the seasons. He still loved her. "Promise me you'll try with him."

My heart swelled with love for my father. Even though he was sick, even though he knew he could demand all of me and I would give it, he was as selfless and wise as he'd ever been. He had released me from my promise to end my marriage. He had unwound the chains of guilt around my heart.

I could not love him more than in this moment.

"I promise, Papa," I whispered. "Thank you."

Chapter Forty - Two

Drake

Guilt was a permanent fixture in my chest. It had taken up root, piercing its blackened thorny branches into every inch of my soul. I clenched and unclenched my hand, the one I found wrapped around her wrist. How could I have done that to her?

How?

Because as hard as you try not to be, you are *just like* him.

It was late at night. I sat in an armchair in the den on the first floor, a masculine room of deep green and wood, and rubbed my face. It'd been a day since I attacked her in the dining room and I hadn't seen Noriko. Truth was, I was hiding from her. I returned home long after she'd finished dinner and had slept in one of the guest rooms last night so

I didn't have to walk past her door.

I should go to her. I couldn't bring myself to look at her face. I was terrified of what I would find. That any affection for me was gone. That all that was left was the rubble of the happiness I destroyed.

My eyes came to rest upon the framed picture—my only framed picture—on the mantle. She was smiling, almost laughing. I had taken that picture in Giverny in Monet's garden. She had been lost in her painting, her features relaxed, her wrist flicking, sometimes wildly, other times moving as gracefully as if she was dancing. I felt invisible and yet honored to witness such an intimate thing. She had been completely immersed—God, and so beautiful that I couldn't help myself—she hadn't noticed when I slid my camera out of the bag I brought and took a candid shot.

I'd brought my old camera with me that day, one I hadn't used in years. I was surprised when it still worked. I used to carry it around with me like a breastplate when I was a teenager.

The world looked simple through the lens of a camera. If I could fit everything into an ordered rectangle, I could somehow make sense of it.

That day in Monet's garden, the world made sense.

Now...

Someone knocked on my door. Noriko. She'd found me. Twin vines of hope and fear wound around my chest. Did she miss me? Did she crave me like I did her? Is she here to pull me into my bed and into her body? Had she forgiven me?

I cleared my throat and called out for her to come in.

It was Loretta instead. My shoulders deflated and I turned back to the picture of my beautiful wife, distant now, like a dream.

"You don't look very happy," Loretta said. It was such an obvious statement I would have laughed if I'd had the energy.

"Didn't sleep well." I was lying to no one. Both Loretta and I knew the real reason behind my morose mood. The walls of the dining room weren't that thick. My staff here weren't stupid.

"I'm afraid I only bring more…difficult news."

My eyes snapped to hers. There was worry in her gray, wrinkled eyes. Worry and…pity. My stomach tightened. What now?

She reached into the front pocket of her apron. "I found the empty packet in her trash can when I was emptying it earlier today. She tried to hide it under used tissues…" Loretta gingerly placed an empty plastic strip on my desk. "I'm sorry, Drake."

Birth control pills.

I was going to be sick.

"What do you want me to do?" she asked. Her voice had gone all fuzzy in my ears as my mind wrapped around this latest development.

The "unproductive wife" clause. The one my lawyer insisted we put into the marriage contract to protect *me*. How ironic. Noriko was using it to make sure she got out of our marriage scot-free at the end of the year.

She didn't want to stay with me.

She was *never* going to stay with me. No matter what I did.

"Get out."

Loretta's eyes widened. "Drake, please, think about what you're going to do before you do it."

My eyes snapped up to hers, my vision bleeding red on the edges. If she didn't get out right now… "Get. The fuck. Out."

Loretta nodded and rushed out of the den.

I stood, my legs wobbling like I was drunk. I turned to the blank wall beside me, the empty wall mocking me, a mirror of my wretched heart.

I thought she…

I just wanted…

But we…

My fist slammed into the wall. I punched it again and again, warm blood coating my knuckles as the skin split, plaster cracking in a shower of dust. The pain in my knuckles was lost under the roaring pain of my rage.

Why was I cursed? Why was I *still* alone?

I graduated summa cum laude from Harvard Business School. I had an MBA from Yale. I turned my father's million-dollar company into a billion dollar one. I was the third richest man in America, for fuck's sake. I had enough power and reach to affect this country's economy. To affect its policies. I was envied by millions. Millions more wanted to *be* me.

But it wasn't enough for her.

I wasn't enough.

Why was it never enough?

Why was *I* never enough?

A glaring ring cried out, cutting through my rage. I spun, glaring at the offending phone, blood dripping from my knuckles. It was my cell phone, not the office phone, vibrating across the side table. I frowned.

A private number.

It must be work. Work I could deal with. Work would be a temporary reprieve from my wreck of a marriage and my sham of a wife.

I wiped the back of my hand against my pants and snatched up the phone. "What?"

"Mr. Blackwell." The unfamiliar accented voice made me frown. Was this another goddamn reporter? How did he get this number? I took pains to ensure only a select few had it.

"Who is this?"

"You asked me to call you if there was any news…from Japan."

My skin prickled. This was the private investigator, local to Shibetsu, Noriko's home town. "I did."

"I'm afraid the news is not good…"

Chapter Forty - Three

Drake

The private investigator hung up and I dropped the cell phone on the table. It slid off to the carpet. I didn't retrieve it. Anger bled out from me as I fell into my chair.

Fuck.

The surgery did not go well.

Noriko's father was dying.

How would I tell Noriko? How do you break the news to your wife that the father she loved may not survive? She'd only agreed to our contract to pay for his cancer treatments. I wasn't stupid. I'd done my own research.

A horrible thought cracked into my brain like a lightning strike. If he was dying…she'd want to go back to see him. If she returned to Japan…she would never come back. Fear's hand tightened around my throat like a noose, trapping the air in my lungs.

I would lose her.

I couldn't lose her. I couldn't. My skin began to itch like ants were running around beneath the surface. My palms and the backs of my knees began to sweat, panic making my heart choke and splutter.

Damn you, Noriko, for showing me a glimpse of happiness with you. Damn you for stealing it away from me.

I wouldn't tell her that her father had taken a turn for the worse. She didn't need to know. It'd only hurt her. He'd get better. I'd make sure he got better.

Which meant she'd stay right here.

You promised her you'd tell her if anything changed. My uninjured hand gripped the arm of my chair and I shoved that voice down.

I was doing this for us. For the greater good.

She'll get angry that you broke your word.

She can't get angry, I argued with myself. *She's my wife, a good wife. This is why I made this investment. So there was no obligation on my part. She knew the deal when she agreed to marry you.*

I didn't want her to be with me out of obligation. Not anymore.

I loved her.

I needed her to breathe.

Your father loved your mother. Look where that got him.

I shook my head. I wasn't my father. And Noriko wasn't my mother.

Still, fear crept into my bones. A pounding tension started in my temple. My eyes flashed to the liquor cabinet hidden behind a panel of mahogany. I only kept a bottle of fifty-year-old single malt Highland Park whiskey that someone gifted me a few years ago. I'd barely touched it.

I could have a drink. Just one. To take the edge off. It didn't mean I was a drunk. I'd never be a drunk. Just one.

I stood up and walked towards the cabinet.

Chapter Forty - Four

Noriko

It had been a day since Drake's confrontation with me in the dining room. I heard his limo crunching gravel. I spotted the flash of his wide shoulders from my window before he ducked into the house. His footsteps never came down the hall.

He didn't go to his bed last night.

He was avoiding me.

Well, I couldn't avoid him any longer. I had to tell him I loved him. Now that Papa had given me permission, now that my heart was no longer torn in two, these words—*I love you, too*—grew swollen and ripe in my chest, desperate to be gifted, to be shared and consumed between us.

These words would fix our marriage. They would be the mortar between these broken pieces so we could create something whole and beautiful.

I wrapped myself up in a robe, my silk negligee underneath, and went looking for him. I'd search every room in the damn house if I had to.

On the ground floor, the door to the den was open a crack, a light shining from it.

"Drake?" I pushed the door open.

My heart squeezed when I saw him sitting in an armchair in the farthest corner. The only light on was the lamp beside him, casting him in an eerie glow and creating sharp shadows across his scowling face. God, I missed him.

"What do you want?" It came out slurred, more like *whaddayawan?*

I blinked, my purpose here momentarily forgotten. My eyes settled on the dried blood on the back of his hand that was wrapped around a glass. "Jesus, what did you do to your hand?"

He didn't answer.

The glass was filled with amber liquid and there was a half-empty bottle on the side table at his elbow. "Are you... drinking?"

"And Mr. Blackwell Senior?"

"He started drinking. He would fly into the most furious rage. He'd start yelling at her, breaking furniture. Eventually, he hit her. His drinking got worse. Then he started to beat her regularly."

I shook these thoughts out of my head. Drake Blackwell *was not* his father.

But the way his eyes narrowed at me, dark and so hateful, made me shiver.

"Come in, wife."

I moved inside the door. Not all the way in. There was something unnerving about the way he was watching me.

Something hard and cruel.

"Have you become frightened of me?"

"No."

"Why are you trembling like a lamb by the door? Come in. I'm not the dangerous one."

I stepped in farther, the sharp scent of alcohol wrinkling my nose. He never drank. Because of his father... Why was he drinking now? "How many have you had? Drake?"

What demons clouded his soul tonight?

He ignored my question, his dark eyes boring into mine. He leaned forward, resting his elbows on his knees as if he was about to share with me a secret. "You put on a good show, don't you?"

"What?"

"You come across all innocent. So fresh-faced and open-hearted. Well," he took a large gulp of his drink, "we both know better, don't we?"

Shit. Had there been another newspaper article? Another accusation against me? "I already told you, nothing is going on between Jared Wright and me."

He let out snort. "Jared Wright is a manipulative megalomaniac, but at least he doesn't hide who he is."

I stared at my husband, my head spinning, my breath going shallow. I had come here to confess my love. To promise that we could make our marriage work. To apologize for being distant.

How had this night gone so wrong?

Why was Drake being hateful? What'd happened? Had I pushed him away so much that our bond was broken? Was everything lost?

"Drake, please talk to me."

"Let's toast." Drake thrust his glass in the air, liquid splashing out over the rim. "To our sham of a marriage."

I gasped. "Drake—"

"To a wife who thinks she can fool her husband. And a husband who will never be good enough for her." He threw back his drink, gulping it all down and finishing it off with a loud smack of his lips before wiping his mouth with the back of his uninjured hand.

Coldness sank into my bones. I couldn't stay here. Not while he was like this. Not when every word he was saying tore pieces off me. When he refused to explain why his love had turned to hate.

"I won't stand here and listen to you carry on until you say something you'll regret. You're drunk."

"And you're a cold-hearted bitch."

His words pierced my heart, tearing holes in it. I tried not to react. I failed, tears already pricking the backs of my lids.

How did we get here? Was it only three weeks ago that we spent that perfect day in Monet's garden? How did we get this hazy, bogged down in the chaos? Why couldn't we raise ourselves up to see the bigger picture?

I turned, my movements wooden, my mind whirring, walking away before I crumbled to ash.

"That's it," he called after me, his voice as hard and bitter as underripe fruit. "Leave. You were going to anyway."

I halted, gasping.

He knew.

He knew my secret.

I didn't have the strength to turn around and defend myself. I had no excuse. I was going to leave him. *Was*.

Until today.

Now he'd never believe me.

I woke late the next morning with swollen eyes from crying myself to sleep. This rift between Drake and me was my fault. I had been taking those pills. I had been planning to leave Drake after one year.

I didn't plan on falling in love with him.

By the afternoon the need to talk to my father again was like an itch I couldn't scratch.

I needed to talk to someone about Drake. About how to fix things between us. Papa would know what to do. He always knew what to do.

This time my sister picked up the phone.

"Tatsumi, it's me," I said in Japanese.

"Oh, Noriko," my sister said, her voice tight and strained.

"What's wrong?" I asked.

My sister broke the silence with a sob. "It's Papa."

"What happened?" I said, my voice getting louder. "Tell me."

"His surgery…" she managed out between cries. "There were…"

"He's okay now, right? Right?"

By now my sister was crying so hard she couldn't speak.

No. My father had to be fine. I'd know it in my heart if there was something wrong. Drake would have told me if there was something wrong. He promised.

"Where's Papa? Put him on the phone."

I heard a crackling and fumbling on the other end. My aunt's voice came on. "Noriko? It's Rumi. I'm sorry to have to tell you this…"

Stop it. Stop right there.

I heard my sister crying in the background, the noise reaching into my heart and slicing it into pieces with every sound.

"There were complications with your father's surgery," my aunt continued, her voice quiet and solemn. "I'm so sorry, little butterfly. He may not have long. You have to come home."

Chapter Forty - Five

Drake

Tonight she was waiting for me in my bedroom. Before I had even closed the door behind me, her voice tremored over my name.

"What's wrong?" I asked, my stomach already sinking under the weight of premonition.

"I need to go back to Japan."

Fuck. "No," I said, a little too quickly.

She bit her lip to keep it from trembling. I hated that she was close to tears. Her pain was my pain. I couldn't let her emotions manipulate me. My mother used to use tears.

Only the weak allowed themselves to be manipulated. And Drake Blackwell was not a weak man.

I steeled myself, looking at something over her shoulder so she remained just out of focus.

"Drake, my father…my father is dying. I need to go back."

She knew. It was over. A bomb detonated in my stomach, shrapnel and fire ripping through me. This would ruin everything. *Everything*.

"How do you know that?" I asked, deflecting, even as I felt the ground underneath my feet shaking.

She ignored my question. "You'll let me go back, won't you?"

"You called them *behind* my back even after I told you not to. How did you get hold of a phone?"

"My father is dying and all you can say—"

"My father is dead. Fathers die."

The gasp that ripped from her mouth felt like it had torn off me. "You can't be this cruel. Please, let me go. I need to say goodbye."

She's going to leave me. She wants to leave me.

"I told you I was keeping an eye on things back in Japan. I told you I'd take care of it."

"You lied," she yelled. "My father is dying and you said nothing to me."

"I was trying to protect you!"

"By keeping it from me? When would you have told me? *After* the funeral?"

If I let her leave, she will never return.

If I lose her, I will die.

I. Will. Die.

Like he did. Just like him. You're just like him. Like father, like son.

This all-too familiar voice rose unbidden this time, choking me, throbbing in my ears like my heartbeat, rattling in my brain until I thought I would go mad.

I felt my body ice up in defense until the blood froze over in my veins and my words came out like frost. "I was trying to figure out how to break the news to you."

"You're lying. You're lying to me." Her arms thrashed out in the air like she was trying to punch my shadow, her voice a mere screech. "You don't want me to go *anywhere* or talk to *anyone*."

"What garbage."

"You won't let me out of this house. You won't let me have friends. I'm a prisoner here. A fucking prisoner."

"Calm down, Noriko."

"Calm down? Calm the fuck down?" She grabbed a vase and threw it at me, a scream tearing from her lungs. "Is this calm enough for you, you son of a bitch?"

It was a wild shot. I moved my head to the side and it flew right past me. It had zero chance of hitting me. But when the vase smashed against the wall, it buried the rest of the emotions left within me. I was now totally cold. I glared at Noriko shaking like a leaf, her mouth distorting into an ugly clownish sneer.

"Please," she threw herself at my feet. "Let me see him. Please, I'm begging you."

"No."

"You can't do this." She clawed at my pant leg, her voice filled with disbelief. "You have to let me say goodbye to my father." The tears streaming down her cheeks were cutting through my shields.

I had to stay strong. I had to hold us together. If I gave in to her, we crumbled.

I crumbled.

I wrapped more steel around my heart until I was stiff and straight from it. My voice was harder to keep steady. "Stay."

Her tears sparkled with fury, with hatred. She launched herself back onto her feet, backing away from me. "Fuck you. I'm going anyway."

I'm going anyway.

Something inside me cracked beneath my fortress walls. Panic overtook all thought.

I could not let her leave me.

I grabbed her arm and yanked her flush against my body. Even furious at her, my body burst into flames at her nearness. My gaze dropped to her lips, parted and pink, breath heaving. God, it felt like forever since I'd kissed her lips. My wife. *My* lips. I leaned in to take them.

Her palm smacked against my cheek, sharp pain radiating through my face. "Let go of me, you *monster*."

"Monster? *Monster?*" I grabbed her with both hands and shook her.

"You're a selfish, heartless beast." She beat my chest, emphasizing each hateful word.

The memory of her betrayal—her birth control pills—flooded my body with fury. "And you're a lying, manipulative bitch. I guess we deserve each other."

She screamed in my face and tried to push me away. I was much stronger than she was. I tightened my grip until she was wincing in pain.

A part of me was screaming, *stop it, you're hurting her!*

Part of me wanted to hurt her for all the pain she had caused me. An eye for an eye. A strip of your heart for all of the pieces you have torn off mine.

The biggest part of me was terrified—so terrified I could barely think. All I could hear in my head was her threat.

I'm going anyway.
I'm going anyway.
I'm going anyway.

She was going to leave me. She couldn't fucking leave me.

I pulled her across the floor, out of my room and towards her bedroom, ignoring her kicking and screaming for me to let go of her, ignoring her feeble attempts to grab onto the doorframe. Fear bubbled across my skin in a simmer, making my brain full of cotton.

She was going to leave me.

She couldn't leave me. I wouldn't let her. I just needed to keep her here until I could fix this.

I thrust her into her bedroom. She backed away from me, her eyes wild, glancing all around her.

I took the small key from the inside of her lock. "You give me no choice." I shut the door behind me and locked it, my heart lurching into my throat as her little body slammed against the other side of it.

The door vibrated as I leaned my palm against it, clutching the door without purchase, a raw, silent sob scraping itself around the insides of my chest at her screams of anguish. Each heartbeat of mine alternated between two thoughts.

You hurt me, too, Noriko.
And,
I can't lose you.

Chapter Forty - Six

Noriko

The sun sank beneath the edge of the Earth, sucking all its light back from between the bars of my prison.

It'd been three days since I'd been locked in my bedroom.

Loretta had been coming in daily with my meals on silver trays, taking away the previous untouched tray, chastising me for not eating.

I wasn't hungry.

I wasn't cold.

I wasn't anything.

I stared blankly at the far wall as I lay in my sheets.

I hadn't been able to cry all day.

There was so much pain in my body that I couldn't tell the difference anymore between pain and no pain.

They say it's a fine line between love and hate. I had no more lines, the two sides bled into each other.

I hated him

I loved him.

I hated that I loved him.

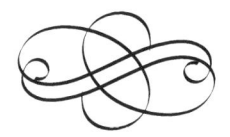

Chapter Forty - Seven

Drake

I walked the lonely path from the top of the stairs to my bedroom. Every time I did I had to pass Noriko's door. As I stepped closer, my heart rate heightened and my palms grew sweaty.

I couldn't walk past without stopping. The space around her door was like quicksand, dragging at my heels and slowing my steps until I was forced to stop completely, staring at the pale decorative door.

I lifted up a hand and touched the cool surface. Somewhere behind this thin separation of wood was the chalice of my remorse. If I could see her. If I could talk to her…

What would I say?

I said nothing. Instead I grasped onto any sounds of life. Sometimes I heard the rustle of sheets as she shifted in bed. Sometimes I heard her crying. I ran the tips of my fingers along the painted wood and gripped the key in my other hand, leaving marks in my palm.

Eventually, I let my fingers fall and continued my journey, alone, except for all my guilt slung around my shoulders like chains of iron.

I was like a wraith. Functioning during the day, working myself longer hours than ever so I didn't have to go home and face...her.

To face...what I'd done.

I couldn't let her out yet.

Because I didn't know how to force us back together. I didn't trust her not to find a way to leave me, to disappear back to Japan.

She wasn't theirs anymore. She was mine. I needed her more than they did. I couldn't live without her.

If you save a life, you're responsible for it.

She saved me. She was responsible for me.

Today as I stopped by her bedroom I heard two voices. I pressed my ear to the door, straining to hear.

"Did you make all these?" I recognized Loretta's voice.

"Yes." My heart tugged at the sound of Noriko's voice.

"Wow, there're so many." What were they talking about? What did Noriko make?

"Nine hundred and forty-two, to be exact."

I needed to see. Just a sliver of her. Just a piece.

I slipped the key that I always carried with me into the lock and turned it slowly. Pushing the door open a crack, I searched for Noriko, my eyes hungry for her.

Loretta and Noriko were standing in front of one of the shelves. It had been empty when Noriko moved in. Now it was covered in what looked like…paper cranes, all in different colors, some patterned, some plain.

Loretta picked one of them up, a blue one, and turned it over in her hands. "Why paper cranes?"

I strained to hear Noriko's answer.

"It's part of the senbazuru legend," she said, barely within my hearing. "Legend says that if you fold a thousand paper cranes you are granted one wish."

"And you're going to fold all thousand cranes."

"Yes."

"What will you wish for?"

"The only thing I want."

"Which is?"

"I want to go home. Where I'm loved."

My heart stabbed. She didn't think I loved her? How could she not feel my love? I'd given her everything to be happy: her own studio, the finest clothes, this beautiful house. What else? What more could I give? Whatever I had was hers.

"Oh, Noriko," Loretta slipped the crane back on the shelf. "You are loved."

Noriko's answer might as well have been a bullet to my heart. "Here, in this mansion, I have everything except love."

I was drinking again.

The world was fuzzy and my pain blunted when I drank.

No wonder my father did it.

The door to my study opened and Loretta stepped in. I think I had been waiting for her.

"Drake Blackwell," she began.

"Loretta Stern," I slurred back to her.

"I have been with you since birth. I have raised you as if you were my own. You have done some questionable things. But this...locking your wife in her room while her father lies dying...this is almost unforgivable."

I winced as her words dug into my skin. I couldn't lose Noriko. I couldn't let her go. Why couldn't anyone see that? "I don't pay you to tell me what's right or wrong."

"Somebody should! And apparently I am the only one who isn't scared to tell you. You are being an ass."

Her words rained against my numbness like arrows. Under the fog, the beast simmered.

"If you don't let her go back to say goodbye to her father, she'll *never* forgive you."

I slammed my glass down on the table. "If I let her go, she will never come back."

"Maybe. Maybe she will. If she doesn't, you only have your terrible behavior to blame."

"No. She stays." It was part of my plan. Keep her here. Fix it. Make her love me.

"What are you going to do? Keep her locked up for the rest of her life?"

"I..." Stupid details. "Just until she promises to stay."

Loretta let out a snort. "Really, boy? For someone so smart you really are stupid sometimes."

"Are you looking to get fired?"

"Let her go. If she is yours—truly yours—she will come back."

"I will not lose her. I can't lose her," I yelled. "She stays."

Loretta shook her head, her eyes filling with pity. "I'm afraid you already may have."

Chapter Forty - Eight

Noriko

I stared at the wall of my colorful paper cranes. My bright symbols of hope.

Nine hundred and fifty-six.

Only forty-four to go.

I knew it was just a legend. But I needed hope. I needed something to hang on to. Or else I would go mad here, thinking about my father dying in a hospital bed somewhere alone.

If only I could become a crane. To fold my body like paper and grow wings. I'd fly across the ocean to my papa. Nothing could stop me.

But I wasn't a crane. I was just a girl and no one could help me.

Oh my God.

I was so stupid. Why didn't I think of it before?

Because I was too numb with pain, too shaky with fury. I ran into my closet and snatched out my secret phone from its hiding place in my shoe. My fingers shook as I scrolled through the contacts and found the work cell number of the only person who had offered me help.

I worried my bottom lip with my teeth as my finger hovered over the call button. Drake hated Jared. Drake would hate that I asked Jared for help. He'd never forgive me.

Well, he shouldn't have locked me in my fucking room. He shouldn't have denied my last chance to be with my dying father. I held onto my anger, because anger was easy to grip. It was solid and dynamic, forcing me into action instead of letting me drown.

"Noriko," Jared answered almost instantly, "I'm so glad you called."

"Jared, please, I need help." My voice came out breathy as if I'd been running for miles. My heart ached like I had been.

"Jesus, Noriko. Is everything okay?"

I let out a sob, a crack in my frozen grief as warm hope—real hope—flooded my body. Once I started talking, I couldn't stop. Not even the thread of unease worming its way through me could stop the spill of secrets once the dam broke.

I told him everything.

Chapter Forty - Nine

Drake

Roger slammed a newspaper on my desk in front of me. "What the hell is this?"

"Good fucking morning to you too," I muttered as I snatched up today's broadsheet. My eyes fell upon the headline and my blood turned to ice in my veins.

The Shocking Truth About Billionaire Drake Blackwell's Wife!
The mysterious Noriko Blackwell has been uncovered! Mrs. Blackwell is a poor teacher's daughter from rural Japan. She agreed to marry the arrogant billionaire, Drake Blackwell, in an arranged marriage in order to pay for her father's cancer treatments. Now that her father is close to death, Drake has locked her in her bedroom at Blackwell Manor in order to

prevent her from returning to her homeland to see him. Mrs. Blackwell has sent out an urgent call for her release. This reporter can only imagine what kind of abuse is happening in the cursed Blackwell Manor. Like father, like son.

"Is this true? You paid her to marry you? You're keeping her locked up?"

I drew my gaze up to Roger, my mind gaping open like a fish. How did this happen? Someone told the papers. Who? Who told the papers?

There were only four people who knew the entire story contained in the article.

Me, and I didn't fucking spill my guts to a reporter.

Isabelle, who would never allow this to get out. The same went for my lawyer who drew up the marriage contract. Both of them were under an ironclad confidentiality contract. Neither of them were stupid enough to burn their bridges with me like this.

That left…Noriko.

I sank back into my chair. Noriko told them. She betrayed me.

"You know what?" Roger said, snapping me out of my thoughts. "I don't care what the truth is. What the fuck are we going to do about it?" He ran his hands through his hair. "Your reputation in this business is everything, you know that. No one is going to want to do business with an abusive husband."

"I am not abusive!" I slammed my fist against the desk, making everything rattle. "I'm insulted at the suggestion."

Roger stabbed his finger at the article. "You are keeping your fucking wife locked up."

My blood ran cold.

I was keeping my wife locked up.

I *was* an abusive husband.

No. No, no, no. That wasn't true. I never hit her. Never. I was *not* like my father.

Roger pushed back off the desk, swear words spit-firing out of his mouth. "Jesus fucking Christ, everything we've worked for, Drake."

"I know," I said quietly.

"We'll run damage control. We'll send out a press release denying everything in this article. We need to get you and your wife out at a public event, a charity event, any fucking event. You two need to be sweet-as-pie, so-cute-I'm-going-to-barf, can't-keep-your-hands-off-each-other lovebirds. Do you hear me?"

"Yes," I said woodenly. I let Roger take control of this situation because nothing in my mind was working.

She betrayed me. My wife—*my wife*—betrayed me. I couldn't even muster any anger at her. *I* had failed.

"Hey, look at me."

My eyes snapped to Roger, who was leaning towards me, his palms flat on the desk. His eyes drilled into mine. "Can you make this happen? Can you be loving with your wife in public?"

Noriko would never agree to it.

Unless…unless I promised to let her go back to Japan.

"Well, Drake? Can you?"

What would it be, Drake? Your company and reputation…or your wife?

Loretta's words came back to me. *"Let her go. If she is yours—truly yours—she will come back."*

I had no choice. This wasn't only my livelihood at stake. Every single employee in my company would suffer if my reputation did.

I had to promise to send Noriko back to Japan if she pretended to love me for one night, for one public event.

She'd do it even though she hated me. Because she

loved her father more. I never had a chance.

"She'll do it."

Roger let out a huge sigh of relief. "Thank God. I'll get our PR department to draw up the press release now. I'll get Sam to find a suitable event to RSVP to for…say, tonight?"

I nodded, numb through my pain. Roger left me alone with my demons, slamming the door to my office shut behind him.

Tonight, Noriko and I would pretend to be happy. We'll hold hands and I'll wave to the reporters on the red carpet and she'll smile at me like I am her world.

God, it would kill me, having her hands on me and knowing it was all lies.

Hadn't it all been lies anyway?

My heart crumpled. I didn't want her to pretend.

I wanted her to love me.

I *needed* her to love me. I needed it so hard it *hurt*. My heart physically ached.

I'd destroyed every chance I had with her. It was clear, written across these pages in black and white.

I'd lost her. I'd only myself to blame. All I had left were pieces of this façade, shards of our sham, blurry dabs of chaos.

And tonight. My one last night with her.

I stared up at the Monet hanging on the opposite wall and my heart stabbed again. I remembered being with Noriko at the charity auction, sliding my hands around her waist and whispering into her ear, sharing our thoughts on painting. I think I started to love her then.

As I gazed at the Monet this time, I couldn't see my way out of the chaos, out of the mess I'd fallen into.

Pain tore through my heart so hard this time it made me cry out.

Oh God. It wasn't just from a broken heart. This was

real pain.

"Sam," I croaked out as I stabbed at the intercom with one hand, gripping my chest with the other. "Help. Me."

My door slammed open and Sam rushed in. "Oh my God, Drake." She ran up to my desk. The next second she was on my phone, talking to emergency services, shouting out the address. "Get here, right now!" She slammed the phone down in its cradle.

Pain throbbed through my left side. I crumpled over my thighs, no energy left to keep myself on my chair. "Don't tell Noriko…don't want…her to see…" I collapsed onto the carpet, the smell of carpet cleaner hitting my nose.

This was it. I was going to die.

You were right, Dr. Tao. It is my heart that will kill me.

Even as my vision started to dim, death seemed to bring a clarity to my eyes. All of my accomplishments, my accolades, all of my money, my beautiful house and my cars and pretty toys, didn't mean shit. These things dissipated like mist in the wake of the last sharp, bright seconds of my life.

Who did I love?
Noriko.
Who loved me?
No one.
Why?

Because I thought private jets and jewels and artists' studios were enough to buy her love. I thought the obligation of marriage, the birth of a baby, the contract we both signed, would be enough to cement us together.

I was wrong.
I thought I had been loving her.
I was wrong.
I thought she was mine.
I was wrong.

They said your life flashed before your eyes before you died. For me, it was only the last four months of my life unfolding before me, where Noriko was a part of it. All those chances I blew to forge a real connection with her shone clearly like diamonds, mapping out a path of gems I had just walked past. If only I had seen them for what they were. If only I had stopped to pick them up.

But it was too late.

It was all too late.

Blackness soaked up through my extremities and I felt death closing in. I could barely hear Sam crying at me to stay with her.

All I could see was Noriko's face. I wished I could have told her that I was sorry. Despite our secrets she parted with, I still loved her. For the first time in my life I understood what that meant.

Her happiness means more to me than my own.

I accepted my death because my death would make her free. With her freedom, I would finally make her happy.

My broken heart beat once more for her.

Chapter Fifty

Drake

Turned out I was a tough old bastard and I didn't die easily.

I opened my eyes with a groan. I heard the beeping of a machine and smelled the sharp scent of disinfectant and sickness. Ugh, I was in a hospital.

There was a blurry feminine figure leaning over me. Noriko?

I reached for her.

"Good to have you back." I recognized Sam's voice.

I dropped my hand.

Sam was sitting beside my bed, her face drawn with concern. She lifted a cup and straw to my mouth and I sipped. Jesus, water was good. She pulled the straw away and I grumbled. "Not so fast." She allowed me a few more sips before placing the cup on the table beside me. "You had a heart attack."

"No, shit Sherlock," I croaked out.

She snorted. "You must be feeling better if you've got enough energy to be an asshole."

I wanted to smile but everything hurt.

I looked past Sam, searching the room for *her*. Noriko wasn't there. My shoulders sagged. She wasn't there.

Sam must have read my mind because she said, "I wanted to call your wife but...you told me not to. Besides, I don't have a number listed for her. You were calling for her when you were asleep."

I would call for her in my death, too.

"Do you want me to call her now?"

Shame filled my aching body when I remembered everything I'd put Noriko through. I couldn't see her.

I didn't want her to see me like this. Close to death. Sick. Fragile.

I had to make things right. I had to let her go. I had to release her.

My chest filled with pain. This time the pain felt *right*. "Call Loretta. I want to speak to Loretta."

As Sam did what I asked, I closed my eyes and sent out my silent goodbyes.

I'm sorry I couldn't love you the way you should be loved. You deserve more than me.

Chapter Fifty - One

Noriko

After I hung up with Jared yesterday I alternated between pacing the room and pressing up against my window, staring at the front gates in the distance. He promised to send help. I didn't know how he was planning on doing that. Maybe he'd send in a helicopter or storm the gates. I had to believe he would help free me. That he would help get me back to Japan.

Rushes of guilt crackled underneath my skin. I could barely ignore it. I shouldn't have spilled my secrets with Drake to another person. I couldn't hold it in anymore. I needed help and Jared was the only one offering it to me. The longer I waited, the greater the chance that I wouldn't get back to my father in time.

Oh, God. What if I was too late? What if he died before I got a chance to see him again?

My fingers shook as I made the familiar folds on a square of blood-red paper. I folded a face and beak. Then his tail appeared. Finally I gave him wings so he could fly.

There. It was finished. One thousand paper cranes.

I placed my little bird in the very center of the other nine hundred and ninety-nine cranes. I closed my eyes and made my wish.

I want to go home. Let me go home.

The door opened, startling me. Loretta entered the room, a solemn look on her face, her eyes red-rimmed as if she'd been crying.

I moved towards her. "Loretta, what's wrong?"

She held up a hand, warning me not to come too close to her. "You are to pack your bags."

"Where am I going?"

Her eyes flashed with something I could not decipher. "Home."

I could scarcely believe it. I was sitting on Drake's private jet flying back home, in the same seat I sat in coming over here less than five months ago. Had it only been four months?

No matter, in less than fourteen hours I'd be with my papa again.

I picked at the expensive nail polish on my nails, a pale pink color like cherry blossoms. I'd never been a nail polish kind of girl. But while I'd been living in the Blackwell Manor, I'd taken to changing my nail polish color every day for something to do. That was, until Drake locked me in my room.

The memory of that day seemed faded in my mind. My rage, the way I yelled, the vase I threw at him. Shame coated me. We had both been animals that day.

The varnish on my nails was chipped, the gloss worn thin. Like my marriage to Drake. When our gloss faded, what were we left with? Lies. Pain. The fight.

I won. I was going home.

I would see my papa soon.

So why wasn't I happy?

As I left the manor, hugging Loretta goodbye, I felt my heart pang. I would miss her, miss this house and…

Why didn't Drake say goodbye to me? I looked for him at the airport—I thought he might have at least met me there to see me off. He didn't even say goodbye. I didn't get to tell him thank you.

Why, after hanging onto me so hard it had become suffocating, did he just let me go?

Was this Jared's doing? It must be. How did Jared get Drake to release me? How did he convince him? Drake hated Jared. He never would have agreed…

Did he blackmail Drake?

In my haste to pack I forgot to bring my phone. I left it behind, sitting in my boot. I may never know.

The tension in my stomach tightened the farther away from Los Angeles—and Drake—I got. I feared…I feared that I had done something irreversible.

I sat at my father's bedside in his private room at Osaka University Medical Hospital. The air was chilled, causing goose bumps on my arm, and smelled of hospital-grade disinfectant and the stale must of recycled air. The machine by his bedside beeped in time with his heart. I latched onto that precious sound. My father looked like a child in the bed, so sunken and fragile that I almost couldn't believe it was him. Someone had stolen my father and replaced him with a shadow.

He mumbled and his lashes flickered. I sat up in my seat. "Papa?"

He blinked several times before his familiar dark brown eyes found me. "Noriko?" he croaked out. It was the sweetest sound.

I shushed him and held up a cup of water with a straw. He drank a few gulps before sagging back onto his pillow. I placed the cup down and took his soft, crinkly hand in both of mine, careful to avoid the IV drip coming out of the back of it. He felt like paper, thin and just as tearable.

His eyes were still hooded from sleep, from the drugs they had him on, things I had no hope of naming. "Nori-chan, is that really you?"

"It's me, Papa." Tears marked hot streaks down my cheeks, sliding over my smiling lips. My happiness tasted like salt. The same as sadness.

I embraced him around the wires and tubes coming out of him.

When I pulled back he eyed me, a smile spreading across his cracked lips. "I'm so glad you're here to say goodbye."

"I am not here to say goodbye." How dare he suggest it. "You're not going anywhere. Neither am I." My voice vibrated with the force of my will. If only my will was enough.

"Hime, they tried to operate. But…the cancer's grown around my spine. The surgeon couldn't get it all out. It's only a matter of time—"

"No!" *Not listening. Not listening.* "There must be something we can do."

MR. BLACKWELL'S BRIDE

"You've already done enough."

My jaw ached from how hard I was clenching my teeth. How dare he. He'd already given up. He couldn't give up. I wouldn't let him. He was the one who always told me never to give up. And now he was lying there being the world's biggest hypocrite. There *had* to be another treatment. Another surgery. Some kind of drug. I'd go to the university medical library and research it my damn self if I had to.

"Can I get you anything?" I said, changing the subject, my voice betraying the violence of my inner convictions. He would not convince me that it was too late. I would find a way to save him. I cursed myself internally for all those wasted hours I spent at Blackwell Manor. I could have been researching his cancer. I could have been finding new doctors, better doctors. I handed over too much power to the health system here and clung too tightly onto threads of faith. "Food? More drugs?"

Before he could answer, I heard hard, sure footsteps coming up behind me. I spun—for a moment, thinking those footsteps belonged to Drake.

Instead it was a woman, a doctor, I presumed from her white coat, but her skin was fair and her blond hair, pulled back into a neat ponytail, was brushed with silver at the temples. A foreign doctor? An oddity in this Osaka hospital.

The doctor smiled at me and nodded to my father. "Hello, you must be Mr. Akiyama and Mrs. Blackwell," she said in English.

"Who are you?" I asked, my hackles rising at her use of my married name.

"I'm Dr. Newton, from Johns Hopkins Hospital."

I blinked as the name sank in. "From the States?"

She flashed me a perfectly white smile as more nurses and orderlies filled up the room. "Yes. I've flown in specifically to treat your father."

"I…" I was too stunned to protest as one of the nurses gently tugged me off my father's bed and to one side, her gentle touch and warm smile confusing me further. They swarmed around my father. I repressed the urge to yank them all away from him. "Stop. Get off him." I turned back to the doctor, anger swirling around my body. Nobody was taking my father anywhere until I understood why. "What are you doing to him? What's going on?"

Her voice was calm despite my outburst. "I don't want to toot my own horn…well, okay, maybe I do," she said with a chuckle. "I've pioneered a new precision surgery. It's the first of its kind. I believe we may be able to save him."

"But… What? How?"

"I agree. It's completely unorthodox. I usually only operate out of Johns Hopkins. But when a man like that makes me and our hospital an offer like that… Well, I can't refuse him."

"A man like…?" I trailed off, my guts twisting.

Dr. Newton gave me a strange look, tilting her head. "Why, your husband, of course."

A brand new hospital wing?

Drake Blackwell offered Johns Hopkins a brand new cancer research wing if this miracle doctor and her team would fly to Osaka and save my father. An entire wing. Not a room or even a corridor or a large, expensive piece of medical equipment. An entire *wing*. Kitted out with all the latest medical equipment.

My first reaction was one of disbelief. Why the hell would Drake do this? He had no reason to.

You were his reason, Noriko.

I shook my head. If he still cared, then why didn't he come and say goodbye to me?

My second reaction was indignation. *I* was going to find a way to save my father—my love was going to find a way—but Drake had to come along with all his damn money and his "everybody do what I say" power. I bet when he died, he'd demand that God send him back to Earth, and you know what? I bet God would. If only to avoid Drake's ego taking up most of heaven for another few years.

I watched my father's frail body disappear between double doors. I felt sick and dizzy, the glaring lights of this ward blinding me. I felt too terrified to hope. Could this surgery actually save him?

I fell into a plastic chair in the waiting room, staring at the linoleum floor—large squares of a sickly green—while the miracle doctor and her team operated on my father. At some point a kind nurse pushed coffee in a Styrofoam cup into my hand.

Once I was able to think a little clearer, I called my sisters and aunt at home to update them on my father's surgery. I didn't tell them that my husband was the one to thank.

My sisters were still in Shibetzu with our auntie, still going to school and trying to have some semblance of a normal life. All the money I received from my marriage contract had gone to my father's treatments. It was almost gone. Until Drake stepped in.

We had no money to spare for a hotel room for my sisters here in Osaka. I wasn't even sure where I was staying. This waiting room was my home right now, I guessed. I hung up with promises to call them back after the surgery was over.

I needed to call Drake and thank him. As I stared at the keypad, I wasn't sure I could make myself dial his home number.

What would I say? God, how badly I'd behaved. He did this for my father anyway.

"Noriko Blackwell?"

I hung up the undialed phone and looked around expectantly. The source of the kind voice was a woman wearing a tailored skirt-suit, her hair pulled back into a bun.

"I'm sorry, who are you?"

She smiled at me. "You've been up all night. You must be very tired. Your father won't be out of surgery for at least six hours. Would you like to rest?"

She must be one of the hospital admin staff. Whoever she was, she was a godsend.

The woman, whose name was Sakuri, escorted me in a black car to a nearby hotel. She checked me into a suite and told me, while I was staring around at this palatial space, that this suite was mine until my father was discharged. She indicated the closet which was filled with brand new clothes, stylish yet comfortable wear, linen pants and cotton blouses, all in my size.

"Mr. Blackwell thought you should be comfortable while you look after your father. The hospital knows to call you here once your father is out of surgery. There's a car on standby to take you to the hospital or anywhere you'd like."

She left me, standing stunned, a strange prickling in my eyes.

I *must* call him now.

I sank into the huge bed and punched in the number to Blackwell Manor in the phone beside it. My heart rate crept up as the calling tone rang in my ear. It crackled when someone picked up and I took in a steadying breath. *Drake?*

"Hello?" A female voice said.

I sagged.

"Loretta, hi, it's Noriko." I asked her how she was, how the manor was and about the herbs she'd planted a few days before I left. I asked about everything other than the one thing I needed to ask…

"So, um," I rubbed the back of my neck. I couldn't delay it any longer. "Is...Drake there?"

Loretta cleared her throat. "I'm sorry, Drake isn't home right now."

"Oh." I looked at the time and calculated that it was not quite dinnertime there. "When will he be home?"

Loretta paused. "I...er, I don't know."

"I'll call later, then."

"Maybe you should let me take a message."

"Oh. Okay. Well...tell him..." *thank you, a thousand times thank you for what he did,* "...tell him to call me."

I hung up. I couldn't express my gratitude through a message, I had to say it to him. It would be better if I could tell him to his face.

Chapter Fifty - Two

Drake

"Noriko called," Loretta said from the doorway behind me.

I winced and rubbed my eyes. I'd been home from the hospital a day and already this place felt empty. I was standing in Noriko's room—her *old* bedroom. It wasn't hers anymore. She was gone—I stared out her window into the night sky. I wondered if she was looking at the same stars. No, it'd be morning already where she was. She was literally on the other side of the world from me; as far as she could get.

I could still smell her perfume in the air. The clothes that I bought her, all hanging in her wardrobe. The books she was reading were stacked up beside her futon bed. And the ghost of her still clung to my heart.

"How did you know I was here?" I asked Loretta without turning around.

"You weren't in your room. Only one other place you'd come…"

I grunted. Was I really that predictable? I suppose I was. Poor little rich boy. Ruined the only thing that was important to him. Broke it by wanting it too much.

"You miss her, don't you?"

"Damn you, woman," I said with no malice in my tone, "can't you leave me to wallow in peace?"

"If you miss her, go to her."

I squeezed my eyes shut and allowed myself to feel—really feel—the ache of wanting to do just that. Then I released the ache as I released my breath. "I don't think that's a good idea, do you?"

"Why not?"

"Why would she want to see her *fucked up* husband again."

"You are not *f'ed up*."

"I didn't let her go out without me."

"You were trying to protect her."

"I forbid her to call her father."

"You…had your reasons."

"I locked her in her goddamn room."

"Yes, well… We've all done stupid things in the name of love."

I sighed. "I can't…" I can't be the man she needs. Or deserves. The best thing I can do is to let her stay there with her family. With her *real* family.

I would never admit it to Loretta, but I was terrified of Noriko. Terrified of loving her so much, I'd turn back into a monster. Only now, with her far away, her hold over me stretched thin. I was able to control the hideous thing inside of me that coveted her, that wanted to keep her all for myself. If she returned, I'd only turn back into a beast. Even if I tried not to, it would only be a matter of time until he reared his ugly head.

Every time I couldn't take being without Noriko anymore, every time the entitled creature inside of me demanded that I go retrieve her, bring her back here where she belonged, all I had to do was look at the thousand paper cranes she made, all so she could wish herself away from me. The beast was silenced once more.

I cringed when I remembered the possessive, jealous creature I became. No wonder she didn't love me.

Like father, like son.

That was why I couldn't bring her back. I couldn't become *him* again. Better to wait here alone until my heart succeeded in killing me.

"She called," Loretta said. "She wants to talk to you."

My heart panged. "I don't want to talk to her," I lied. I had no idea what hearing her voice would do to my willpower.

"Is this really what you're going to do? Stand there and do nothing? Let her slip through your fingers?"

"I'm glad you understand the plan."

"Ingenious."

I let out a sigh. "Just let this go, Loretta. She'll never forgive me."

Chapter Fifty - Three

Noriko

My father and I returned home from the hospital six weeks later. The surgery was deemed a success and radiation seemed to have gone well. He had to keep returning regularly to do tests to make sure, but for now he was in remission.

Remission!

Drake saved my father's life.

He still hadn't called back.

Now I knew why.

My sisters came to Osaka a few weeks ago to visit Papa and me while he was still in the hospital. It felt so good to have them with me in that giant bed in the suite, our feet touching, their warmth on either side of me as we sat huddled together in bed.

"We heard your husband wouldn't let you speak to us, Nori-chan," Emi said in a breathless tone, her eyes wide in the glow of the bedside lamp.

"Yeah," added Tatsumi. "We heard he locked you up in a dungeon like a princess in the tower of his castle."

"What?" I cried out in shock. "Who told you this?"

They glanced at each other before training their eyes back on me. On the hotel room tablet, they showed me the articles in English and in Japanese. It seemed that the Japanese media latched onto this "news" from the States concerning one of their own. Headline after headline drove like nails into my chest, making it hard to breathe.

Japanese Beauty and the American Beast

The Beast and His Japanese Bride

Billionaire Beast Locks Away His Japanese Wife

As I read article after article, my blood drained from my limbs.

Oh my God.

Jared played me. He used what I told him, what he swore he'd keep secret, to make Drake look bad. Publicly.

I betrayed Drake. In the worst possible way.

I imagined this news hitting Drake. I felt every throb of his pain, his anguish, when he found out that the woman he desperately loved had done this to him. The knife that would have twisted in his heart now twisted in mine, his blood still warm on the blade.

Drake hated me.

I had his love and I destroyed it.

No wonder he sent me back without saying goodbye.

No wonder he wouldn't speak to me. I remembered his words from our fight.

"It doesn't have to be a fucking reporter. Anyone with a fucking camera phone can sell pictures of you. Anyone can twist anything you say into a story. I fucking told you they're all vultures. Now they know. Now they have a juicy story to run with. Now they've got somewhere to dig. Oh yes, and dig, dig, dig they will, those little worms. They'll dig and they'll use whatever they find to try to tear me down."

Drake knew the public was waiting to turn on him. It was what he feared. I had played into it perfectly, my careless, angry words spinning a flawed man into the nightmare creature of fairy tales right before the public's eyes.

This could not get any worse.

I spotted this article… And realized it very well could.

Billionaire Drake Blackwell Forced to Resign as CEO

Chapter Fifty - Four

Noriko

I felt sick. I felt like my insides had been ripped out. What had I done? Blackwell Industries was his life. I destroyed it. With one careless slip of my tongue.

I kept reading the article.

After the public outcry over the negative press concerning his alleged horrific treatment of his Japanese mail-order bride, Drake Blackwell, CEO of Blackwell Industries, has been forced to step down. It seems these allegations have been a fatal blow to his already cold and calculating reputation in the business world. It has been reported that Mr. Blackwell has sent his wife back to Japan to avoid the local media from getting her side of this fairy-tale-turned-nightmare. Sources say that she is being paid to keep quiet.

My insides twisted into knots. This was why he paid for my father's surgery. Not because he still loved me. He thought it would keep me quiet.

Oh, Drake, I wouldn't have said anything. You didn't have to pay for my silence, you just had to ask.

"God, Nori-chan, you were lucky to get away from him," Emi said.

"How did you?" asked Tatsumi.

"Yes, how did you get away from the beast?"

"He's not a beast!" I cried.

My two sisters blinked at me before trading looks.

"But the articles—"

"I don't care what the newspapers say. They don't know anything." I flung myself out of the bed and rushed out onto the balcony, the cool breeze whipping around outside. I didn't stop running until I'd slammed my hands along the railing, heaving in breath.

What had I done?

I'd ruined his life.

How could he ever forgive me?

How could he ever love—

"Nori-chan?" Tatsumi called from behind me.

"Are you okay?" Emi said, her voice all small.

"I'm fine," I lied. No one could ever know the truth of a marriage except for the two people in it; sometimes, not even them. "I just need some air. Go back inside. I'll join you soon."

I could feel their weighted stares on my back. I could sense the questions they were holding back like a pack of wolves.

"Go inside," I commanded in a tone that sounded so

much like Drake's that it sent a stab through my heart.

I heard them retreating, their hushed whispers, the door click signaling that I was alone.

And alone, I was.

The last of the fog in my vision cleared. I saw each gnarled root or jagged rock Drake and I had stumbled across over the last five months. I felt the weight of my sins and his like a single being. This was what a marriage was, I realized. It wasn't his fault, it was ours. It wasn't my mess, it was ours. When life got heavy, it laid across both our shoulders.

The ones we let in close, get close enough to see the cracks in our armor. And with our love we hand them a knife. By trusting them with our secrets, we show them where to aim.

Drake and I had both wounded the other. We were both to blame. Both wrong in so many ways.

Our fault. Our mess. Our marriage.

Was it even a marriage anymore?

Here was my chance to cut ties with Drake before the year was up. Was that what I still wanted?

It felt strange to be back here at our small house in Shibetzu. Like a shoe that'd become a tad too small. I found myself wincing at the noise of my sisters bickering as they tumbled over each other to get ready in the mornings. I found myself scrunching my nose at rice with every meal, missing the variety of foods I was served in the Blackwell dining room.

I missed the quiet and solitude of the manor. I missed my studio, filled with everything I needed. I missed the gardens where I'd often take my paints. Mostly, I missed the way my heart would kick-start when the gravel crunching outside told me that my husband was home.

I'd outgrown this place. Like a tree that had been replanted into a different shaped pot, it could not fit back into the old pot.

Papa found me sitting alone early one morning underneath the cherry tree. He lowered himself onto the grass in front of me. "Nori-chan, it's good to have you home."

"Yes, Papa," I said. I didn't lift my eyes to his.

"What of your husband? When do I get to meet him and thank him for what he has done for me?"

My husband. In the last six weeks, Papa had been silent about Drake. This was the first time he'd asked about him.

"I…I don't think he's coming." *Ever.* My chest squeezed around each jagged word.

"He must come for you. You are married. You love each other."

I shook my head as tears pricked the backs of my eyes. "Oh, Papa. I have ruined everything with him."

"How could you ruin anything? It is not possible."

I let out a sob-laugh. "Trust me, I am very capable of making a huge mess of my life." And my marriage.

"You still love him?"

I squeezed my eyes shut as the creeping realization that I'd been trying to ignore could not be denied anymore. I nodded.

"And you've told him?"

I shook my head. I never got the chance.

That's a lie, Noriko. You had the chance, several of them, you were too scared to take it.

I had used my promise to my father as an excuse. I had been too scared to make a life of my own outside of the safety of my family home. I had been too scared to give my all to my marriage. Now this house I once called home had become its own sort of prison.

Months dragged by… Autumn came again and for the first time it felt like an old friend, like the only one who understood what I felt inside. Leaves turned red like they were bleeding from the inside, before curling into their dry, brittle bodies, straining, hanging on by their fingers until they gave up and let go, swirling and falling to the ground and finally crumbling to dust. The air chilled and the bony branches shivered.

Then the snow fell and the world looked clean and white. A new year. A new start. If only there could be such a thing for my marriage.

Finally spring arrived with her new buds and her hope, a sentiment I no longer believed in. It had been almost eight months. Eight months without a single word from Drake.

It was a Saturday morning. My father and sisters were sitting huddled under a blanket as I stirred our breakfast congee, a rice porridge, on the stove. There was something about today, something nagging the edge of my mind about today. I couldn't figure it out.

My thoughts were interrupted by the sound of a car pulling up outside. I froze. Our visitors were usually from the village and they walked. Nobody we knew owned a car…

I ran through the house, my bare feet pounding on the straw mats. I slid open the front door, my eyes searching, my hope soaring…

A large black car had pulled up outside our gate, a figure climbing out of the back seat. Those familiar wide shoulders. The dark shock of hair. That air of power.

Drake.

Drake had finally come.

Chapter Fifty - Five

Noriko

I took a wobbly step down the stairs towards him. He was here. After all these months, why was he here? Could he be ready to forgive me? Could he be here to take me home? Hope fluttered like a crane in my chest.

I heard my sisters gasp from the front door behind me. "Papa, that's Mr. Blackwell!"

My papa shushed at them, instructing them to go and wash their faces and put on better clothes. He was buying me time to speak with Drake alone before my family crowded him. My heart sang silently with gratitude.

I didn't turn around because all I could feel was him.

He was more handsome than I remembered: full, defined lips, intense stare, dark stubble darkening his strong jaw. His hair had grown longer, curling over the collar of his brown sports jacket.

Drake pushed open the low gate before he looked up, our eyes catching. He froze. I stopped walking on the path, only now realizing that I hadn't put shoes on, gravel poking into the soles of my feet.

My stomach flipped. Everything I wanted to say, everything I'd wanted to say for the past eight months choked into my voice box like swallowed ash.

As I stared, I noticed heaviness in the corners of his mouth, the touch of shadow under his eyes. He looked tired and world weary.

Losing your own company will do that to you.

I shoved down my rising guilt, or at least I tried to. Perhaps he wasn't here to talk but to rage at me instead.

I certainly deserved it.

Something that looked like longing flashed in his eyes. It was gone before I could be sure. "Noriko," he said on an exhale.

My heart was drumming so hard I wasn't sure I could speak without my voice trembling. "Drake."

We stood there looking at each other, waiting for the other to speak first.

"How are—?" I asked at the same time as he said, "I was just—"

He allowed a smile to tug at one side of his lips. "Please, you first."

"What are you doing here?" I asked.

"I'm here on business. Well, not here exactly, but in Tokyo."

I nodded. Before I could thank him for coming, my sisters raced up behind me and crowded me, clinging onto my arms as if they were holding me back from being devoured by a lion.

"What is he doing here?"

"We won't let him take you, Nori-chan."

"Girls," I chastised in English. They knew enough English to be able to speak it. "Don't be rude."

I'm sorry, I mouthed at him.

He smiled and shook his head. To my utter surprise he bent down until he was eye level with the girls.

"I have heard a lot of good things about you two," Drake said to them in accented Japanese.

They both gasped. I smiled. I never did tell them that he could speak Japanese.

"In fact," he continued, *"I have gifts for both of you."*

"For us?" they both exclaimed, looking between Drake and each other.

Drake looked over his shoulder and motioned to his driver with his fingers. The driver, a young boy with a terrified look on his face and a wonky haircut underneath his chauffeur's cap, stumbled up the path carrying two gift boxes, which he set down beside Drake.

"Thank you, Hideki." Drake said to him.

Hideki nodded before racing back to the car.

My two sisters looked at each other, giggling. It didn't matter what they'd read about Drake, it seemed they were already being swayed by his good looks and the charm that he'd turned on for them.

Drake placed one box in front of Emi and one in front of Tatsumi. "I hope you like them."

Emi tugged open the box and cried out with joy as she tugged out a slick designer cream leather *randoseru* with a cute-looking skull with gems for eyes across the flap. Oh God, this backpack could have cost at least a grand. At the same time, Tatsumi pulled out a framed No Doubt poster autographed by none other than Gwen Stefani. Both girls squealed, jumping up and down on their toes, a chorus of thank yous in both Japanese and English coming from their mouths.

Tears pricked at the corners of my eyes. I spoke of my sisters once to him. He remembered.

He remembered.

Surely there was hope for us.

"Drake, it's too much," I said.

"No," he said quietly as he straightened, "it's not. It doesn't come close to making up for the months that you were taken from them."

I frowned at his choice of words.

"I'm afraid I don't have anything for you, sir," Drake said, turning to my father.

Papa looked at him with surprise. "Son, you've done enough for this old man. You saved my life and sent my daughter home to me while I recovered. There is nothing more you can give me. Perhaps there is something you want from me?" He raised his eyebrow and glanced at me.

I felt Drake's eyes on me, too. When I glanced at him I caught the brief look of pain in his eyes.

"*Now, girls,*" my father said in Japanese, "*come take your gifts inside. Let's leave Drake and Noriko alone for a minute so they can catch up.*"

They stumbled noisily into the house, both talking at once, carrying their gifts. I was left alone with Drake.

I knew we weren't really alone. The paper walls in the house were thin. Papa and the girls could hear everything from inside without too much trouble.

"Won't you stay for breakfast?" I said, aware that the congee may already be burnt. "Maybe we can go for a walk together afterwards." *I have so much to say to you.*

Drake looked surprised at my invitation, and longing flashed before it disappeared behind the mask he wore so well. "I, er…thank you, but no. I have to be off."

"Oh." My stomach dropped. "So soon?"

"I have something for you, too."

A present? For me? As quickly as it had dropped, my heart became a feather caught in an updraft. He reached into his jacket and pulled out an envelope, handing it to me.

"What's this?" I turned it over in my hands, opening the flap and pulling out papers. I read the headline and the rest of the text blurred.

Divorce papers.

He didn't come for me. He came for a divorce.

There was no hope for us.

I gripped the cursed papers, my hands shaking with the need to rip them apart.

Here was proof. He didn't love me anymore.

"Read over them, then sign them," Drake said. "I've included an addressed envelope in there for you to return them to me."

There would be nothing easy about signing these papers. God, how I wanted this before, and now it was the last thing I wanted. "So that's it then?" I said, trying to keep the bitter disappointment out of my voice.

"That's it."

"Oh…"

"Goodbye, Noriko." He leaned in, his familiar cologne rushing around my head, making me dizzy. His lips brushed mine, as softly as they did that morning after we first made love. That first kiss was a hello. This one…

This was goodbye.

His presence left my side so suddenly that I swayed.

His feet crushed the gravel as he practically ran from me, as if he was desperate to leave.

As if being near me gave him pain.

Of course it would.

As he slid into the car, my poor heart stuttered, crying for him to come back. My soul tried to rip itself out of my body to chase after him as he disappeared from sight in a cloud of dust. I couldn't make my feet move. My vision became a whirl of color, of blurry dabs, like a Monet too close up.

I realized what was special about today.

It was our one year anniversary.

I waited, glaring at the divorce papers sitting in the corner of my room every time I passed them. I didn't sign them. Not yet.

I hadn't reapplied to study, I hadn't looked for a job. Because I didn't think I'd be staying.

I still clung to him.

It wasn't over.

It couldn't be.

He'd be back. Once he realized I wouldn't sign them. He'd realize his mistake and come back. He'd miss me and want to sort things out and he'd come back.

One week turned into two. Still no sign from Drake.

I couldn't deny the truth anymore.

We were over.

I pulled the papers in front of me on the low dining room table one afternoon when I was alone at home. Drake's signature was already on the bottom. It was just like him, all aggressive and sharp lines, indents in the paper where he'd used a heavy hand. I traced his name with my finger and let out a huff.

How did my sacrifice turn into my salvation? How did my salvation turn into my sorrow?

I let go of the last strains of hope. I lowered the pen slowly to the paper.

Gravel crunched outside.

Oh my God.

That sound.

Drake.

Before I knew it, I was flying, sprinting so hard my heart felt like it was going to burst out of my chest. I tumbled out the front door. A black car was pulling up outside the gate. The windows were tinted. I couldn't see in.

Drake. Drake came back.

The door opened. My stomach jammed up into my throat.

Then dropped.

It was Hideki, the same driver from when Drake came. Where was Drake? Hideki hurried towards me as I rushed towards him. We met in the middle of the path.

"Hideki?"

He held out a phone to me.

I grabbed it and held it to my ear. "Drake?"

"Noriko?" It wasn't Drake's voice that answered. It was a female voice, one I didn't recognize. "You and I have never met," she said in English. "My name is Sam, I'm Drake's personal assistant. We need you to come home."

"But..." *home*, "I am home," I said slowly.

"I know you haven't signed the divorce papers."

I stiffened. "What business is that of yours?"

"Drake needs you. Please, if you still carry any affection for him. He's... He's had a heart attack."

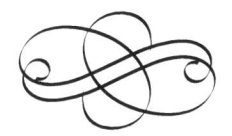

Chapter Fifty - Six

Drake

That annoying beeping broke through my darkness. Stupid alarm. Or was it? It sounded familiar. I attempted to get my eyes open. They were stuck. My body ached. As I came to consciousness I could feel the scratchy material of the bed underneath me.

What had I been doing before? What was the last thing I remember?

Oh right. I was in the limo on the way to a meeting. I'd been talking to Felipe when…

The flash of pain echoed in my left side and my left arm tingled.

Damn, heart. Stop messing around and just kill me already.

Finally my eyes peeled apart. My corneas stung as too much light flooded into my sensitive pupils. God, why do they have to make hospitals so damn bright and white?

There was a blurry figure by my side, slowly coming into focus.

Noriko.

My heart skipped a beat and I swear I heard it in the machine.

I was dreaming. Or perhaps I truly was dead.

"Drake?" her sweet voice trembled around my name. "Can you hear me?"

More of the room came into focus; the machines by my side, the table opposite covered in loud, obnoxious flower arrangements, more crowding the floor. I could smell the sickly-syrup scent of lilies as if I were at a funeral.

This wasn't heaven. I wasn't dead.

Which means *she* was really here. I refocused on Noriko. Her hair was loose around her sweetheart face, her eyes looked red and swollen, and she worried her bottom lip with her tiny white teeth. She looked as stunning as the day she stumbled into my limo and into my world, as precious as the day I handed her divorce papers.

Longing ripped through my heart as violent as the attack that put me in this hospital bed. I winced, my fingers curling into the sheets so I didn't reach out for her. The beeping of the machine beside me increased in pace, making my reaction at seeing her again obvious. Sweat appeared, cold on my forehead. I felt raw and vulnerable. Why didn't I strip naked down to my heart in front of her and throw myself under her feet? Why didn't I hand over my fucking soul for her to crush again?

Her eyes welled with pity—*pity*—and anger turned to a boil inside me. Look at me, the great Drake Blackwell, reduced to a pathetic weak pup in a hospital bed. Look at the envied Drake Blackwell all alone and unloved in his hospital room, the only person guilted into being by his side was his *ex-wife*. Screw her. I didn't need her pity.

"Get out," I growled, my voice cracking over my dry throat.

Shock flittered over her delicate features. "Drake, I—"

"I said get the fuck out." I tore my eyes away from her. I couldn't stand to see her tears. They were like ice shards, cutting open my veins. I looked to the wall to my right, my eyes landing on a replica of a famous impressionist painting of a couple having a picnic by a lake. Bitterness surged up inside me, mixing with my own wretched self-pity. "Nobody wants you here," I yelled as loud as I could, my insides feeling like they were being torn to shreds, the fast beeping like a warning alarm. I wasn't sure whether I was yelling at her or at myself.

The bed shifted as she yanked her weight off the edge. I heard a single pain-filled sob before she ran out of the room.

The instant the door clicked behind her, I sagged into the pillows, guilt and regret tumbling over my relief. Already I ached for her to return. But I couldn't. I just couldn't. It was too hard to look at her and know she was never really mine. It almost killed me handing over those divorce papers. I'd rather be alone than to suffer in her presence.

Why was she here? Who contacted her?

Loretta. I knew it already. That meddling woman couldn't keep her nose out of anything. Thought she knew what was best for me. How did she manipulate Noriko into coming here? Did she guilt Noriko into coming? Likely, Loretta begged. *Please, Noriko. Drake has no one else. And he still loves you—so pathetic, I know—so you need to come because no one else will.*

Fuck her. Fuck them all. I didn't need anyone.

But the boy inside me knew that I was lying. My heart ached again, a long, lonely cry.

Chapter Fifty - Seven

Noriko

I jarred my wrists slamming on the door as I raced out of Drake's hospital room.

Why did I come here? He didn't want me here. He didn't care. Sam was mistaken.

Firm hands grabbed my upper arm, forcing me to stop. Loretta was standing in the hallway outside his door, blinking at me. "What's wrong?"

"Sam told me to come. Told me…" I heaved in a breath. "H-he doesn't want me here."

"Trust me, Noriko, he wants you here. He's been calling out your name in his sleep."

"He screamed at me to leave."

She narrowed her eyes at me. "During the day he sits in your studio among your finished paintings, just staring at them. He's been sleeping in your room in your bed."

"Then why…" *Nobody wants you here,* "why is he being such…"

"An asshole?" Loretta said this with no malice in her voice. "Are you really surprised?"

My shoulders dropped. "No," I said quietly. I was an insecure fool. This was how Drake reacted when he was scared. When he was hurting. Like an injured animal, protecting the open wound in his bleeding heart, lashing out at those closest to him, clawing those who tried to get near him.

Loretta clicked her tongue. "I've been watching you two dance around each other for almost an entire year. Avoiding the truth about how you feel, *not* communicating with each other, acting like two children, dammit. The problem is that neither of you is prepared to throw yourself wholeheartedly in first."

"Why do I have to be the one who moves first?"

Loretta raised an eyebrow. "Because you have a family who loves you. You had parents who loved each other. He never did. He doesn't know what a good relationship is supposed to look like. *You do.*"

Tears clouded my vision as Loretta's words poked large holes in my stubborn pride. But…it wasn't enough. "I don't know, Loretta."

Loretta let out a low breath. "He's too damn stubborn to tell you, but you need to know something. This isn't his first heart attack. He was here in this hospital when he gave the order to send you home."

I gasped as the cracks of my heart filled up with realization. That's why he didn't come to say goodbye. He was here. If only I'd known he was hurting. He never told me.

Why didn't he tell me?

Because he couldn't stand for me to see him this way. Just like right now. Oh, Drake, you and your silly swollen pride. I don't care about that.

I remembered a line from Sun Tzu's *The Art of War*.

"*In the midst of chaos, there is also opportunity.*"

I let out a shaky breath. "What do I do? He doesn't want me in there."

"That boy doesn't know what he wants," Loretta said sharply. "Noriko," she grabbed my shoulders and looked right into my eyes, "do you love him?"

I nodded, because I couldn't speak.

"Then you go in there and tell him that you're *not* leaving."

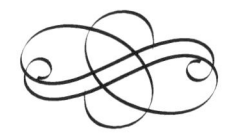

Chapter Fifty - Eight

Noriko

I took a steadying breath before I pushed open Drake's hospital room door. He was in one of the larger suites on a quiet floor reserved for the hospital's VIP guests. He lay in bed with his eyes closed as I padded up to him, his bed tilted up so he was sitting rather than lying.

His eyes snapped open. They widened before they narrowed. "I thought I told you to—"

"I know what you said. What's even louder is what you're not saying."

His Adam's apple bobbed. He tore his eyes from me. "What the hell do you want? More money? The alimony wasn't enough for you, huh? You want more?"

"I'm here, Drake. I'm not leaving."

"Stubborn, girl," he muttered. "Are you looking to get another scoop for your friend Jared?" His reminder stabbed at me. I refused to budge. "Poor Drake, lying in a hospital on the verge of death while his poor abused wife takes pity on him."

"I'm here for *you*. And you're not dying. Although," I mused lightly, "I wouldn't put it past you to die just to annoy me."

His eyes snapped to mine. I swore I saw hope bobbing on the surface before it was drowned in fear. "Yeah, well, I don't want you here. Get the fuck out."

"I'm not going."

"Didn't you hear me?" His voice rose, shaking with emotion. "I don't want *you*."

I brushed his barbed words off me with a steadying breath. "I'm not going anywhere."

"Get the fuck out of here. Go back to where you came from, you greedy gold-digger."

"I'm not leaving. I'm not leaving you." I kept repeating these words, my voice and my resolve getting stronger and stronger with every repetition.

In life you choose to be the water or the rock.

Today, I would be the rock.

I would be the rock until he melted into water.

I could see him fighting the rising tide of grief, a grief so old and deep it stretched back to the darkness of his childhood. I saw all of him, the sad, lonely boy who became a scared, confused teenager who grew up to be a cold and ruthless man. I loved every part of him. I accepted every single piece. I promised each fragment of him that I was not leaving, every word of mine a battle chant. He was my home and I would die fighting for him. I would bleed to protect him. I would love him until my dying breath.

Trust me.
Believe in me, Drake.
Let me love you.

As my strength grew, his fury weakened. Yes, he still fought. And how he fought. But I would win. Because I was rock and I was love and love *always* won.

I had one last move saved up.

I threw open the gates to my soul. I dropped all shields around my heart. I let him see right into the very center of me, palms open, showing him that there was no judgement here. No conditions. Only love.

The last of his shields collapsed, his army spent. He sagged back like a broken soldier on his pillows, his arm flung over his face.

I reached for him, placing one hand on his cheek, rough with stubble, and the other on his poor heart, broken from too much sorrow. Give me your fears, husband, and I will shield you with my love. Hand me your sadness and I will dry it like tears in the sun.

"I'm right here, Drake. I'm right here and I'm not leaving."

His arms moved so quickly I could barely react. They wrapped around me and pulled me against him, crushing me to him with more strength than I thought possible in his state.

"I'm staying," I whispered as his arms closed around me. "You hear me? I'm not leaving you."

I held him as he shook in my arms, the beeping of his heartbeat increasing in pace along with mine. My promise trickled down to the one who needed it most, the boy inside of him who just needed someone to *stay*.

Chapter Fifty - Nine

Drake

It hurt so fucking much. I felt like I was dying.

I was drowning in a deep ocean, my lungs burning from taking on water. I couldn't swim to the surface. I couldn't breathe.

As I suffered, as I kicked and pulled, I heard her words, *I'm staying*.

I felt her soft, warm body in my arms, her heart knocking against mine as our chests pressed together. She was hope filling my lungs like oxygen. She made me buoyant.

Slowly I rose up.

This was not the end of my darkness. It was part of me, I knew. But for the first time since I could remember, I saw light dappling on the surface.

I brushed my hands over her hair, her face, her shoulders, to make sure she was real. "Are you sure I'm not dead? This feels a lot like Heaven."

She let out a laugh even as tears escaped those end-of-me eyes, or perhaps they were my beginning. I leaned in and licked each precious salty one, the taste of happiness and sadness. When I pulled back her eyes were hooded, her gaze on my mouth. Heat roared through my body and I tugged her closer.

"Excuse me?" I was vaguely aware of the nurse at the door. "You can't be in here. Family only."

Noriko snapped her left hand up to the air, the gold band glinting in the light, her eyes still on me. "I *am* family."

She still wore her ring. Did that mean...? "We're not divorced?" I dared to ask.

She shook her head, her hair falling about her cheeks. "I couldn't sign the papers. Did you not know?"

I shook my head. "I told my assistant Sam to take care of it. I told her not to tell me when it had been done."

"Sam was the one who called me."

"Excuse me, sir? Miss?" A voice called from the door. "Visiting hours are over."

"Go. Away," Noriko yelled out.

There was a gasp, then a grumble before the door swung shut.

I smirked at my wife. "You've become very bossy, you know?"

"You're rubbing off on me."

"I like the sound of that," I joked, before everything in me grew serious. There was so much to say. "I missed you all these months. God, how I missed you." I weaved my fingers in her hair, pulling her forehead against mine, inhaling her sweet breath.

"Why didn't you come?"

"I did."

She shook her head, her hair falling about us. "Why didn't you come and bring me home?"

I squeezed my eyes shut for a second. Home. She said *home*.

"I thought you didn't want to come back. With what I did to you and the pills—"

"Oh God." She buried her face in her hands. "I'm embarrassed about the pills," it came out muffled. I tugged down her hands, forcing her to face me. "I have no excuse for the pills."

"It's okay, you don't need—"

"I do need to explain. It *was* my plan to leave after one year. I made a promise to my father I'd come back. But I fell in love with you, Drake, inconveniently and irreversibly, and I wanted to stay…"

The words unspoken were clear…*until you locked me up and refused to let me see my father*. God, when I looked back at my behavior now, I felt sick. I could hardly believe that *he* and I were the same man. I felt justified at the time. I felt *right*.

"I know it doesn't excuse what I said to Jared," she continued, "I was desperate. I just wanted him to help me get back to Japan. I didn't think he'd sell our story to a reporter."

"I know, Noriko. I don't blame you for that."

She shook her head. "But the fallout of my careless actions. How can you ever forgive me after I took your company away from you?"

I couldn't help but laugh. "Noriko, you did the best thing for me."

"What?"

"I stepped down as CEO, yes. But I still sit on the board of directors. I still have a say. Blackwell Industries has been good to me, but I don't owe it my life anymore. I don't want it to be my life. I want to figure out who I am and what I really want to do. Thanks to you, I now have the time to do that." I cupped her face and searched her eyes, fear already tumbling around my stomach. "Noriko, I want to be a better husband. I want to be your perfect husband. I am far from it. I'm going to fuck up. I'm going to fuck up a lot, I imagine. Most of the time with you, I don't know what I'm doing."

She smiled like the Mona Lisa. My Mona Lisa. "I don't know what I'm doing either. We can work it out together."

"You and me."

"Yes."

"Are we really doing this?"

"Yes."

I couldn't take any more air between us. I pulled her mouth to mine and kissed her with all the strength of everything I felt but had never been good at saying. With every lap of my tongue, I promised her that I would try to be the man she needed, I would fight to be the husband she deserved. The beeping increased again as need rushed through my blood.

She giggled against my mouth.

"Damn this machine. I am at a disadvantage."

She pulled away a little, her eyes twinkling. "I like hearing how I affect you, Mr. Blackwell."

"Don't get smug, Mrs. Blackwell."

She grabbed my hand, the one without the IV drip, and placed it on her heart. "Now we're even," she whispered.

Chapter Sixty

Noriko

After Drake was discharged from the hospital, he and I barely let go of each other as we rode in his limo home. Loretta had gone ahead to get the house ready for us, and she greeted us at the door with subdued happiness.

Drake and I were silent as we climbed the stairs, my eyes darting around, soaking in the place I had come to call home. Had it really been eight months since I left?

Drake paused at the top of the stairs and I followed his line of sight towards the dark hallway of the west wing. Unease bunched in my stomach as he pulled me towards the abandoned rooms.

"Drake?" I tugged back on his hand. "You don't have to."

He looked at me with a heaviness in his stare. "I want to. I need you to know...*everything* before you decide that you're staying."

"I'm staying—"

He held up a hand to silence me. "Don't make promises you might not be able to keep after you hear what I have to say."

I nodded, my mouth going dry.

"You know he killed his father? It was deemed a suicide. Surprising how there was no note."

"Drake wouldn't murder anyone."

"Wouldn't he? Even to get revenge for the murder of his mother?"

Was this what Drake had to reveal to me?

He led me into his mother's bedroom first. That cream and yellow room I entered without permission a year ago. We held each other among the dust and her ghost and he told me about his mother's drug problem, about the men she pulled into her bed, how his parents fought, how it got violent. All things I knew. Hearing it from *him*—his voice cracking as he spoke—hearing the scared, silent boy inside finally getting to speak, tore shreds off me. I knew it must be hard for him to speak of the darkness in his past. It warmed my heart that he was sharing it anyway *with me*.

I watched as slowly, bit by bit, the chains of his childhood fell away. Not all of it. Perhaps never all of it. We always carry the past with us, as much a part of us as our blood and our cells. But the healing started today.

We left his mother's room. When I paused at the doorway, glancing back, I swear I *felt* her watching me, sending me her wishes. *Look after him. Because I wasn't able to.*

Drake walked me farther into the west wing, to the next room.

Oh my God. His father's bedroom.

I rubbed my palms on my skirt. I held my breath as Drake pushed open the door, indicating for me to enter first.

I did so, my entire body tense.

The room I stepped into wasn't a bedroom.

It was a man's study covered in a thick layer of dust.

I felt Drake suddenly at my back, his breath on my neck. "My father died here."

Chapter Sixty - One

Drake

Sixteen years ago…

"You're drunk. Again." I glared at my father, a broken mess in an armchair in his study. I turned to get the hell out of this room that stank of sweat and the sharp tang of addiction. I could barely watch as my father, the once great Pierson Blackwell, became a sniveling, cowering wisp of a man those last few months after she died. I couldn't fucking watch him destroy himself. "Clean yourself up," I said over my shoulder, my voice hardening. I felt relief when my insides froze over the pain, hiding it from me as if through a thick sheet of ice. I paused at the door and turned to stare at him once more. My lip lifted in a sneer. "You're disgusting."

My father mumbled something into his hands.

"What was that?"

His admission came out between his fingers like a hiss. "I killed her."

I froze, my hand clenching into a fist around the door handle. "You…"

"If it wasn't for me, she wouldn't have needed those drugs. If she didn't need those drugs, she wouldn't have taken too much that day and…and…"

My lungs released a fraction. He hadn't actually killed her. He blamed himself for what she did to herself. The same thing he was doing to himself with that fucking bottle.

I strode towards the side table and grabbed the half-empty bottle of Macallan. He grabbed the other end and the liquid sloshed onto my wrists.

"Leave it," he begged, his acrid breath wafting all around my face.

This close I could see how the alcohol had made his once vibrant face soft and sallow, yellowed his eyes and corroded his teeth with decay. I felt bile rising in the back of my throat. I snatched the bottle away from his weak hands, stepped over to the partly open window and threw it out. He moaned like he was in pain as it flew out across the lawn and landed somewhere among a bed of lilies. My mother's favorite flowers.

I turned back to him, pouting at me like a sullen child in his armchair. "Why did you do that?"

"Pull yourself together, old man." *For once be the father you should have been.*

I began to walk out again. I knew it wouldn't fucking help, taking away that bottle. He would just pull out another one from his myriad of stashes around the mansion. Why did I even try?

"Please, don't leave me like this," he begged. "Take this. End my suffering."

At that, I spun.

He had a gun, a fucking gun in his hands, holding it towards me like an offering. "Let me be with her in Heaven." He fell towards me, his knees hitting the floor before he crawled towards me, the gun handle out.

Dear God. Kill my father. How could he beg me, his only son, to do such a thing? Did he think I could actually do it? Did he think I actually would? As payback for all those years of tears and bruises? How I hated him, but I could never kill him.

I shoved him back, his sniveling sending a mix of repulsion and disgust and pity through me, the taste of it bitter in the back of my throat. "I'm not going to kill you."

"Please, I can't do it myself. I can't..."

"You don't deserve death. You deserve to live with *what* you are and what you've done."

"I can't. She won't let me rest. She's everywhere, in my dreams, in the shadows, whispering, blaming me."

"Jesus Christ..."

"If you loved me you'd do it." His watery eyes pleaded with me. Trying to guilt me, manipulate me into taking the gun.

"I don't love you." I spun, determined now to reach that door and get the fuck out of there. How far my father had fallen, and it scared me to watch him.

"You son of a bitch," he snarled behind me. "You were always such a fucking disappointment." I knew he was trying to anger me, to get me to turn around and snatch that gun off him. His words fell against my deadened heart and slid off. "You know you were never really mine. You're a bastard belonging to one of your whore mother's lovers."

I flinched, but I kept walking. Perhaps it would have been a relief to think that I wasn't really his. But I looked too much like him for there to be any doubt.

I paused at the door, my repressed anger sliding down my throat like a pill, and I said the words I would die regretting. "Maybe you're right. Maybe you should just kill yourself."

He didn't respond. I stepped out of the room and closed the door behind me, the clicking sound of the lock releasing a flood of guilt at the words I said to my own father. *I am a terrible son.* I should go back in there. Apologize.

My pride won out. He had hurt me too many times. I was too fucking weary from our fights, our arguments that never would resolve anything.

I let go of the door handle and took a step away.

That's when I heard it.

Bang.

I'd never forget the sound a gun made when it went off, the sharpness inside your ear, the pressure against your eardrums, the way it seemed to penetrate your skin with electricity, making your body flinch. Even muffled through that wooden door.

I'd never forget running back into my father's study, seeing the spray of blood all over the back of the armchair and the wall behind it. I collapsed by his side and I gripped his shoulders.

And all that blood on my hands.

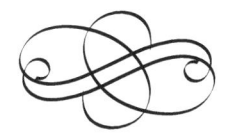

Chapter Sixty - Two

Drake

I searched her face when I finished my story. I saw no judgement there. No accusations. Only love.

She took my hand and led me out of the darkness of the west wing and to her bedroom, filled with light.

We stood in the center of her room just as we did a year ago. My heart was in my throat as she slowly undressed me, starting with the buttons on my shirt and pushing it off my shoulders. She commanded me. She owned me. Even after I grabbed her, my need snapping apart my control, *she* possessed *me*.

My redemption.
My salvation.
My wife.

"How…" I whispered, when we lay together afterwards, "how can you love someone like me?"

She looked at me with those beautiful eyes and smiled. "*Kintsugi.*"

"What does that mean?"

"In Japan we repair broken pottery using lacquer made of gold," she traced right across my heart, "because we believe our flaws, our cracks, are precious. There is no need to disguise them or try to hide them. They are part of your history. Part of your beauty."

A love so ferocious rose up to swallow me. I reached for her hand, my fingers shaking. "Marry me."

She cleared her throat. "I hate to be the one to tell you this but…we're already married."

I shook my head. "You married me because you needed the money. Marry me again because you need *me*."

She let out a sigh. "No."

No? The word looped around my throat and threatened to strangle me.

"I'll marry you because I love you."

Happiness unlike anything I've ever known surged through my body. Could it be possible? Could this happiness belong to me? Was it mine? To keep? To hold?

She shot me a smirk. "Besides, you owe me a proper wedding."

I chuckled. "That I can do."

She raised an eyebrow. "One where you actually show."

"I'll get Sam to put it in my calendar."

She poked my ribs with her free hand.

I grabbed her hand so she couldn't do it again. "You and your family name the date," I kissed each dainty knuckle, "you tell me where and what and how and I'll make it happen." I pulled her over my naked body, my hardness nudging at her entrance. "But right now? I want to make babies with you."

For once, my wife didn't argue.

Epilogue

Drake

Nine months later...

"Just one more push. Come on, Noriko," the doctor said.

My wife, still stunning even covered in sweat, bore down and grit her teeth with her effort.

I hung back behind the wall of nurses, my insides feeling like they were winding around and around a spool.

I thought of all the changes I'd made over the last nine months. I converted my bedroom into a nursery and now Noriko's bedroom was *ours*. The guest bedrooms opposite our room were reserved for Noriko's sisters and father when they came to visit during every school holiday. I cleared out the west wing, dusting off those old ghosts and letting the light back into each corner, and turned it into a children's paradise with bedrooms and a huge playroom, our kids getting their own wing when they were older.

Noriko had plans to open up a gallery in the next few years. I taught business part-time at a local university and was taking photography lessons for fun.

None of this felt like it meant anything at this second.

I was going to be a father.

I had never been more terrified in my life.

I had my father's blood in my veins. I had his blood. I'd made different choices. Would it be enough? The fingers of my past reached out for me like ghostly arms.

Noriko let out a cry and another smaller cry joined hers.

Our baby.

She did it.

My wife did it.

She gave birth.

"Congratulations, Mr. and Mrs. Blackwell, you have a healthy baby boy." The nurse placed a swath of cloth into Noriko's arms.

I still couldn't move. The panic gripped me like vines wrapped around a tree. Oh God, what have I done? I couldn't do this. I couldn't—

"Drake?" Noriko called to me.

Only then did I move, drawn to her side by her voice just like I had been drawn to her since the very beginning. She handed me our boy, pushing him into my stiff arms. He was as light and fragile as a doll. I could barely look at him. Oh God, what if I—?

"Look at him, Drake. Breathe."

Reacting purely at the authority in my wife's voice, I forced my eyes down. In my arms, wrapped in a pale blue blanket was my son—our son. The room faded away, until it was just Noriko's hand on my back and this—this miracle.

He had a tiny squished-up face, with dark hair—mine—and olive skin—hers—and a set of Mona Lisa eyes that locked onto mine. A jolt like lightning snapped through my body, evaporating all my doubt. For the second time in my life, I fell in love.

"Hey little Mason," I whispered to him, our first father-son moment. "I'm your papa. I'm here to tell you that you don't need to worry about anything. You have the most incredible mama. She is kind and patient and the depth of her love is as endless as the universe. You are so lucky, my boy."

I looked up to see Noriko watching me, a satisfied smile on her face. If it was even possible, my heart felt like it grew twice as large, swollen with more love than could fit in this galaxy.

Tears pricked my eyes and I turned back to my son. My boy. "As for your papa? Well, your mama has made him a better man. He will be an even better man for you. You'll be proud of him, I swear, like he's already proud of you." I leaned in to press a kiss to his smooth, tiny forehead.

"I'm staying," I whispered just for him, "I promise."

The End

Dear Readers,
It was only after I published Girl Wife Prisoner (the novel this story was born from) that I realized the *real* main character was Drake. He was the most complex and broken character. He had the most to learn. His growth was most interesting. And the countless messages from you guys telling me that he was your favorite character just confirmed it.
That's why I unpublished Girl Wife Prisoner. So I could rewrite the story and give Drake and Noriko the story they deserved.
I hope you enjoyed it!
Keep reading to see what's coming up next.

xoxo Sienna

Too Young

Irish Kisses #1

Sienna Blake

Saoirse
I wanted him since the day I met him. Long haired, tattooed and tall as an Irish giant.

He was the only one who ever truly cared. The only one who ever saw past my indifferent façade and saw *me*.

I could be anything I wanted, he said.
Except his.
Because I was too young and he was my Juvenile Liaison Officer…

Diarmuid
It's been years since I last saw her. With a body like a woman now, I hardly recognized her.

She was the only one who ever silenced the ghosts of my past. The only one who got past my asshole facade and understood *me*.

She could be anything she wanted.
Except mine.
Because she's only seventeen and I'm trying hard not to fall for her.

If I give in, she will ruin me.

*This is not erotica. This is a slow-burn love story spanning across a nine-year time period. There is no underaged sex between the two main characters.
Although this book is part of a series, it is a standalone novel.

Coming early 2018

Beautiful Revenge

A Good Wife Novel

Sienna Blake

My name is...*was* Alena Ivanova.

Five years ago, I made a mistake. A big one. One that cost me the only man I will ever love.

Now, in the lonely moors of north England, I live with my cold, cruel husband. My only friend is his daughter from a previous marriage. At least I didn't starve to death during the bitter Russian winter.

When my husband arranges for a potential investor to stay with us, a mysterious self-made millionaire by the name of Mr Wolf, imagine my shock when *he* walks in...

My name is...*was* Dimitri Volkov.

Until she broke me.

Five years I've worked for this moment.

Five years I've dreamed of revenge.

Bit by bit, she will watch her charmed life crumble to the ground.

Then when she needs me the most, when she is desperate, scared and alone like I was all those years ago...

I will destroy her.

Although this book is part of a series, it is a standalone novel.

Out Now

Love Sprung From Hate

Dark Romeo 1

Sienna Blake

I didn't know she was a detective, the only daughter of the Chief of Police.
I didn't know he was a mafia Prince, heir to the Tyrell's bloody empire.

It was only supposed to be one night.
God help me, I can't stop thinking about that night.

So when she walked into the interrogation room, my heart almost stopped.
I can't believe he might have tortured and killed someone.

I have to avoid her at all costs.
I will be his downfall.

So begins a deadly game of cat and mouse, of blood and lust, of love and duty, and of an attraction so fierce the consequences are inevitable…

Inspired by Shakespeare's Romeo and Juliet, this is a retelling for mature audiences. Don't enter the Underworld if you're scared of the dark.

Out now

Get your FREE ecopy of Paper Dolls!
Join my Reader Group for your free ecopy of my full-length, standalone romantic suspense, Paper Dolls. You'll also get access to exclusive giveaways, a sneak peek into what's coming up next, vote on covers and blurbs, and interact with me personally.
http://bit.ly/SiennasDarkAngels

Or sign up for my Newsletter
for new release, sales & giveaways alerts:
www.siennablake.com

Did you enjoy Beautiful Revenge?
The best way you can show me some love is by posting a review at your retailer! Don't tell me, tell the world what you think. (Then message me so I can thank you personally.) It really helps other readers to decide whether my books are for them. And the number of reviews I get is really important. Thank you!

If you're a Blogger,
please signup to my VIP Bloggers List for ARC opportunity alerts:
http://bit.ly/SiennaVIPBloggers
Blogs will be verified.

Stay sexy,
Sienna
xoxo

Stalk me! I like it

www.siennablake.com
www.facebook.com/SiennaBlakeAuthor
www.instagram.com/SiennaBlakeAuthor

Books by Sienna Blake

Bound Duet
Bound by Lies (#1)
Bound Forever (#2)

Paper Dolls

Dark Romeo Trilogy
Love Sprung From Hate (#1)
The Scent of Roses (#2)
Hanging in the Stars (#3)

A Good Wife (Standalone Series)
Beautiful Revenge
Mr. Blackwell's Bride

Too Young ~ *coming early 2018*

Acknowledgements

Firstly, thank you to everyone who read Girl Wife Prisoner and took a chance on this new "version" of their story. Thank you for emailing me to tell me that Drake was your favorite and the most interesting character. You were right. You had me rereading GWP with new eyes. And inspired me to rewrite it with Drake as the centerpiece. I hope you loved his story as much as I do.

My dearest Kathy of Book Detailing. You already know how much I love you. You are the doctor of my stories when they are sick and broken. So I turned you into a real doctor in this book.

To Terrie of Just Let Me Read. Thank you for keep the machine running so I can focus on my writing.

To my Reader Group. Thank you for your input on my title, cover and blurb. Love you all. This group is my online safe haven.

To my fabulous early reviewers and book bloggers. You guys are the heartbeat of the indie world. Without your unwavering support, I'd be no where. Thank you from the bottom of my heart.

Thank you Romacdesigns for that beautiful cover. On point as always.

And thanks to Christie of Proof Positive for your eagle eye and manuscript feedback.

Last but not least, thank you to my FlexHuddlers. You are my daily support, motivation and source of the best craic in all of Ireland!

About Sienna

Sienna Blake is a storyteller & inksinger, wordspinner of love stories with grit, and alter ego of a *USA Today* Bestselling Author.

She loves all things that make her heart race—rollercoasters, thrillers and rowdy unrestrained sex. She likes to explore the darker side of human nature in her writing.

If she told you who she really was, she'd have to kill you. Because of her passion for crime and forensics, she'd totally get away with your murder. *wink*

Printed in Great Britain
by Amazon